REVIVED

The Unexpected Series

S.E. ROBERTS

s.e. roberts

revived

the unexpected series
book one

Revived

Copyright © 2018 by S.E. Roberts

Formatted by: Jessica Ames

Cover design by: Sly Fox Cover Designs

Edited by: Kim Deister at The Story Tender

Edited by: Trenda London at It's Your Story Content Editing

Proofread by: Andrea Galante

REVIVED PLAYLIST

Follow Me~ Uncle Kracker
Jumper~ Third Eye Blind
Brown Eyed Girl~ Van Morrison
Single Ladies~ Beyoncé
To Make You Feel My Love~ Garth Brooks

These songs are used in a fictitious way and the author
does not claim ownership to any of them.

Dedicated to my BFF Amanda. Love you!

PROLOGUE

CLAIRE

The roaring gusts of wind thrust my small car around the wet street. It's difficult to see too far in front of me, so I'm driving significantly under the speed limit. This severe weather is common for spring in Chicago. I really shouldn't complain after the horrendous winter we just had.

I should be focusing on keeping myself safe, but I'm eager to tell my husband about my news. Our son Brady is only eight months old which means he and his sibling will be close in age. My brother Evan and I were four years apart, which made it hard for us to bond, so I always wanted my children closer together.

Trevor told me he would be working late tonight, so my best friend Shayna is babysitting while I surprise him with dinner at the office. I got him his favorite, Charlie's, on my way. I've missed him this week, as he's worked late every night.

When I pull into the narrow, vacant parking lot, I quickly get out of my gray Honda Civic and open the back door to collect our food and drinks. I'm eager to spend some alone time with him, even if I'd rather it be somewhere else.

The torrential downpour is causing drastic flooding on the sidewalks, so I am careful not to fall. I cautiously balance everything in my hands, trying not to drop anything. I'm clumsy, but right now would not be a good time for that to transpire. I set the takeout bags on the sidewalk to open the door but find that it's locked. *Strange*. I guess it makes sense because the office is closed. I know he doesn't like stragglers walking in, especially after hours.

"Trevor?" I call out, unsure if he'll be able to hear me over the rain beating on the roof.

After what feels like several long minutes, I try again. "Trevor?" I yell, starting to become irritated because now I'm soaked. Of course, I'm wearing a white shirt today, of all days.

I'm standing under the awning in front of Davis Chiropractic, but it isn't doing me much good at this point.

Finally, I hear something on the other side of the door and I'm relieved to know that I'll be inside soon. But then I hear a voice that isn't Trevor's.

"Trevor!" *A woman's voice. What the hell is going on?* I rattle the handle harder but still get no response. I quickly run around to the back of the building and bang on one of the windows. I see another window is slightly ajar. That's when my world comes crashing down on me.

I can't breathe.

My husband, my world, is thrusting in and out of his

assistant, Nicole. His fingers run through her stringy, boxed-blonde hair.

I'm going to be sick. How could he do this to me?

I can't seem to pull myself away from the window fast enough, but when I do, I run. It's the only thing I know to do. I abandon the food sitting on the sidewalk and sprint to my car.

I'm only a couple blocks from Shayna's, so I head in the direction of her house. I know she'll be able to calm me and I need to see my son. This was supposed to be one of the happiest days of my life, but it is now possibly the worst.

"CLAIRE, what the hell is wrong with you?" Shayna asks as soon as she swings the door open. I know I'm a mess with mascara running down my face, my clothes drenched from the rain.

"He. He." I can't get the words out because I'm crying so hard. My chest hurts. I can hardly breathe.

"Okay, babe, you need to calm down. Let's go sit and I'll get you a drink. Want some lemonade?" I nod as I climb onto a stool at the bar in her kitchen. Before getting my drink, Shayna brings me a bath towel to wrap myself in.

I'm appreciative of the silence and I start to calm a little as I sip my drink. Finally, Shayna speaks.

"What happened, Claire?" She looks at me with concern in her eyes.

"I just caught Trevor with Nicole," I whisper. Saying it

aloud makes it more real and causes me to lose my composure once again.

My hands start to tremble uncontrollably and I have to put my glass down before I break it.

"I'm going to be sick." I sprint to the bathroom and lose the contents of my stomach. The horrid taste of bile in my mouth making me want to throw up again.

I hear the faucet on the sink turn on. In the midst of my breakdown, I didn't notice Shayna had come into the bathroom.

"Here, this should help you feel a little better." She pats at my forehead with a wet cloth. Thankfully, it does help some as I had started breaking out in a sweat.

"Thanks." I croak. I know that this stress cannot be good on my baby, so I really need to calm the hell down.

Once I'm confident that I'm not going to be sick again, I lay on the bathroom floor. Typically, this would gross me out as Shay has hairspray stuck to it, but right now I couldn't care less. I welcome the coolness against my skin.

Moments later, once my breathing is back to normal, I grab onto the toilet as I carefully stand.

"You wanna go lay on my bed?" Shay asks. "Brady is playing in the living room and I'll watch him as long as you need."

I wipe my mouth on the back of my hand. "No, I think I'll be alright." I then wipe my sweaty hands on my skirt, which of course does nothing, considering my skirt is still wet.

"Okay, well, at least let me get you some dry clothes." She heads toward her bedroom as I stare at myself in the mirror above the sink. My makeup is completely washed off my tear-streaked face, my eyes red and puffy.

He cheated on me.

I'm still trying to wrap my head around this new bit of information. How could he do this to me after everything we've been through together?

"Here." Shay hands me a pair of yoga pants along with a New Kids on the Block shirt. If I wasn't so devastated right now, I'd probably laugh at her.

Once I'm left alone, I slide down the door and as my ass hits the floor, the emotions take over again. I can't seem to catch my breath and now I've given myself a raging headache from all the crying I've done in the last hour. I'm not sure how it's possible that I still have tears left.

After several moments, I'm finally able to change.

I walk toward Shay's kitchen to fetch a plastic bag for my wet clothes and hear my son babbling in the next room. I manage to form a small smile on my face. My heart aches, but the little guy still needs his mother. Somehow, I'm going to have to figure out how to move forward from this. *Is that even possible?*

When I get to the living room, I lift my son from the floor as Shayna gives me a worried look.

"Shay, I just need to hold him." She nods in understanding and leaves the room to give me some privacy.

Brady is very much a mama's boy. He's the calm to my storm and I wish that I could sit here all night like this with him in my arms. I lean in to kiss the top of his head. The aroma of his lavender shampoo hits my nose, and I immediately become relaxed by the familiar scent. He rests his head on my shoulder as if he knows exactly what I need in this moment.

I look over at the coffee table that holds my phone and

see that it's lighting up. I had shut the ringer off on my way here so I wouldn't have to deal with Trevor. I'm not ready yet.

Not a minute later, I notice it ringing again but quickly send it to voicemail. I know I'll break again when I hear his voice. I don't want to hear his excuses or lies. If I had more of Brady's things with me, I would ask Shay if I could crash on her couch tonight. I'm not sure what awaits me at home.

I lay on the couch and massage my sons back which soon puts him into a deep slumber. I know I need to get home before I also become tired. *Who am I kidding?* I'm exhausted. Mentally and physically.

When I catch myself dozing off, I decide it's time to gather Brady's belongings. I need to stop putting off the inevitable. Maybe he won't be home, so I can avoid him a bit longer.

"Come on, Mama. I'll walk you out to your car," Shay says as she buckles Brady into his seat for me. Mindful not to wake him.

"Babe, I've been trying to call you for the last hour. Where have you been?" Trevor asks as I walk through the front door. *Is he serious right now? Does he have no idea what I just saw?*

I silently begin weeping again but disregard his question as I lift Brady from his car seat and carry him upstairs for bed.

Trevor now runs my father's chiropractic office after he and my mom were killed by a drunk driver two years

6

ago. Actually, our dads had owned it together for years. His dad died the year before my parents, from cancer.

I love my family, but I've always hated their way of thinking. Nobody was ever good enough in my father's eyes. He and my mother always snubbed their noses at people who didn't have high-society professions like them. My husband is no different. I guess that's why he fit into our family so well.

Once I have Brady changed and, in his crib, I head downstairs, hoping to get some laundry done. I'm quiet as I go down the stairs because I'm assuming that Trevor is in our bedroom, but I couldn't be so lucky.

"Claire, what's going on?" That's when I lose it.

I can't speak at first, over the tears. "What's going on?" I choke out. "What the fuck do you think is going on?" I'm seeing red as I lean against the mocha brown wall and sluggishly slide down it because I feel like I may be sick again if I don't sit.

My sweet, loving husband doesn't seem to care that I'm devastated. I can tell he's only probing because he feels he has to.

"I have no idea, but would appreciate it if you'd fill me in. Where have you and Brady been all night?" He's either a complete moron or he's good at playing dumb. I can't decide which. I press my face into my hands, refusing to look at him.

"Shayna's," I clip as I snap my head up in his direction.

"Okay, so why didn't you answer my calls?" He asks hesitantly.

"Because I didn't feel like talking to my cheating husband." I stand and head toward the basement so I can start laundry, but I'm quickly halted when he grabs my arm.

"What the fuck are you talking about?" He seethes, looking guilty *and* pissed. *Sorry, Trev, your secret is out.*

"I'm talking about how I saw you laying on top of Nicole when I brought you dinner!" I scream. I can't keep it together any longer as my knees begin to buckle underneath me.

We're now standing by the basement entrance and as I swing the door open to head down, he grabs me by both shoulders and begins to shake me.

"Claire, I've been so stressed with work and then having to come home to you needing my help. I'm exhausted and just needed to let off some steam." He says this as if it's no big deal. He's still holding on to my shoulders, but the next thing I know I'm stumbling backward and everything goes black.

❦ I ❦

RYKER

THREE YEARS EARLIER

I double-check my coat pocket, making sure the tiny, black, velvet box is still there, as I ride in the back of a London airport bus. It's been six months since I've seen my girlfriend Monica and I am ready to get to her. She has no idea I'm coming, but I've been planning this trip for months to surprise her for our two-year anniversary. I just hope she's in her apartment when I get there. I know she doesn't work today, so my chances are decent.

I've never been here before, so I try to enjoy the sights we pass, but I'm too anxious to pay much attention. Monica is only a few miles from the airport and I probably could have walked but didn't want to chance getting lost. I booked a bed and breakfast that I plan on taking her to tonight after my surprise for her is on her finger.

After what feels like hours but is probably only a few minutes, the bus finally stops at the end of Monica's street. I grab my suitcase from overhead and make my way towards the love of my life.

I was so worried that we wouldn't be able to handle a long-distance relationship, but we've made it work. Don't get me wrong. It fucking sucks that I haven't seen her in so long, but at least we get to talk over FaceTime every night. We're halfway through her internship and then I plan on making her my wife shortly after she gets home. She'll want an extravagant wedding, but I don't want to postpone it longer than we need to.

These apartment buildings look more like old houses. I have to double-check her address since they all look the same. Once I'm sure I have the right building, I open the door and am immediately hit with the strong smell of fresh paint. This place is extremely worn down and it's going to take more than a coat of paint to help it. I head to the flight of stairs directly in front of the entrance and start the lengthy trek up to the fourth floor where my beautiful girlfriend is. It's loud as hell in here with the airplanes flying over the building, causing the stairs to vibrate. I don't know how anyone handles the noise all the time.

I lightly tap on the third door on the right. I stand there for a moment without an answer and can't hear her on the other side of the door, so I knock again. Still no answer.

I try the knob and it's surprisingly unlocked. I'll be sure to tell her to make sure she keeps it locked. She's in an unfamiliar city and, honestly, not in the most pleasant area.

I walk in and still see no sign of her. The apartment is small but has plenty of space for only Monica. It is decorated just as I would expect from her. The walls are a dirty white color, but the couch is decorated with gold and brown throw pillows, giving the space some character. I spot a flowery candle, burning freely, sitting on the coffee table. She must be home because she'd never leave a candle burning.

"Monica?" I call out but don't get an answer.

I head toward what I assume is her bedroom. Maybe she fell asleep and doesn't hear me.

I push the door open and my heart halts in my chest. There lies *my* girl between another man's legs. I need to throw up, but the rage takes over instead.

"What the fuck?" I roar. Monica flies off the bed with a look of shock on her face. I look over at the douche bag and he looks terrified. *Good. That's what you get for screwing my girlfriend.*

"Ryke?" Monica asks innocently. I'm not an idiot. "What are you doing here?"

She doesn't even act regretful as she stands, covering her body with a sheet like I haven't seen her naked figure before.

"I should probably be asking *you* that question." I can't see straight.

Now the douche stands from the bed, ass naked, and starts towards me like he can actually do something to me.

"Who the hell are you?" The douche asks. He's still walking toward me and I decide the best move would be to leave the room so this naked ass guy doesn't try to assault me.

I make my way to the door, but before I can leave, Monica stops me in my tracks.

"Ryke, I can explain!" She sobs. Apparently, she thinks if she cries I'll actually believe the bullshit she's about to spew at me.

I turn around and once again my heart stops.

"You're pregnant?" I croak out.

She hurriedly shields her stomach as if that'll cover the large bump.

"Goodbye, Monica." I don't give her a chance to explain as I slam the door behind me.

I'm currently in a foreign city with nothing but a goddamned broken heart.

2

CLAIRE

I shoot up in bed so fast I nearly fall off the edge. I'm drenched in sweat like any other night. My long, curly hair sticks to the side of my face. Between having to feed Brady and trying to survive these horrible nightmares, I hardly got any sleep. *When will things get better?*

All little girls have dreams about being an adult. I dreamt of marrying my Prince Charming and living in a beautiful white house with a picket fence and a huge yard where all five of our children would run and play. I'd sit on the porch and sip on my morning coffee while enjoying the sounds of their joyful giggles.

Trevor Davis is the furthest thing from Prince Charming.

I flew into Phoenix late last night with my son Brady. We're staying with my brother Evan and his wife Avery. They are seriously a godsend. As soon as we walked through the door, Evan was asking questions. I told him we'd talk about it later because I was worn out and not ready to talk. He doesn't know that I left my husband.

Avery gave me a knowing look as if she could read my mind. She's like the sister I never had.

I look over to my left at the blue and purple plaid playpen my parents used for me and Evan. Little coos come from my son.

"Hey, little man, are you hungry?" I ask Brady. He, of course, says nothing back, but instead kicks his chubby little legs and swings his arms in the air. "I'll take that as a yes." I give his soft cheek a kiss while I lay him on the bed to change his diaper. He is such a sweet baby and has always been extremely laidback. This chubby little boy with dark brown curls and icy blue eyes always knows how to make me smile. He motivates me to keep going every day.

I lay next to Brady on the bed after I mix up his bottle. It's nice that he can hold it on his own now. He fists my long hair in his hand as he sucks away. This is something he's always done since birth. It seems to be a comfort for him. *I love you too, little man.*

This past year was one of the best *and* worst years of my life.

Trevor and I were together for seven years and getting ready to celebrate our third wedding anniversary in a couple months. Everything seemed so perfect until I caught him cheating on me last month. I wanted to leave him right away but confronting him turned into a fight which caused me to trip and fall down the stairs backward. Not only did I break my tailbone, I lost my unborn child. Trevor didn't mean to hurt me, but that night he ruined me. I never told him that I had a miscarriage. I knew that he would try to guilt me into believing that it was my fault.

"Hey, sis, is it okay if I come in?" Evan calls from the other side of the door.

I roll my eyes in frustration, ready to get this conversation over with. I lay Brady back in his bed and then swing the door open to see my brother on the other side.

"You doing alright?" Evan asks me as he gives my cheek a kiss. He's probably four or five inches taller than me, which intimidated all the boys when we were younger.

"Yeah, I'm fine. What's up?" I ask, not wanting to discuss my reason for being here yet.

"You do know we have to talk about this, right?" He asks as he raises his dark eyebrows at me. Brady got his dark, curly hair from my brother and I. Evan usually keeps his short, but right now it's becoming a bit unruly.

"Talk about what?" I ask, trying to act naïve.

"Sis, you know exactly what I'm talking about. You and Brady are welcome here anytime, but what's going on? Where's Trevor?"

"He's in Chicago still. I left him." I try so hard to keep the tears from coming but fail.

"Come here." He wraps his large, muscular arms around me and lets me sob into his chest. He is all I have now, besides my son. "What happened?" He asks gently.

"He had an affair." I sniffle and wipe the tears from my face. "I feel like such a fool." By now, my cries are coming out hysterically and I've lost all control. I'm positive that Avery can hear me from the other side of the house.

"How is that even possible?" He asks, shocked. "He's always working, especially since he took over the practice." He searches my eyes for answers. "I'm going to kill him for doing this to you." He scowls as he clenches his fists.

"Evan, calm down. I'm fine. And it's very much possible when he's sleeping with his assistant." I don't want to talk about this anymore. I don't even know if Trevor has slept with anyone else. But honestly, it doesn't even matter now.

"Look at me, sis." He grabs my chin so I can't look away from him. "You're going to get through this. You and Brady can stay here as long as you need."

"Thanks, Bub." Evan grins at the nickname I gave him as a kid. "I don't want to be a burden, so I'll try to get us out of here as soon as possible."

"Don't be ridiculous. We love you both and we're glad you came, no matter the circumstance." He leans in and gives me another kiss. "I'll take Brady while you get showered."

I couldn't tell my brother that Trevor caused me to lose our baby. It doesn't matter if it was an accident. Evan would hop on the next flight and kill him with his bare hands.

Evan and Avery have a four-bedroom house. The guest bedroom Brady and I are staying in has an attached bathroom, so it allows for some privacy. I step into the scorching hot water and let it relax my body. I don't think a shower has ever felt so good. *How did things get so bad?* I know my body changed from having a baby, but I tried every day to get back to my pre-pregnancy size so I could look good for Trevor. I did the best I could by eating healthy and going to the gym every night. Apparently, I didn't work hard enough. Although, I've lost a bunch of weight over the past month from all the stress. Evan didn't notice because he hadn't seen me in months.

Isn't being a new mother supposed to be an enjoyable time? I was blissfully happy until last month when everything fell apart.

When I get out of the shower, I realize that I forgot to wash my hair.

"Damn it," I mumble to myself.

I guess I'll be wearing my thick hair in a messy bun today. I don't have anyone to impress anyway. I stare at my reflection in the mirror and see that my dark brown eyes look tired. *I am tired.*

When I step back into the bedroom, I put on clean yoga pants and my Illinois State University workout tee. I'm not planning on working out today, but I'm all for comfort.

Once I'm dressed, I go in search for my phone that I haven't looked at since I got off the plane last night. Once I finally find it at the bottom of my purse, I see there are three missed calls from Shayna and eight text messages.

Shayna: You better be dead if you can't even text me to say you made it.

Her final text reads. I shake my head. She's crazy.

Me: Thanks for your concern. I am alive and well. Love you.

I met Shayna several years ago at the daycare we both worked at. She was the reason I stayed there so long. Other than all the times we went out with Trevor's coworkers, I didn't have much of a social life. Even though I hadn't seen her much outside of work, Shay had always been my rock.

She is engaged to her son Koda's father, Dennis. They've been together for five years, but he just proposed last year. They are set to get married this fall.

My stomach rumbles, so I head for the kitchen, but my phone rings in my pocket.

"Hey, bitch, what are you doing?" Shayna asks as soon as I answer.

"Well, hello to you too." I roll my eyes. "I was trying to eat some breakfast before I was so rudely interrupted." I laugh.

"I wouldn't have to bother you if you'd answer your damn phone." I feel bad because I know she's really concerned.

"I'm truly sorry, Shay."

"You're forgiven." She sighs. "How's my baby?"

"I'm good, thanks for asking." I snigger.

"You know I mean sweet little Brady. Is he doing okay? Are you doing okay, mama? I've been worried about you guys since I dropped you off at the airport."

"Yeah, we're both fine. I told Evan this morning I left Trevor and he said it's alright to stay here as long as I need."

"You found out your husband was cheating on you and now you've moved across the country. You deserve time to relax."

"I know, I will. I just don't want to bum off of him, ya know?"

"Well, I'm sure he doesn't think that's what you're doing. He's been begging you to move to Phoenix since your parents passed, so I know he's glad you're there. Even if it is because of the douche canoe." She chuckles. Shayna has always been able to make me laugh in a cruddy situation. I'm not sure how she does it, but I wouldn't have her any other way.

"Thanks, Shay."

"But, seriously, let me know if you need anything at all and I'll be on the next flight out there." I know without a doubt she'd do anything for me or my son. Even though she has her own family to worry about.

"I know you would. But I have to go or I'm going to starve to death. Love you and I'll text you later."

I hit "end" and walk to the kitchen and notice Evan watching me.

"What?" I ask, not meaning to snap like I do.

"Why are you limping?" *Shit, think quick.*

"I, um, fell down the basement stairs while I was working on laundry." *Well, it's the partial truth.*

"You are such a klutz, sis." Evan laughs. *Thank God, he bought my lie.* My tailbone still hurts like hell, but I've got to remember to try to walk straight, at least around Evan.

Avery strolls into the kitchen with a babbling little Brady.

"Look at Aunt Avery's favorite little guy!" I love seeing her and Evan with my son. Unfortunately, they haven't gotten to be a big part of his life since we lived so far apart. I'm glad we now get to make up for lost time. At least there is some good coming out of this nightmare.

"Hey, bud." I take Brady from Avery as I kiss his pudgy little cheeks. "How's Mommy's boy?" He giggles and kicks his feet. He's the number one reason I came to Phoenix. I wanted to start a new life for him where he can be around the people who love him most.

"Hey, Claire, I talked to my mom this morning and she offered to watch Brady tonight if you want to go out with us and some friends." Ugh. The last thing I want to do today is put real clothes on and face a bunch of strangers.

"Thanks, Av, but I honestly want to be lazy today with Brady. I might take him to the zoo later, but I don't want to leave him yet."

"Aww, come on. You deserve a night out and you know Brady will be in good hands. Pa-lease?"

"Okay, okay. Fine." I huff and roll my eyes in annoyance, but how can I say no when they are letting us stay with them?

"Good!" She cheers. Why is she always so damn chipper?

"I don't even have anything to wear. Where are we going?" All I brought in my suitcase was yoga pants and a few pairs of jeans and t-shirts. I couldn't bring all my clothes because I was in a rush to get everything packed before Trevor got home from work. He knew I was coming to stay with my brother but doesn't know I plan to stay long-term.

"Don't worry. We're the same size, so I'll find you something in my closet." *Dear Lord, help me.* She is a lot less conservative than I am. I'm now extremely scared about what she'll possibly pull out for me.

"Okay, but remember I'm a mother and my girls are bigger than yours." I wink at her.

"Eww, your brother and kid are in here!" Evan yells as he sweeps Brady out of my arms. "Us guys will be in the living room watching the sports network, away from this nonsense." We both chuckle at him.

I sneak back into my bedroom while Evan has Brady. I'm already worn out from pretending to be okay. I'm not the outgoing girl I acted like in front of him and Avery. I crawl back into bed. I feel like I'm slowly losing myself.

३ ॐ
CLAIRE

I wake once again breathless. It takes me a second to remember where I am. Phoenix. Evan's house. *Where's my baby?* I look at the clock. 3:00 PM. I fell asleep while Evan entertained Brady.

I gaze at myself in the mirror over the dresser and I look awful. It's clear I haven't been sleeping or eating well. I see puffy bags under my eyes. I have cried enough tears to fill the Nile River and I haven't been sleeping well at night.

I spray myself with my vanilla-scented body spray and reapply some deodorant. I feel like I need another shower, but this will have to do for now.

I open the bedroom door and still hear nothing in my brother's house. I can't remember anyone trying to wake me. I'm suddenly nauseous. *Where is my son?* I'm being overprotective, but Brady needs me. When I walk into the kitchen, I see a note sitting on the table next to an ink pen.

Hey Sis,

We took Brady to the zoo with us and to get some dinner. You looked peaceful, so we didn't want to wake you.

P.S: Avery left some clothes for you on our bed.

Bub

My stomach clenches. Why would they take my child to the zoo after I told them I wanted to take him? I'm livid and it's best I found out like this instead of them telling me face-to-face. They're helping me and offered us a place to stay, but I'm envious. My baby is all I have now. I run to the bathroom and splash cold water on my face.

Once I finally gather myself, I head toward my room to get my phone I left when I went in search of my family. I need to ask Evan when they'll be home. He's also going to get a piece of my mind.

Me: You should have woken me up.

My brother is notorious for not answering his texts, so I decide to unpack more while I wait. I hang a few shirts I brought for myself. I really need to go shopping. When I'm finished, I fold all of Brady's little outfits and put them in the set of drawers Evan moved into our room. It's a lot warmer here than it is in Chicago, so I'll need to get him some things as well.

After fifteen minutes, my phone finally dings in my pocket.

Evan: Sorry, sis, but Brady is fine. We'll be home around six, so be ready.
Me: Fine, but I don't want to go out tonight.
Evan: Come on. You need to meet some new people if you're going to stay here.

Damn him. Why does he always think he can decide what I do? I really don't want to go out, especially after he took Brady from me all day. But he is letting me stay at his house and I really do need to meet people. I hate admitting that he's right.

Me: Fine, but only this time. You owe me.
Evan: We'll see.

I huff and fall back on the queen-sized bed. Avery is an interior designer and doesn't mess around when it comes to their house. The walls in here are a beautiful lilac color and all of the tables and picture frames are ivory. She put a down comforter on the bed, a lighter color purple with ivory flowers. It's like the decorations were made for this room. I wouldn't be surprised.

After wallowing in self-pity, I remember the clothes Avery set out for me. Their room is done in different shades of green with a stunning white comforter. Sitting on the bed, I see a skimpy, leather skirt and a gorgeous sequined, purple tank top. *Why in the world does my sister-in-law want me to show my ass off to a bunch of strangers?* I pass on the skirt but grab the tank and head back to my room to try to look like a human again. I pull on a pair of skinny jeans with the tank top and slip on a pair of wedges from Avery's closet. It's nice having someone to bum clothes off of, especially after only having a brother. I sit on the bed but fly off immediately when an awful pain shoots through my tailbone. Sometimes I forget I'm supposed to be gentle on it. Some days it's fine, while others it hurts just to sit.

I pop a couple pain pills and soon the pain becomes

tolerable. I curl my hair and apply minimal makeup. I'm not going out to impress anyone tonight. I might have a drink or two, but I also want to have a good time and try to get my mind off of everything. Maybe this is just what I need. I won't be telling Evan that, though.

Since I'm not expecting anyone home for a while, I decide to head to the mall to get a few outfits. I don't want to keep borrowing clothes from Avery. Plus, I'm in desperate need of some new bras and panties.

I'm not used to driving in Phoenix traffic. It isn't as bad as Chicago, but all the snow birds are still here, so I'm about to lose my damn mind on the 101. Thankfully, I find the shopping center without any problems.

I stop at Alfredo's for Italian before I head to the Baby Gap to get some clothes for Brady.

It's strange shopping for me, though. Trevor made sure I always wore the best of the best when it came to clothes and jewelry, because what kind of doctor's wife wouldn't have the top-of-the-line of everything? But I'm used to buying everything according to what he wanted, not because I liked them.

He always wanted me to be conservative, yet sexy. *What the hell does that even mean?* But it was important to him that I always looked my best in case we ran into anyone he knew while we were out, which was almost always. Chicago has a lot of chiropractors, but Trevor still manages to keep a decent number of clients. We often saw other doctors from around the area. All the chiropractors in Chicago get together several times a year for different benefits, plus I was forced to spend time with those he considered friends. I always felt way out of place with their snooty wives, who always pretended to be friendly.

Once I'm satisfied with my selections, I head back to the parking lot with my bags. I really wanted to get my hair done while I was out, but I'm exhausted. It seems that the simple task of only running errands has become a huge challenge for me. I just want to go back to Evan's and sleep. I'd love to sleep the rest of the day, but it doesn't look like that will be happening. I know my brother is only trying to help me by keeping me busy, but right now I just want to hide away from the rest of the world.

4

CLAIRE

W hen I get back to Evan's, I'm once again alone, so I decide to lie down and read a bit before I'm forced to face the public again. I love my brother, but he doesn't comprehend how drained I am.

"Hey, Sis." I fly out of bed at the sound of Evan's voice. "Shit. Sorry, I didn't mean to scare you. I didn't expect you to be sleeping again." He eyes me skeptically.

"I dozed off while I was reading." I wipe the drool off my face with the back of my hand.

"It's okay. You needed rest and Brady was good for us."

"Good. I'm glad, but it would have been nice if you told me you were taking my child somewhere. Didn't you know how worried I'd be?" I say as I stretch my arms above my head. I didn't realize how tired I was.

"Claire, I'm sorry, but we were trying to help you. You've been through a lot lately, so we thought you could use a break." *Great. Now I feel like a bitch.*

"You're right, thank you. I'm an overprotective mom. What can I say?" I half smile.

Evan laughs. "Lucy will be here soon, so hurry if you need to get yourself ready." He starts to pull the door shut, but I stop him.

"Wait, Evan," He pushes the door back open and looks at me questioningly. "I think I'm just going to stay in with Brady tonight." I know he's not going to fall for my bullshit, but I really don't want to do anything but sleep. I know I'll have to care for Brady, but once he's in bed, I can join him.

"What the hell, Claire? No, get your ass up. We're leaving soon." Who the hell does he think he is? Now I'm furious.

"No!" He stops in his tracks and slowly turns back toward me. "Evan. I am *not* going out." I know he's going to argue with me, but I'm not letting him win this one. I know I told him I'd go with him and Avery, but I don't think I can handle it right now.

"You're being ridiculous. Get up."

My composure snaps.

"Goddamn it, Evan! I'm fucking staying home." Now I have tears running down my face. I know I'm probably overreacting, but the thought of being around people, makes me want to throw up.

"Sis, what's going on?" Evan walks toward the bed and sits on the edge. "You seemed fine earlier. What happened?"

"Nothing." I really don't want to talk about this with my brother. He could never understand what I've been through. Hell, I'm not sure I understand how I'm feeling right now. One minute I'm fine, but the next all I want to do is cry and sleep. I know I sound dramatic, but I don't think I've ever felt so awful in all my life.

After several minutes, my brother finally leaves me alone.

ONCE EVAN and Avery are gone for the night, I feed Brady one of his frozen toddler meals and then mix up a bottle. I rock him in the living room until he drifts off to sleep. I'm envious of how carefree he is. *To be an innocent child again.*

Tonight, I could tell that Evan was pissed that I wasn't going with them. He was angry with me because Lucy had volunteered to help with Brady and I had refused her offer.

I kiss Brady's cheek as I run my fingers through the dark ringlets on his head. Holding my son, feeling him, seems to lessen my anxiety and makes me feel a bit better.

"WHAT THE HELL, Claire? Brady has been screaming for ten minutes. Are you going to get your ass out of bed?" Evan's voice is muffled as I try to come to. I rub my eyes with the back of my hand and then I hear my son wailing at the top of his lungs. *My head feels like a fucking train hit it.*

I look over and see my brother getting Brady out of his bed, as he shoots daggers at me with his eyes.

"Claire, I don't know what the fuck is going on, but you have got to get your shit together. I know Trevor obviously did a number on you, but you still have your child to care for. You're being a self-centered brat."

Without saying anything else, Evan strolls out of my room with my son in his arms.

I grab my phone off the side table and see that it's 8:00 AM. *Fuck. Brady was probably starving.* But I know that Evan is now taking care of him, so I roll back over in bed and sleep is quick to find me again.

―――――

I WAKE to the sound of clattering coming from nearby. *Who the hell is being so loud?* I sit up in bed and then see Evan emerge from my bathroom.

"What the hell are these?" He asks with rage in his voice.

"Are you going through my things?" I jump out of bed and grab the bottle from his hand. How dare he invade my privacy?

"Why are you taking Codeine? Are you trying to fucking kill yourself?" He yells.

The next moment Avery is standing in the doorway of my room.

"What's going on?" She asks hesitantly. I can tell she doesn't want to get in the middle of whatever is going on between me and Evan. My sister-in-law has always been a great friend to me, but I know she also adores my brother. I can respect that, but right now, I hate him.

"Claire is taking Codeine. That's what's going on." Evan answers his wife without taking his eyes off me. I've never seen my brother like this and, I have to admit, it's kind of terrifying. I know he's only worried but fuck him. I'm an adult and it's time he starts treating me like one.

"Fuck you, Evan." I walk to the bathroom and slam the

door behind me. I probably shouldn't be treating their house like this, but he makes me want to fucking scream. What does he know? He has no idea how I'm feeling right now. It's not like I'm trying to overdose or anything insane like that. Evan didn't bother reading the bottle to see that my damn name was on the label. He doesn't know why I need pain meds and it's not like they aren't prescription. The fact that they help me sleep is an added bonus. I feel ashamed for acting the way I did in front of Avery, but Evan has managed to piss me off in the last day in more ways than I can count.

My HEART SPRINTS in my chest, feeling like it's trying to climb out. I'm pretty sure I was hit in the head with a brick and my right-hand hurts like hell. *Where am I?* I slowly ease my eyes open, but nothing comes into focus right away. I can recognize the outline of a few figures. It looks like there are people standing around me. *Oh. My. God. Am I in the hospital?*

I try to sit up but am halted by restraints attached to both my wrists. *Was I kidnapped?* I feel helpless, as I have no clue where I'm at right now.

"Ms. Davis?" I hear a voice in the distance ask but can't tell where it's coming from. *How do they know my name?*

"Ms. Davis, I'm Dr. Stanton. Do you know where you are?" *Okay, so I wasn't kidnapped.*

When I don't answer, he goes on. "You were brought in by ambulance last night after your brother found you passed out on the floor. You were very close to overdosing from your pain medication." He gives me the look of a disappointed father. *What the fuck did I do?*

"I'm sorry, w-what?" I barely manage to get out. My throat feels like blades are gouging it. I start to cough and, in the next instant, there's a straw in front of my face.

"Here. Have a drink." I take the offered liquid and immediately find relief.

My vision finally comes to focus and I am definitely lying in a hospital bed.

"Claire, I know you just woke up, but we need to discuss what's going to happen next." I must give this man an odd look because he goes on to explain. "Your brother just finished filling out the paperwork for you to be admitted to the Ahwatukee Mental Health extended stay facility." *He has got to be fucking kidding me.*

"What? No. I'm not going to a psych ward." I once again try to sit up but am quickly reminded that I'm strapped to the bed. "Can you please get these things off me?" I ask nodding my head toward my wrist. "I want to go home. I need to see my son." I'm immediately hit with fear. *Where is Brady?*

"Ms. Davis, I'm truly sorry, but we can't allow you to go home at this time. We worry that you are a danger to yourself right now and it's imperative that you're monitored around the clock."

I yank at the restraints and start kicking my legs like a toddler. I'm pretty sure my nine-month-old acts better than this.

My throat feels like it's closing up and my eyes begin to burn with the tears I desperately need to let fall. *How is this my life?*

"I wasn't trying to kill myself, doctor. I broke my tailbone last month and it was bothering me, so I took some Codeine. I have a prescription for it." I know he's not believing a word I'm saying as he stares at the clipboard in front of him. "I swear to you. I'd never do anything like that to myself. My son needs me too much." I'm being completely honest with him.

"I believe you, but you've become extremely ill from taking it. You got very lucky." What he doesn't realize is that I've also lost a significant amount of weight in the last month. Most of my clothes seem to swallow me whole.

I hear the door swing open and in walks Evan, but then I see my husband behind him. I can tell Evan isn't thrilled about seeing Trevor, but then why the hell is he here? I'm seeing red. He has no right to be here in Phoenix. He needs to go back to his whores and stay the hell away from me. He's done enough damage to me to last a lifetime.

"What the hell is he doing here?" I yell but then regret it as I flinch in pain from the ache in my throat.

"Sis, Trevor is going to take Brady back to Chicago with him while you're in Ahwatukee." The look on his face shows how nervous he was about telling me this. *Over my dead body!*

"No fucking way!" I'd grab my throat if I could, but they have me strapped to this damn bed like a freaking prisoner. I'm not a threat to myself, but I'm about to become a threat to them if they don't let me go.

"Claire, Brady isn't safe with you right now." This comes from fucking Trevor. Evan shoots him a look saying *shut the fuck up*, but right now I want to kill them both.

"Isn't safe with me? What the hell do you know about

taking care of our child?" There is no way I'm letting him take my baby away from me. "No, he's staying with me. I'm going back to Evan's and so is Brady."

Everything in the room becomes a haze, as my eyes can't seem to focus on anything. I can't get enough air into my lungs.

The pain only lasts a short moment. I'm suddenly relaxed before everything fades away.

5

RYKER

"Hey, what's up, man?" I haven't talked to Carter in some time, so it's kind of strange that he's calling. We used to hang out a lot, especially growing up, but life got crazy and shit happened.

"Hey, I've got a bunch of people coming over tonight for drinks. You off?" I honestly couldn't tell you the last time me and Carter got together to hang out. But it was nice we could always pick up where we left off. We weren't a couple of pussies that had to hold each other's hands through everything.

"Yeah, I'm off. What time should I come?" I've been so busy lately with my bar, that a night out sounds exactly like what I need.

"Just come whenever. Everyone is coming at seven."

I click "end" to disconnect the call and go to my small kitchen to retrieve a beer from the fridge. I probably shouldn't be drinking yet because God knows that's all we'll do tonight at Carter's. It's a miracle we aren't both alcoholics after all the beers we've consumed over the years.

Being a single father, my dad always let us get away with shit that I'm sure Carter's parents would have been pissed about. It sucked not having my mother around, but he made up for it the best he knew how.

I let my shih tzu Grizzly out and then quickly change into some worn jeans and a form-fitting t-shirt. After I let Griz back inside, I slip my shoes on and head out the door.

CARTER HAS LIVED in this old, worn-down neighborhood on the west side of town, for as long as I can remember. His house is white with chipped paint on the side of it and a roof that should have been replaced years ago.

"Hey!" Carter yells towards me as I enter the house. He's clearly been drinking for a while as he's already making an ass out of himself.

We give each other a bro hug and then he hands me a cold beer from the fridge.

He introduces me to a bunch of people I've never seen before and I see a few I have. Unlike me, Carter never stayed in touch with anyone after high school.

The smell of stale beer and cigarette smoke permeates the air. Even being the owner of a bar, the smell of cigarettes gives me a fucking headache. I tried smoking once in school and choked so bad that I never picked another one up. Carter, on the other hand, either always had one in his mouth or behind his ear.

I vaguely remember my mother, but I do remember

her coming home with alcohol on her breath. I can still see her yellowing, discolored teeth from the rare moments when she smiled, unmistakably the result of always having a cancer stick in her mouth.

I finish the last sip of my Corona and toss the bottle in the garbage can under the kitchen sink. I lean into the fridge to grab another but then feel a hand rubbing my ass. I immediately get a fucking hard-on. *So, sue me.* I'm am a twenty-eight-year-old single man. A single man who hasn't gotten laid in God knows how long.

I stand up straight and when I turn around, I'm greeted by a blonde girl who is possibly an entire foot shorter than me. Her golden locks just barely hit her shoulders, her eyes the color of grass. Not freshly watered grass. No, more like the color it becomes here in Phoenix after a long summer's drought. She's hot. I'll give her that.

"Hey, darlin'." I give her my signature *let's fuck* smile and I can tell that she's thinking the exact thing I am. It seems that we both have one thing on our minds tonight.

She giggles. It's fucking obnoxious, but my raging dick couldn't give two fucks about her laugh. "Hi, I'm Vanessa, but you can call me Van." She giggles again as she runs her long, fire engine red nails down my arm.

"Ryker," I whisper as I lean into her ear. "Want to get out of here?" I'm fucking horny as hell and if this girl turns me down, I'm going to have to find another one, quick. Or I'll be getting myself off in Carter's bathroom with my hand, which has been the norm lately.

"Yes," she says in a breathy voice. I use that as an invitation to grab her hand and lead her through the house. I have no intention of taking her back to my house, but I better figure out where I'm taking her fast, or I'm going to blow a damn load in my pants.

We make it out to Carter's backyard and there are several other people out here, sitting around a fire that is slowly losing its flame.

"Let's go this way," I say as I lead Vanessa to the run-down storage building at the end of the yard.

"You want to fuck me in this old thing?" Vanessa asks as she waves her arm in the air, looking at the outdated structure.

"Yes, is that alright? I don't think I can wait another second to be inside you." At that, she seems to be appeased.

I grab her hair and crash my lips to hers.

The sex is certainly nothing to write home about, but it at least sated my hunger a bit.

❦ 6 ❧

CLAIRE

I'm not sure how long I've been staring at the gray, textured wall in front of me. It feels like hours, but I'm sure it's been less than ten minutes. The strong scent of hand sanitizer makes me want to heave the bland lunch of ham and potatoes the nurse just brought to my room. Okay, so it could have been much worse, but hospital food always tastes repulsive.

Soon after my anxiety attack at the hospital last night, I was discharged and brought to Ahwatukee Mental Health. The doctor and nurses here are slowly losing their patience with me. I've refused to speak to anyone because they won't let me call to check on Brady. I'm sure that if any of these people have children at home, they'd also be livid if they were kept from them for the unforeseeable future. Not only am I being kept from my child, Trevor is the one who is taking care of him right now.

The hospital is observing me while my body is apparently detoxing from the Codeine. I'm sure the way I'm acting is only prolonging my stay here, but right now my biggest concern is my son.

The door swings open and in walks one of the young nurses who I met last night. I think her name is Tasha. She's probably fresh out of nursing school as she looks like she's only twenty. Behind her comes another young girl with shoulder-length, curly, black hair. I can tell she wants to be here as much as I do.

"Claire, this is your roommate, Sierra." *Just great.* "Sierra, your bed is on the left," Tasha says with very little enthusiasm before she turns to leave the room. I'm now alone with this stranger. I'm not even sure what to say to her. I guess I'll continue my silent game with her too.

Sierra lays down on her bed and turns her back toward me, facing the door to our room. I wonder what her story is, but if she's like me, she probably doesn't want to talk about it.

I decide to lay back on mine as well and end up dozing off for a bit. I'm mentally exhausted. The only time I find any kind of relief is when I'm sleeping.

We're both interrupted from our sleep when nurses come in and out of our room. There's no such thing as privacy in this hell hole. Apparently, they're worried that we'll shoot up or try cutting ourselves with our nonexistent weapons. We literally have nothing in this room besides the clothes on our backs. And by clothes, I mean the seafoam green hospital scrubs we were given. All of our toiletries have to stay in the communal bathroom and we can only use them when we're supervised. I seriously feel like a prisoner.

After being bothered several times, I decide I should try talking to my new *roomie*. Who knows how long we'll be stuck in here together? I should probably not make enemies with everyone I come into contact with in this place.

"So, you're Sierra?" I ask feeling stupid because, of course, I already know her name. But I'm not sure what else to say to her to strike up a conversation.

"Yeah," she says as she turns to look at me. "How long have you been here? Please tell me this shit gets better."

"I just got here last night and, so far, it's been pretty sucky. Do they think you're suicidal too?" Once the words come out of my mouth, I feel bad because I have no idea what brought her here. "Sorry, that was really insensitive." I turn toward the small window in our room. A window that is only about a foot wide and doesn't open or close. A window that doesn't have any kind of blinds or curtains on it. It's obvious that the hospital is very cautious about what their patients are around. Besides the two beds, there are only two small desks with chairs that are mounted to the floor. We don't have lamps, only the obnoxious florescent light that buzzes above our heads. This is the closest I've ever been to being in a prison cell.

Sierra chuckles next to me. "Nah, don't apologize. I'm here because my *wonderful* mother-in-law thinks I'm an unfit mother because I have postpartum after having my son last month. What kind of witch pulls a mother from her newborn child?" I look over at her and can see her eyes glossy with unshed tears. I'm all too familiar with her pain, but I can't imagine being taken away from my newborn.

"Oh, my God," I gasp. "I'm so sorry. Couldn't they just put you on an anti-depressant to help you?"

"I've been taking something since Auggie was born,

but it wasn't helping. I think Glenna is only punishing me. She's angry that her son missed out on the birth of his child so I should have to suffer, apparently." My heart breaks for her. Did her husband die?

I'm not sure if I should probe, but I ask anyway. "Why did he have to miss the birth?"

"He got deployed the week before August was born. We had no idea it was going to happen and we don't know where he's at now."

"I'm so sorry. I can't imagine having a newborn all by myself."

She chuckles. "I wish I had gotten to do it all by myself, but Glenna made sure she was there every single second of every single day. I felt like she was smothering me."

"Does she have your baby now?" This poor girl must feel so lost right now.

"Unfortunately, yes. I don't have any family here, so she was my only option. Miles was contacted by the military about me being here, so I'm sure he'll come home as soon as he's allowed. I have no idea how long that could take, though." She runs her fingers through her short hair and then sighs. "So, what's your story?"

I don't respond right away as I really don't want to talk about my issues.

I finally tell her what brought me here. She's the first person I've told how depressed I became after everything happened with Trevor. It's nice to talk to her, even if she's practically a stranger.

EVENTUALLY, Sierra and I are allowed to shower before heading to the cafeteria for yet another meal of tasteless slop.

"So, how did you meet your husband?" I ask Sierra as I scoop a bite of mashed potatoes into my mouth. I haven't stopped worrying about Brady since I got here, but having someone to talk to who can relate helps me feel a tad bit better.

She gives me a small smile. I can tell their love is strong. Jealousy immediately hits me. I had that once, or at least I thought I did.

"We were high school sweethearts. We got married right after graduation before he was deployed for the first time." She stabs at the meat that lies on her plate. I can tell she's just as thrilled about the food here as I am. I should call Evan and make him bring us some real food. It's the least he could do for making me live through this hell.

"That's so sweet." I may be envious of the love her and her husband share, but I'd never wish the agony I've gone through on anyone.

Once we're finished with dinner, we're told that we will be having group counseling next. *Great.*

"Don't be afraid to share your story with your new friends. We're all here because we're struggling with something." *What the hell have I gotten myself into?*

As much as I want to blame Evan for my being here, I really have nobody to blame but myself. I should have left Trevor as soon as I caught him cheating. I knew I was going to, but it was hard for me to function after the accident. Thank God Shayna helped me because my husband was pretty useless. She had her own son to take care of, but she stepped up and did what she could for us. Trevor was hardly ever home, so at least I was left alone most of the time.

7

CLAIRE

"I'm Susan. I've been sober for the last twelve years. Not that long ago, I was sitting in the same chairs you're in now. I know it's hard to imagine, but one day soon you'll be sharing your story with others who are struggling."

This lady is nice enough, but I have to admit she's a bit annoying. She's only about five feet tall and wears her gray-streaked, black hair down to her butt. She honestly kind of looks like a witch, minus the wart.

"Who would like to introduce themselves first?" Of course, no one volunteers. "Okay, how about you?" She says and, as luck would have it, she's pointing right at me.

"Oh, um. I'm Claire." I give a slight wave and then put my head down because I feel weird having everyone staring at me. I feel like I'm being interrogated.

"It's nice to meet you, Claire. What brings you here?" I'm about to lose my fucking mind. It's none of their goddamn business why I'm here.

"I'm sorry. I can't do this." My chair squeals as I push it across the floor when I stand from it.

45

"Claire, you don't need to be embarrassed." I hear her saying this behind me as I dart out of the room. I'm immediately halted when strong, burly arms wrap around me.

"Ms. Davis, you need to go back in there. Everyone is required to participate in group therapy." This comes from a man nearly twice my age. He obviously hits the gym every day. I could only dream of being that fit when I'm fifty.

"I'm not feeling well," I lie, hoping he'll let me go back to my room. When I look up at him, it's obvious that he isn't buying my bullshit.

"Ms. Davis, you won't be allowed to make your phone call today if you don't go back in that room." I'm so fucking tired of being treated like a child, but I guess I better listen so I can call Trevor later to see how Brady is.

I reluctantly turn back toward the large room and, once again, see about twenty sets of eyes looking at me. I never was one who cared for attention from others and right now is no different. I anxiously gnaw on my right thumbnail as I find my seat again next to Sierra.

"Hey, you okay?" Sierra asks as she leans in toward me.

I give her a slight nod.

"The guy over there," she points to a man across from us with long, dark, dirty-looking dreads. "He's here because he nearly killed his wife's boyfriend when he caught her cheating on him. After doing time in prison, he's required to be here as part of his probation."

If Susan cares that we're talking while she is, she doesn't let us know. *Good. I'm tired of being treated like I'm five.*

"The girl at the end of the row with the pink hair...

she's here because of a drug addiction. Her ex-boyfriend is two seats down from her." She chuckles. "Wouldn't that suck? Being stuck here with your ex?" This makes me chuckle.

"Yeah, that would suck."

After a few minutes, the conversation is unfortunately brought back to me.

"Claire, would you like to take your turn now?" Susan eyes me, probably expecting me to dart from my chair again.

"Sure." I nod. "I'm Claire. I'm here because I almost accidentally overdosed from my painkillers. I fell down my basement stairs last month and broke my tailbone." Suddenly, the ties on my hospital pants are fascinating.

"Thank you for sharing that with us." She clears her throat and then goes on. "Now that everyone has had a turn to introduce themselves, we'll call it a night. Tomorrow night, we will discuss different coping strategies that you'll be able to use once you're home and don't have the support of the hospital staff."

We all shuffle from the large room and head back toward our rooms. It's only seven PM, but nothing is expected of us after our meetings. *Thank God.*

SIERRA HAS BEEN GONE from our room for the past twenty minutes on her phone call. I was told that as soon as she returns, I'll be able to make mine. I really don't want to talk to Trevor, but I need to hear my son. Even if it is only baby babble. I just need to be reassured that he is alright.

"You can go now," Sierra says as she comes back into

the room, looking rather upset. I should make sure she's alright before I leave, but I'm anxious to make my phone call.

"Ms. Davis, you have fifteen minutes." An older gentleman with ghost white hair hands me a cordless phone and then sits in a chair in the corner of the room. I'm basically in an interrogation room and, needless to say, getting no privacy.

"Thank you." I nod as I dial Trevor's number.

The call automatically goes to voicemail. "Hi, you've reached the voice mail of Doctor Trevor Davis. I'm unable…" I click "end" and lay the phone on the table.

Damn it.

I run my hands through my hair, forgetting that it's in a messy bun on top of my head. I'm sure it now looks ridiculous, but I can't bring myself to care. I'm not in a psych ward to impress anyone.

I pick the phone back up from the table and once again try dialing Trevor. *God damn it!* Evan told him that I'd be calling him, so why the hell isn't he answering his fucking phone?

After trying a third time, with still no response, I hand the security guard the phone and head back toward mine and Sierra's room.

Sierra is sound asleep. I can't say I really blame her though. There is nothing for us to do here. I'm bored out of my fucking mind. If people aren't crazy already when they get here, I guarantee they will be by the time they leave.

I'm busy counting the white tiles on the ceiling when I hear a knock on the door. I don't want to wake Sierra, so I get up and answer the door.

"Ms. Davis, you have a visitor." *Who the hell would be visiting me? If it's Evan, I'm going to kill him.*

"A visitor?" I ask, most likely with shock etched on my face.

"Yes, your husband is here."

"TREVOR, what the hell are you doing here?" I hiss at him as I take the seat across the table from him.

"Now, is that any way to talk to your husband who came to visit you in the psychiatric ward?" He chuckles. It pisses me off that he even knows I'm in here.

"What do you want?" I ask with a venomous tone.

"I just wanted to check on my wife." Who the hell does he think he is? After everything he put me through, he doesn't get to call me *that* anymore.

"Where's Brady?" I had no idea that he was still in Phoenix. I figured they took the first flight back to Chicago last night.

"He's with your brother. He and Avery wanted to spend time with him before we leave for Chicago in the morning." I'm about to lose my fucking mind.

"Just leave him here." I don't know why I'm trying to tell him what to do. He's not going to listen. He doesn't care what I want.

"What kind of father would I be if I left him when his mother is mentally ill?" He sneers.

"Trevor, I am *not* mentally ill and you fucking know that." I hiss. "I got addicted to Codeine after I fell down the fucking stairs while you were arguing with me. Did you forget about that?" Now, I'm practically laying across

49

the small table, as close to his face as I can get without touching him. I know there's a security guard watching me from across the room, so I have to be careful.

"Claire, you are so dramatic," he states nonchalantly. I want to punch him in the fucking throat.

I've had enough of his bullshit for one night, so I start to stand from the chair.

"I have to get back, but please answer your phone tomorrow night when I call."

Without letting him say another word, I walk toward the door and nod at the guard on my way out, letting him know I'm leaving.

Why the hell did my brother agree to watch Brady, so my stupid ass husband could come see me? He doesn't love me and I'm not sure if he ever actually did. How was I blind for so long?

8

CLAIRE

It's been exactly sixty-two days since I came to Ahwatukee Mental Health, but today I "graduated" from the program I've been in since I got here.

Soon after I was admitted, I found out that I only had to be here thirty days. After that, it was up to me if I wanted to stay or not. After the first month of being here, I was already making huge strides but decided to keep going so I didn't relapse as soon as I left.

My depression became less and less every day and if you asked others, they'd probably tell you that I actually became somewhat pleasant to be around. *Somewhat.*

Sierra just left two days ago. I was thrilled for her, as she hadn't seen her baby since she got here. Speaking of babies. I've missed my son more than I can express. Evan agreed to fly to Chicago to get Brady for me, so he could be here once I get discharged.

"Hey, babe!" Avery yells as she runs around her car to give me a hug. She's definitely parked in the fire lane, but I've never been happier to see her.

"Hey, Av. Thanks for coming to get me." I squeeze her tight before throwing my bag in the backseat. I only have the few items I came with.

"Of course. Evan and Brady's flight gets in at seven. Want to grab some dinner while we wait?" she asks as she pulls onto the 101. It's so nice to see the sun again. Occasionally, I would go outside and sit on the back porch of the hospital, but we weren't allowed to leave the premises. I willingly stayed as long as I did, but it still sucked not being able to leave for the past two months.

"Sure, but I really want to shower and put some *real* clothes on," I say as I stare down at the pajama pants that I wore when I was taken by ambulance to the hospital. It's hard to believe that everything went down just two months ago.

AVERY and I walk into Martin's, one of her and Evan's favorite diners. It smells delicious in here with the scent of warm cinnamon wafting through the air. They are famous for their homemade cinnamon and pecan rolls.

"Screw dinner. I'm eating a huge ass cinnamon roll."

I chuckle at her, but I really can't disagree. "That sounds amazing. I want the same." I stick the menu back behind the salt and pepper shakers. We place our orders for two *huge ass* cinnamon rolls and two cups of coffee. I'll probably be wound for sound tonight, but at least it'll help me stay awake to see my son. *God, I've missed him.*

It's hard to believe that he's now eleven months old. In just one month, we'll be celebrating his first birthday. It makes me sad to think about how much I've missed since we've been separated, but I plan on making up for lost time as soon as he gets back to me. I have no idea how Trevor has done with him, but I do know that he temporarily enrolled him back in the daycare I worked at with Shayna. That made me feel a lot better, knowing that she'd be with him most of the day during the week. I only talked to Shay a few times over the last couple months, as I wanted to talk to Brady every night. We were only allowed one phone call a day.

We visit for the next hour until it's time to pick Evan and Brady up from the airport. Evan hates flying, so I can only imagine how he did with a toddler in tow.

I SPOT my son as soon as he and my brother enter the airport. I waste no time running toward them.

"Whoa, sis!" Evan laughs.

"Hi, baby!" I reach for my son, but he lays his head on Evan's shoulder, unsure of what to do. My heart cracks a little in my chest. *Did he forget about me while he was gone?*

"Brady, it's me, Mommy," I coo at him, hoping he'll realize who I am. He slowly lifts his head up and takes me in for a minute, right before he starts to cry.

Evan rubs his back and whispers reassuring words in his ear. In the meantime, my heart feels like it's going to explode. *How could I have left my son for so long?*

"Claire, he's been through a lot lately. Just give him time." *Yeah, easy for him to say.*

I numbly walk beside Evan and Brady toward the luggage claim. Avery retrieves their bags and then we head toward the parking lot for the lengthy hike back to Avery's car.

I slide into the backseat by Brady and grab his hand as I scoot next to him in the middle seat.

"Hi, baby," I whisper at him. He finally gives me a small smile as he grabs onto my thumb with two of his fingers. "I've missed you, sweet boy."

"Mama!" Brady yells after several minutes into our drive. My face immediately breaks out with probably the biggest smile I've ever managed to give. With all the hell I've faced over the past few months, that's saying a lot.

"That's right. I'm your mama." I lean down to his level and kiss him on his little button nose.

He's changed quite a bit since the last time I saw him, but only because he's gotten bigger. Without having access to my phone, I wasn't able to receive any pictures of him from Trevor. Thanks to Shay, though, I had one picture of him that she snapped at daycare about a month after he got to Chicago. I slept with it under my pillow, counting down the days until I got to see him again.

IT'S BEEN three weeks since I've been back to Evan's. A couple days after being discharged, I started seeing my new therapist, Desiree. At first, I was a bit reluctant to talk to her, but honestly, it's been nice to talk to someone new. I got a lot of help in Ahwatukee, but there I felt like I was just another patient. With Desiree, I get her undivided attention. She doesn't judge me for how I handled everything with Trevor. Actually, soon after I started seeing her, I found out that she went through a bout of depression after her divorce a few years back. She decided to go into counseling after all the help she was given.

"Hey, how are you doing today, Claire?" Desiree asks as we walk back toward her office. When I started coming here, I noticed how warm and welcoming this place is. It doesn't look like any other doctor's office I've ever been in before. The walls are mostly covered by bricks, but the small parts that peek through are painted a dark purple. In the middle of the waiting room sits a fireplace. I never understood why anyone needed to have such a thing in Arizona, but it does make the building look even more inviting.

"I'm actually doing pretty good," I say as I take a seat across from her. The small room is cluttered with picture frames of her family, the walls covered with all of her certificates. She's in her forties and, before working here, worked as an interior designer. I know she would get along great with Avery.

"Are you still taking your medication?" When I nod, she goes on. "I think you're doing great in your recovery. I know this has all been difficult on you, but in just the few weeks we've been meeting, I've noticed a huge improvement."

Hearing her say this makes me feel good because I really have worked hard at taking care of myself. Desiree has helped me realize that it's okay to take time away from everything. Yes, Brady is still my first priority, but I also have to take care of myself. Evan and Avery have really stepped up to help with him. Even if I only run down to the coffee shop, it helps to keep my head clear.

"Thanks. I feel a lot better. I seem to have a lot more energy and find that I'm enjoying things a lot more now."

"I am so glad to hear that." Desiree smiles.

We continue to talk for the rest of my session and then we plan to meet again the next week. She tells me that after our next appointment, I'll only need to come bi-weekly. I know that it's a good sign, but my visits with her have become like a security blanket to me. I just hope I'm ready.

After my appointment, I decide to stop at The Espresso Bean for an iced caramel coffee. As I'm standing in line, I hear someone calling my name.

"Claire!" I turn around and am greeted by the bright smile on Sierra's face. A smile I didn't get to see much while in Ahwatukee. Honestly, neither one of us smiled a lot while we were there.

"Sierra!" I say, matching her enthusiasm. "How are you? You're looking great." I look her up and down, noticing that she has more color in her face and she's lost a bit of weight, just since I saw her a few weeks ago.

"Thanks. My doctor recommended I join a gym to take out my stress. It seems to help and it gets me away from Auggie for a bit. I love being a mom, but it's exhausting. Well, duh, you know that." She smiles as she leans in to hug me. "How's everything going for you? How's your little guy?"

I order my coffee and then join her in a booth at the back of the shop.

"He's really good. Getting so big. His birthday is actually next week." I pull out my phone. "Here he is," I say as I show her the screensaver. "He's got a tooth coming in, so he's been super fussy lately, but other than that, he's at a really fun age." I put my phone back in my purse. "How's Auggie?"

She smiles. "He's really good. Still getting up several times a night. I loved nursing, but I have to admit, now that I'm not, it's so much less stressful." She blows on her steaming coffee.

"Girl, I completely understand." I had nursed Brady for several months and it got to be overwhelming at times. "All that matters is that he's getting fed. You're doing a great job." I slurp at the rest of my drink.

"Thanks, that means a lot. Hey, Glenna is taking Auggie to meet one of her friends on Friday night. Want to hang out? I went to Ryke's Bar with some girlfriends awhile back and I loved the live music they had there. I have to admit the owner there is pretty hot too." She winks.

"You're such a hussy," I joke. I've never heard someone talk about their husband the way she talks about Miles. I hope that he's able to come home soon to finally meet their son.

She laughs. "I may be married, but I'm not blind." She sets her mug on the table and then works on the blueberry muffin in front of her. "So, what do you think? Want to go out?"

"I'd actually love to. Evan and Avery already kicked me out of the house that night. They informed me that I need to get a life." I chuckle.

"Well, then let's go find you a life," Sierra jokes.

9

CLAIRE

I stand in front of the full-length mirror in the bathroom looking at myself. I twist from side to side to make sure I look good from all angles. Since I got back to Evan's, I've started gaining back some of the weight I had lost. I wasn't heavy before, by any means, but I'm glad I'm not skin and bones anymore. I had barely recognized myself when I looked at my reflection.

Brady and I went shopping with Avery this afternoon in downtown Phoenix. She has Fridays off, which is nice, so we can spend alone time together. I love my brother, but he can be a real pain in my ass at times. Ever since I was hospitalized, our relationship has been a bit awkward. Don't get me wrong. I know he was right for admitting me to Ahwatukee, but since then, I feel like he looks at me like I'm brittle. Like I might crack at any moment. No matter how much I've improved, he still treats me like I might go off the deep end if he says the wrong thing to me. I'm so sick and tired of him tiptoeing around me.

Tonight, I'm wearing a new knee-length, rusty orange skirt with a black, low-cut tank-top. It's hot as hell outside. I'm also wearing a light coat of makeup, but I'm not sure why I even bothered when I know it'll most likely melt off my face as the night goes on.

I'm looking forward to seeing Sierra again, but I'm a little hesitant because we're going to a bar and I'm not supposed to drink. Alcohol mixed with my antidepressant would be bad news. Plus, Desiree said it would be best that I didn't while I'm still recovering. I'd hate to be set back because of one night of fun.

"Here's your mama!" Avery says as she brings Brady into our room. I look at him in the mirror as I put my gold stud earrings in my ears and see that he's been crying.

"What's the matter, baby?" I ask as I take him from Avery. "I didn't hear him crying."

"He was playing and hit his head on the coffee table." I then notice the small bruise that's starting to develop on his forehead. At my attention, his bottom lip starts to quiver.

"Aww, baby, I'm so sorry," I say as I kiss his ouchie. Brady's words for it, not mine.

Over the last couple weeks, he's been talking a lot more and it makes me so proud to see how much he's learning.

I slide my black wedged sandals on and take Brady into the living room so I can rock him before I leave. I feel bad that Evan and Avery are always helping me out, but most of the time, they insist that I go and do something for myself.

Before everything happened, my brother thought I

was a selfish bitch, but now it seems like he can't get me out of the house fast enough. Don't get me wrong. I spend most of my time with Brady now that I'm back.

I still haven't found a job yet, but not for a lack of trying. I've applied at several daycares in the area and even a few office jobs. My brother assured me that it's fine if I don't work right now, but I feel completely useless. I want to be able to help them with things around their house. At least for mine and Brady's food. I thankfully have most of my parent's inheritance left, which I hadn't needed to dip into until now. Even with that, Evan refuses to let me use it. He tells me that I should keep the only money I have to my name. Thank God, I had it in a separate account from mine and Trevor's, so he didn't have access to it.

"Hey, girl," Sierra says as she hugs me the moment I climb out of Avery's car. It's so nice seeing her so carefree. She's still the girl I met a few months ago, but she's different in the sense that she's much happier. I guess we both are.

"Hey, you look adorable," I say as I grab her shoulder to spin her around so I can take in her outfit. She's wearing a turquoise skirt paired with a yellow shirt and a white jean jacket that goes over it. She's obviously from the desert because there's no way in hell this midwestern girl would be wearing something like that in this weather.

"Thanks. I never get to dress cute anymore, so I decided to take advantage of our night out." She links her arm with mine as she leads me toward the bar. Like I mentioned before, I love seeing this side of her. She has quickly become another one of my best friends and I'm grateful that I've had her.

THE DOOR CREAKS SHUT behind us as we enter Ryke's. I have to admit that I'm surprised at how nice it looks inside. The outside of the building looks pretty worn down, but most of the work has been visibly invested in the interior. Every inch of every wall is covered with old record covers. I wonder if the bands on them are favorites of the owner. But with a name like Ryke, I find it hard to believe that the guy is old enough to know who half these groups are.

It's clearly an old building, but there is a lot of pride and care put into its appearance. Each table that sits on the floor is made of black painted wood. Above each hangs a light that appears to be made from old car parts. There's definitely a unique vibe in here.

Surprisingly, the smell is different than any other bar I've been to. I'm not hit with the strong, stale scent of cigarette smoke or the overbearing scent of alcohol. No, instead it smells more like the smoke from a pipe. The sweet, warm aroma engulfs me, making me want to relax instead of giving me the anxiety I've found lately in most social situations.

Being Friday night, all of the tables are taken, so we find two empty stools at the bar.

A young guy who appears to only be in his early twenties greets us. When we tell him we only want water, we receive an odd look from him. We both giggle as he walks away from us and we turn toward the small stage in the center of the open room.

The guitarist starts to sing. It's a song I recognize but couldn't tell you what it is. I'm guessing this guy isn't much older than twenty-one. Or maybe it's just the way he carries himself or the unruly hair that falls to his shoulders. You can tell he really doesn't care about his appearance, if his torn jeans and week-old scruff on his face are any indications.

His first song comes to an end and then he starts playing Uncle Kracker's *Follow Me.* It doesn't seem like that would be a song you'd hear in a bar, but it seems like anything goes here. The atmosphere is inviting, mostly because it's very laidback.

Mr. Shaggy finishes playing and steps off stage as an older guy around my age shakes his hand and gives him a half-hug. You know, the type that guys always give each other?

Unlike the guy before, this one has my breath escaping from my lungs. He has dark, unruly hair that makes me want to run my fingers through it. Usually, I'm not a huge fan of facial hair, but his is very well kept. *What the hell, Claire?* I clearly haven't gotten any in a long time if I'm letting this complete stranger affect me from only the sight of him.

His outfit consists of faded, form-fitting jeans and a button-down red, plaid shirt. A white t-shirt peaks out of the top.

He takes a seat behind the mic as he slips his guitar over his head. *God, this guy is sexy.*

"Hey, guys," he starts and I feel like my panties are going to explode underneath my skirt. I'm not much for sex toys, but tonight it would probably be good to have one because I'm acting like a freaking horny teenager right now.

"Have you enjoyed all the music tonight?" The crowd hoots and hollers. Once everyone finally settles down, he continues. "I'm glad." He smirks. "I don't usually play, but I've had a few requests tonight, so what the hell, right?"

"That's Ryke, the owner," Sierra whisper yells as she leans into me. "Isn't he hot?"

I don't answer but instead continue to look straight ahead, waiting for him to play.

The crowd goes wild again, but when he strums the guitar, all that's heard is him. At least, for me.

His voice is incredible. Manly, but smooth as silk at the same time.

Again, not a song I expected to hear, but I've always been a fan of the band. Hearing it takes me back to junior high when all I had to worry about was if Johnny Filmore liked me or what color I wanted my braces to be for the month. Maybe that's why I've always liked music like this. Because it reminds me of a simpler time.

He finishes the song and then all of time seems to stand still. At first, I'm sure that he's staring at someone behind me, but then I realize that he is looking right at *me.* Suddenly, it feels like I'm in this building alone with this stranger. *Very sexy stranger.* The bar isn't big, by any means, so we're only about twenty feet from where he's playing. He grins at me and then starts to play again. Nobody else seems to be affected by him like I am. Sierra doesn't even realize the moment we just had. *You have lost your damn mind!*

I really should go outside for some fresh air. I start to stand from my seat, but I'm quickly frozen in place when I hear the lyrics of *Brown Eyed Girl*. Chills run down my spine as he sings.

A ridiculous part of me wants to believe that he's singing this about me, but there's no way he can even see what color my eyes are. Yes, we're not far from each other, but it's still dark in here.

I haven't even consumed any alcohol tonight, but I seem to be drunk. I *really* need to get out of here.

"Hey, you okay?" Sierra asks as I stand up. "You're not leaving, are you?"

Now I feel bad because this is supposed to be a fun night out for her as well and I'm trying to bail on her.

"No, I just really need to pee." I head toward the bathroom and when I enter, I splash cold water on my face.

I don't know what's come over me, but I've never let any man, besides Trevor, affect me like this. I'm not sure I like it. The last time I opened myself up to someone, he ruined me.

Claire, all he did was look at you and sing a song about your eyes. He did NOT propose!

Once I'm done giving myself a pep talk, I decide to head back out to visit with Sierra. I wonder if she has any idea what that Ryke guy just did to me. Of course, she doesn't because he didn't do anything besides play a couple songs while sounding sexy as sin.

"Woah, sorry." This comes from a rough, masculine voice that is accompanied by a strong hand on my arm.

I look up at the mysterious person to see the most

gorgeous set of ocean blue eyes I've ever seen. I'm not even exaggerating. His eyes alone could be my undoing.

"S-sorry. I wasn't watching where I was going." *Oh, my God!* I sound like such a fangirl. As if I were at a Keith Urban concert, not at some dive bar.

I seriously want to run back to the bathroom and hide in one of the stalls for the rest of the night.

10

RYKER

She's fucking adorable.

I caught sight of her and her friend as soon as they walked through the door tonight. The other girl was nice enough to look at, but this one? She's absolutely stunning. I know I sound like a complete pussy, but fuck, I don't even care.

"It's no problem." I smile down at her. I would say she's average height for a woman, but still a good six inches shorter than me. "You're not from around here, are you?"

She gives me a questioning look. "Sorry." I run my hand through my too long hair. "It's just that I've seen your friend in here before but not you."

She gives me a half smile. One that tells me she's still embarrassed about running into me.

"Yeah, I'm new to Phoenix." She leaves it at that and then starts to walk away from me.

"Can I get you a drink?" I call out to her retreating back. *What the fuck am I doing?* Vanessa is going to be here any minute and here I am, offering a drink to another woman. *A woman.* Unlike Vanessa, she seems to be in her later twenties, not fresh out of high school. Not that she looks old by any means, but I can tell that she's more mature than my girlfriend.

No, Vanessa isn't really just out of school. She's totally legal. But she's experienced a lot less of life than I have. She has no idea what it's like to struggle, as she's obviously been handed everything to her from her daddy.

"No, thank you. I was just heading out."

I don't even catch her name before she vanishes from the hallway I'm still standing in. Now, by myself. I completely forgot why I even came down here in the first place. This mystery woman has been distracting me since I first laid eyes on her an hour ago.

"I DIDN'T GET to hear you play," Vanessa pouts as she sticks her bottom lip out like a fucking toddler. Seriously, what adult woman does that? Vanessa, that's who.

"It's okay. I'm sure I'll play again soon." I take a swig of my beer and then catch myself looking around the bar unconsciously.

"Who are you looking for?" Vanessa asks as she rubs my arm seductively.

We've been together for the last three months. I can't even say we've been dating because that would mean we've actually spent time outside the sheets together.

Tonight is one of those rare nights that she decided to come see me at the bar. Her friend Bianca is tagging along with her because, as I've been told, women *always* travel in pairs. Her friend is almost as annoying as she is. *Almost.*

67

"Nobody," I finally answer her when I realize I haven't responded. She stares at me like she knows I'm lying, but then lets it go.

"What time are you off?" she asks as she sits on my lap. I fucking hate it when she does this shit while I'm working. I'm all for PDA, but she irritates the hell out of me. *But if the mystery girl was sitting on my lap...*

I have got to stop thinking about her.

"Not until eleven." I'm short with her, hoping she'll stop talking.

Here's the thing. Years ago, I promised myself that I'd never get into another serious relationship, not after finding my girlfriend in bed with another guy. Don't get me wrong. I've slept with plenty of women, but it has never gone further than a few rolls in the hay.

Until Vanessa. I mean, yes, most of our relationship, if that's what you want to call it, has revolved around sex. But until her, I hadn't spent more than a few nights with one woman.

I guess I felt like she was safe, though, because I would never see myself spending the rest of my life with someone like her. She's not the settling down type. At least, not for a long time. I know that I can be a huge ass to her at times, but I guess that's my way of keeping her at arm's length.

I mean, I'm not a complete asshole. I don't yell at her or anything like that. But I think I've done a pretty damn good job at letting her know not to expect anything long-term with me.

IT'S NEARING 10:00 and I'm beat after working my ass off behind the bar. Vanessa finally went out to the makeshift dance floor with Bianca, so I feel like I can actually breathe. A part of me thinks that I should just end things with her now, but she knows that I don't want anything serious with her, or anyone.

I look out to the floor and see her dancing with some douche who appears to be in his forties. It's fucking disgusting, but, honestly, it doesn't really phase me. I should probably care, but if she goes home with him, I'll be off the hook. She knows that I won't fuck her again if she's with anyone else, so I guess that would be my easy way out. Cut me some slack. I have *some* standards. I'm not willing to catch some disease. I value my manhood way too much for that shit.

"Hey, baby." I hear Vanessa on the other side of the bar as I'm drying a clean glass. I finish what I'm doing and then turn toward her.

"What's up, Van?" She leans over the counter, her tits practically in my face, and bats her fake eyelashes at me.

"I'm *really* horny, Ryke," she whines at me. *Jesus, this woman is ridiculous.* And she doesn't give a fuck that people nearby are staring at her.

I look around and see that everyone is now minding their own business and then lean toward her so I'm nose-to-nose with her.

"Van, this is my fucking workplace. You cannot say that kind of shit to me while I'm here. Got it?" I snap and then step back from her, shaking my head.

"But, Rykey." *What the fuck? Is she five?* "Are you embarrassed by me?" She pouts, trying to look cute. Instead, she looks fucking ridiculous.

I see that I don't have any customers wanting drinks right now so I walk around to stand closer to her. She takes this as an invitation and rubs my arm with her long, fake nails, the other hand working its way toward my dick. I won't lie and say that it's not a turn on, but I've had e-fucking-nough of this girl's bullshit.

I look down at her and sneer. "Vanessa, stop." When I straighten myself back out, that's when I see her. *Mystery girl. Brown-eyed-girl. I thought she left an hour ago.*

I stare at her for a brief second as we make eye contact and I realize that she's giving me a dirty look. *What the hell did I do?*

She turns on her heels as fast as she can, as if her ass is on fire. *What the hell?*

I'm just standing here with my girlfriend. Minding my own damn business. *Is she jealous?*

"Hey, man." I turn at the sound of Austin's voice. "Why don't you take off with your girl?" He chuckles, knowing damn well I do not want to go home with Vanessa tonight. "I can close up shop if you want."

"No, it's okay. You stayed late last night." By now, I'm shooting daggers at him. *If looks could kill.*

"No, really. I insist." *Asshole.*

"Yay!" Vanessa starts jumping up and down like a fucking two-year-old, flapping her arms. "Now, I can have my way with you." She stands on her toes to give me a kiss and then runs off toward Bianca. Because, of course, she can't go anywhere without her bestie.

"I hate you," I say to Austin as I walk back behind the bar. "I seriously fucking hate you right now." The asshole has the balls to laugh even though I want nothing more than to put my fist through his goddamned face.

"You can thank me tomorrow after Vanessa *has her way with you.*"

Why do I keep this guy around?

Austin has worked for me since I opened two and a half years ago. He really is a great guy, when he isn't pushing me off on annoying women.

He does all the hiring when we need extra help and we trade off on who closes each night. I guess you could call him my assistant. Right now, I *really* want to kill my damn assistant.

"Fuck you, man." I grin at him. He's right. At least, I'll be getting fucked. Although, for some reason, I'm really not in the mood for it tonight.

"Hey, you alright?" Sierra asks as she catches up to me and grabs my arm. "You looked super pissed back there." She eyes me suspiciously, waiting for me to answer.

"Yeah, I'm fine. Just needed some fresh air," I lie.

"Ya know, Claire, we haven't known each other but a few months, but I can totally tell when you're *not* fine." She stands with her hands on both her hips, challenging me to argue with her.

"Ugh! Okay. That bar guy was totally giving me the creeps. *Happy?*" I huff, completely full of shit. I'm so pissed at myself for thinking there was some kind of chemistry between me and that stranger. *Why the hell would I think such a thing?*

"What? Ryke? Claire, he may be a player, but I promise you he's no snake." When I don't say anything, she continues to pry. "Ohmigawd!" she yells loudly, not caring that everyone else out here is now staring at us. She doesn't typically seem the type to like attention, but right now, she doesn't seem bothered by it. "You've totally got the hots for him, don't you?" she screeches.

"Seriously, Sierra? Are you thirteen?" I laugh at her. "But to answer your question, no. I do *not* have the hots for him. I'm still married anyway." I start to walk toward the parking lot but then feel her cold hand on my arm again. How is she cold? I'm over here sweating like a whore in church.

"Claire, I know you're still married to that asswipe, but you deserve to be happy too. Hopefully, your divorce will go through quickly and then you won't have to deal with him anymore." What she doesn't realize is that I haven't even filed for divorce yet. That would require me to go back to Chicago and, frankly, I have no desire to see Trevor right now. *Or ever.* "Why don't you come stay with me tonight? Glenna has Auggie until the morning. Your brother is watching Brady, right?" I have to say I'm extremely surprised that she'd agree to leave her baby again so soon, but she deserves the break.

"Yeah, okay." I nod at her. "I need to run to Evan's to get some things though."

I program Sierra's address into my phone and then we part ways. I could certainly use a night away. Brady will be asleep the whole time I'm gone anyway and I know my brother won't care.

"Claire, Brady will be just fine. Go." Avery says as she practically shoves me out the front door. *Well, geez.* It's super strange having all this freedom since leaving Chicago. I never had help like this when I was with

Trevor, other than when my mother-in-law Lynn would help with Brady.

"Knock. Knock." I say as I open Sierra's front door. I can't believe she left it unlocked. Not that she lives in a super shady area or anything, but any yahoo off the street could walk into her house if they wanted to.

"In here!" She hollers from the other room. I slip my flip-flops off onto the rug and make my way toward her voice. Her house isn't big, but I'm guessing she and Miles pay an arm and a leg for it. That's Phoenix for you.

When I step into the living room, I see all of Auggie's things scattered around. His animal print swing, along with a matching bouncy seat. Brady lived in his when he was that age. In the corner of the room sits an oak changing table that holds a set of drawers underneath it.

She is unquestionably not a neat freak, as there are dirty dishes laying around on the coffee table and empty soda cans on the floor next to the couch. I remember how stressful being a new mother was, but I know Trevor wouldn't have put up with me not keeping up on our house. *He's such an ass.*

"Hey," I say as I join her on the couch. "Whatcha watching?" I ask, pointing to the small TV in front of us. I have to be honest… this looks more like a bachelor pad than a family home. But in a strange way, it's very alluring.

"Just catching up on the last *Walking Dead* episode." When I raise my eyebrows at her, giving her a look that says *really?* she goes on. "What? Miles got me hooked on it before he left. It's the shit." She reaches for her can of Mountain Dew that sits on the table in front of her. I love this carefree side of her. She reminds me a lot of myself.

Like a hormonal, pregnant woman, I start to tear up at the thought of how thankful I am to have her.

"I've never seen it," I say as I reach over and steal some of the popcorn out of the bowl on her lap. "Really? Skinny Pop?" I snigger at her.

"I'll have you know that Skinny Pop is the bomb, thank you very much. Plus, it won't go to my ass like that buttery shit would."

I shake my head at her and then turn toward the TV, knowing that if I keep watching this garbage I'm guaranteed to have nightmares. Why is this entertaining?

"So," she starts when the show goes to commercial. "What the hell happened with you and Ryke tonight that had your panties in a bunch?" This girl reminds me so much of Avery *and* Shay. *God, I miss my best friend.*

"Nothing happened." I pop more of the skinny goodness into my mouth, trying to avoid her question. She, of course, doesn't let me off the hook that easily.

"Spill it, mama." She says as she pulls the bowl out of my reach. "If you want my Skinny Pop, you have to give me answers first." She squints her eyes at me, trying to give me a dirty look which just makes me laugh.

"You're nuts. You know that?" I shake my head at her before leaning over her lap to get the bowl out of her hand. In the next second, the bowl goes flying out of both our hands, sending popcorn into the air.

"Damn you. This stuff is like gold, Claire." She's now on her hands and knees like a damn dog, trying to pick up all the kernels off the floor. *I* will *not* be eating that now.

"Why don't you just vacuum it up?" After asking, I know that was obviously the wrong thing to ask as she throws the offending snack at my head.

"And waste a perfectly good bowl of popcorn? No way." She continues on the floor. "But don't think you get out of my question, missy. What the hell happened tonight?"

I inwardly groan. "Nothing really happened tonight besides the fact that I ran into him like a fucking loser when I came out of the bathroom." I'm sure my face is ten shades of red right now, thinking about how embarrassed I was. I just saw possibly *the* hottest living male and had to act like a buffoon in front of him.

"Did you talk to him? He seems like a great guy. Always has a different chick on his arm when I see him, but can you really blame the guy? I mean, you saw him."

The guy is for sure a man whore. I know I really shouldn't judge him since I don't even know him. But he practically undressed me with his eyes while he was on stage tonight and then again outside the bathroom. Then he was all over that skanky looking bitch not long after that. The blonde bimbo appeared to be not a day older than eighteen. I'm guessing he wouldn't bring an underage girl into his bar, but she looked way younger than him.

"No, not really. I mean he offered to get me a drink, but I turned him down."

The show is now back on, so I try to pretend that I'm actually interested in it now.

"Nuh uh, girl." She clicks the TV off with the remote and turns toward me on the couch. "Why the hell did you turn him down?" I'm not looking at her, but I know that she's looking at me like I've lost my damn mind.

"I can't drink, remember?"

"One drink wouldn't kill you and you know it." She

stands to take the bowl into the small kitchen off the living room. The only thing that separates us is a tiny half wall, decorated with picture frames. I recognize her in many of them from when she was younger. I also spot one of her and Miles on their wedding day. She wears an ivory strapless dress with a train that goes on for days. She looks absolutely exquisite.

"Sierra, I'm not even going to entertain that idea. Once again, I'm *still* married and I do *not* need to get mixed up with someone like him.

"Whatever!" She hollers from the kitchen, slamming cabinet doors.

"What are you doing in there?" I ask as I stand to join her.

We're interrupted by the ring of her phone, coming from the coffee table.

"I'll grab that for you." I walk back to the living room and as soon as I see it, Miles' name comes into view. I rush to the kitchen so she can answer it before it goes to voicemail. I know she doesn't get to talk to him often.

"Here." I practically throw it at her. She gives me a questioning look until she realizes who's on the other line.

"Hey, baby," she answers and I suddenly feel like I'm intruding.

I quickly write out a note to let her know I'm going out to grab food. I suddenly have a huge craving for chocolate eclairs. I have no idea where the hell I'm going to find them this late at night, but I'm on a mission.

I slide my shoes on and quietly pull the door shut behind me, not wanting to interrupt Sierra's conversation.

12

RYKER

I'm exhausted and really just want to have a damn beer and then fucking sleep, but Vanessa seems to have different plans as she fondles my dick through my jeans.

"Van, I'm really tired tonight. Can I give you a raincheck?" I know I'm being a total douche right now, but I really can't get in the mood to fuck her. Why couldn't she have gone home with the old man she met tonight?

"Come on baby, *please?*" she begs, which has my dick shriveling up even more.

Before I can answer her, my phone pings in my pocket. *Why the fuck is she texting me?*

"Who is it?" Vanessa asks, leaning over my arm to see who it is. She's so damn nosey.

"Monica," I grumble. I don't even care if she's jealous because maybe that'll make her leave. I've only talked about her a few times to Van. She knows Monica is the reason I don't do serious relationships anymore.

"Let me call her." She grabs for my phone, but I'm quicker than her, raising it in the air out of reach.

"No," I snap.

"But, Ryke, I'm your girlfriend now and she needs to know that." Oh, my God. This girl is relentless.

"Van, if you do that she'll just keep bothering me. Just leave it alone." I stand to put my phone in the kitchen, out of Vanessa's sight. I feel like a fucking teenager, hiding something from my parents. Or a parent who's trying to keep their child away from something forbidden. That's more like it. Vanessa acts like a damn kid.

Before I leave my phone, I punch in my password, curious to know what the hell the bitch wanted.

Monica: Phil left me. Can we talk?

Ugh. Every goddamn time something goes amiss with her and the asshole, she comes running to me. Why the hell does she think I care?

I walk to the fridge to get a Corona and toss the cap into the garbage. My phone chimes on the counter after I had completely forgotten to shut it off.

"What?" I bark an answer.

"Ryke? It's me." Like I don't fucking know who she is.

"What do you want, Monica?" There's malice in my tone, but I want to make it damn clear that I don't want to talk to her. Now or ever.

She hiccups. "Phil left me and Kayla." She sniffs and I don't feel one drop of sympathy for her. She's a bitch and deserves all the bullshit that's thrown her way.

"And why are you calling me?" I spit. "When you decided to hop in bed with the asshole, you became his problem, not mine." I run my hands through my hair, realizing I'm in desperate need of a damn shower. I reek of smoke every night when I come home from the bar, so a shower is a must before I even consider sleep.

"You don't mean that." She sobs and I am so close to grabbing a steak knife out of the drawer behind me, wanting to stab my eyes out with it. She makes me that fucking nuts.

"Yes, I do, Monica. Now, leave me the hell alone. I've had enough of your bullshit for one lifetime." I disconnect the call and this time make sure I shut the damn thing off.

Is there a fucking full moon tonight? Because all these psychotic women are driving me up a damn wall.

"Was that Monica?" Vanessa asks as she comes into the kitchen, nearly giving me a heart attack at the young age of twenty-eight. She's always sneaky as shit. You'd think I'd be used to it by now, but no.

"Yeah." I don't feel like I should have to explain myself to her. I didn't do anything wrong. She's exasperating.

"I'm your girlfriend. Did you forget that, Ryker Allen?" *Here we go again.*

"No, Van, I did not forget." I walk toward her and wrap my arms around her waist and inhale the strong citrus scent of her shampoo. I instantly sneeze. God, why does she use that godawful stuff?

"Are you getting sick, baby?" She asks completely oblivious to the fact that I'm allergic to her hair.

"I'm fine." I kiss her on the nose, trying to stay on her good side. Who am I kidding? She doesn't have a good side. Well, unless you count the sex part, but really, I could do without it. "You don't need to be jealous." I kiss along her neck, trying to get myself turned on, but doing a shit job.

I still can't get my mind off that gorgeous, brown-eyed, mystery girl.

Holy shit.

Just the thought alone gives me a fucking hard-on. I've never in my life let a complete stranger affect me like she has.

Vanessa's long fingernails trail up and down my jean-covered dick.

Our clothes start soaring through the air in the middle of the kitchen and, not wanting to take her to my bed tonight, I lift her onto the counter. She shrieks when her bare ass hits the cool granite.

Just as I'm about to push inside of her, my stomach becomes queasy. I have no idea what the hell has gotten into me, but this is the second time tonight I haven't been able to follow through on fucking her. God, if any of my friends got wind of this, they'd take away my damn man card.

"I'm sorry, Van. I can't do this tonight." I start gathering my clothes off the floor, but when I stand back up, I feel the sting of her goddamn hand on my cheek. *Fuck, that's gonna bruise.*

"What the hell was that for?" I yell.

"That's for getting me horny as hell tonight, several times, and then backing down. I know you're older than me, but damn. I didn't think you'd start losing your sex drive for a few more years."

This girl is fucking insane. Does she honestly believe that men in their thirties don't have sex? I have absolutely no response to her stupidity.

When she sees the dumbstruck look on my face, she continues on with her bitchiness.

"It's alright. I'll call Rick. I'm sure he'll put out for me." She finishes buttoning up her shirt and then quickly puts her tight ass pants back on. She honestly looks like a cheap hooker.

"Okay, well, then I guess this is it." I didn't realize I'd get off the hook this easy. "Ya know, because I told you we had to be exclusive for this to work."

"Well, if your fucking old man dick would stop shriveling up every time we try to fuck, this wouldn't even be a problem." *Old man dick? Bitch.*

"Vanessa, get the hell out of my house." I walk toward my bedroom, letting Griz out to roam the house freely now that she's leaving.

"Ohmigawd! Get him away from me!" Vanessa shrills when Griz starts sniffing her leg like he wants to piss on it. She hates my dog and I guess, in a way, I was trying to piss her off even more. It's working.

"Vanessa, this is his house, not yours. Get out."

"Ugh!" She throws her arms up in the air. "Fine. We're through!" She says this as if I hadn't already told her I was finished with her. But if she wants to think it was her idea, so be it.

The front door crashes behind her while she's in the middle of her outburst. I know I'm being a dick, but I couldn't care less about what just happened with Vanessa. She'll go find someone else's dick to get off on, and she'll move on just fine.

"Come on, Griz. Let's go to bed." I lead him into my room, where his kennel sits at the end of my bed.

He growls at me like the little shit he is, but then quickly falls asleep.

Me, on the other hand, not so much. I can't get a certain brunette out of my mind and it's making me fucking irrational.

After lying awake for God knows how long in my smoke infused clothes, I decide to get up.

I don't know where I'm going, but I need to get out of this house to free my damn mind.

❧ 13 ❧
CLAIRE

I t's blazing hot out tonight, but I roll the windows down. The summer's breeze hitting me in the face, instantly relaxing me. As miserable as it's been with this weather, I'd take this over Chicago's winters any day.

Sierra lives just a couple blocks from Ryke's Bar, so I have to drive by to get to any grocery store. The speed limit is only thirty-five here, unlike other areas where it's forty-five. As I'm passing Ryke's, I see a figure out of the corner of my eye. It's dark, so, at first, it's hard to realize that it's a person. "What the hell?" I slow down just in case the moron decides to run out in front of me. This person is visibly inebriated. I just want to get out of here.

I'm almost at a standstill now, trying to make sure they're alright. I know better than to approach a stranger in a big city, much less a drunk stranger. But I really hate to leave them out here if they need assistance.

I'm trying to focus on the road in front of me, but then I hear a loud grunt through the window, coming from the offender.

"Ow, shit."

I quickly pull Avery's car over and, without shutting it off, run to where the stranger is. *Oh my god. It's him.* What kind of sick joke is this? Where's his girlfriend? Shouldn't she be here making sure he doesn't do something completely idiotic?

"Um, are you okay?" I ask, poking at him as if he's a dead animal on the side of the road. He groans again. "Do you need a ride home?" *What the hell am I thinking?* Sierra says he's a nice guy, but for all I know, he could be a serial killer. What if he gets in the car with me, but then ends up slicing my body into tiny little pieces? *You have lost your fucking mind, Claire.*

He's finally able to sit, so I reach my hand out toward him to assist him in standing. Although, it's not like I can actually lift this bulky man off the ground. He's got to be a good two hundred and twenty-five pounds. Not because he's overweight, but because he's got muscles of steel that cover his perfect form. Obviously, he takes care of himself, even if he's acting like a negligent prick right now.

"I can stand on my own," he huffs as he slowly finds his way off the ground. But right as he's trying to find his balance, he hurls all over the ground in front of him. Thankfully, missing my open-toed shoes. I have to look away before, I too, lose my dinner. I've never been able to stomach others throw up, but coming from this big, burly man, it's even more repulsive. Most likely from the atrocious smell of whiskey mixed with it.

"Alright, buddy. Get that out of your system before you get in the car with me." I start walking toward Avery's car again, but then I hear his voice.

"Thanks for your help," he grumbles. He's obviously not a very pleasant drunk. He was totally different earlier tonight when I embarrassed the hell out of myself by running into his stupid ironclad frame. Now, he gets to be the chump. Although, I'm not sure he'll really care how he acted tonight when he wakes up in the morning. Well, he'll care, with the hang-over from hell he's going to have, but I'm sure he doesn't become easily humiliated like I do. He appears to be a real cocky son-of-a-bitch.

"Yeah, no problem. Just finish that shit up before you get in. My sister-in-law will murder me if you spew in her car."

I sit in the driver's seat, checking Facebook, and, after several minutes, I hear a tap on the window.

I click the doors unlocked and Ryke climbs in. He looks worse for wear, but at least he's done losing his insides.

He gives me his address, but as soon as I program it into my phone, I hear whistling coming from his nose. Yes, his nose is fucking whistling like a damn tugboat.

Thank God, the drive isn't long because this guy has me wanting to pull my damn hair out. Tonight, at his bar, he had me feeling things I hadn't in a long time. For a stranger, nonetheless. But he went and quickly ruined that by hanging all over Bambi and now this shit.

"Ryke, we're here." I elbow him in the side, trying to wake him, but he isn't budging. I rest my hand on his arm just to make sure he's still alive.

"Just great." I slam my head down on the steering wheel which sends the horn wailing.

"Jesus Christ!" my drunk companion yells. I'm pretty

sure I just woke his entire neighborhood, but at least I got his reckless ass up.

"You're home," I say as I unlock the doors for him. The sooner I get this guy out of the car, the faster I can find my damn eclairs. My stomach grumbles at the thought.

He tries to stand from the car but staggers to the ground, catching his elbow on the cactus that sits beside his driveway. Oops, perhaps I shouldn't have pulled over so far.

"Fuck!" he hollers, bringing his elderly neighbor out to her front porch.

"Ryker Allen, what the hell are you doing out here so late, causing a ruckus?" The old lady flails her cane in the air and I have to admit, even I'm a bit terrified of her.

I go around to Ryke's side of the car and address the woman. "Ma'am, I'm so sorry. I'll make sure he doesn't disturb anyone else tonight."

I grab him by the arm, now coated in blood and try to yank him to his feet. Not surprisingly, he doesn't budge from his position on the ground. What the hell am I going to do with this guy? I guess I could just leave him here and hope I don't accidentally run over him on my way back down the driveway. *Fuck.*

"Ryker Allen, you get your ass off the ground right now!" I resort to using my mom voice, treating him like a child. He's acting like a fucking child right now and I really don't want to deal with this shit tonight. Why the hell didn't I just leave his ass back at the bar? Let him be someone else's problem? Who fucking knows, but I need to get back to Sierra's. I'm sure I've missed several calls from her while dealing with this dip shit.

"Damn woman," he grumbles as he finally stands to his

feet. "Who are you?" He squints his eyes at me, obviously not remembering me from just hours ago. *Why does that bother me?* It shouldn't bother me because this guy is a complete good-for-nothing moron.

"I'm your savior," I say without emotion in my voice. "Go inside before you act like even more of an idiot in front of your neighbors tonight."

I head back to the car once I think I'm finally off the hook. But, of course, I couldn't get so lucky.

Ryke makes it all the way to the porch but is now retching into the rose bush next to him.

Thank God, I'm far enough away from him this time, so I can't smell that godawful shit. My stomach can only tolerate so much in one night.

We finally make our way into his small house and he stumbles through the hallway, toward what I assume is his bedroom.

I collapse onto the couch, but then I hear him retching. Again. I don't think I can deal with this guy anymore tonight.

"Are you alright?" I ask, standing in the doorway of the bathroom, not wanting to get too close to his nasty ass.

"No," he moans as he lays his head on the toilet seat. The thought makes me cringe, but from experience, I know the coolness feels good when you feel like you've been hit by a train.

I hesitantly walk toward him. "Let's get you to bed."

He thankfully doesn't argue and stands from the floor and leads me in the direction of his bedroom.

"Y-you wanna fuck, brown-eyed girl?" This guy has lost his damn mind.

"Uh, no, sorry. You are definitely not my type."

I search through his dresser for some clean clothes for him and then pull the door shut behind me so he can change.

MY PHONE PINGS from somewhere in the distance, but I can't find it when I move my hand in the direction of the sound. After several moments, my vision finally comes to focus and it takes me a minute to remember where I'm at.

Fuck.

I had plans of going back to Sierra's once I got Ryke settled, but he couldn't stop puking and I really didn't feel right about leaving him. Not that I should care.

The thought of his bed makes my blood boil. *Why the hell do I care who he's had in his bed?* Well, I know exactly who it was. Malibu Barbie. I'm not jealous or anything, I swear.

I finally find my iPhone which had fallen between two of the couch cushions after I fell asleep.

Sierra: Babe, where are you? I'm really starting to worry about you.

I close out of the text to check the time. Two in the morning. *Shit.*

Me: I am so sorry. Something came up and I had to go home.

I decide to lie so I don't have to hear about this from

her later. I know she won't respond now because, surely, she's sleeping, but at least she'll see it when she wakes up.

I set my alarm to get up in a few hours, knowing Ryke will most likely sleep until noon. I really don't want to be here when he wakes.

❧ 14 ❧

RYKER

Beep. Beep. Beep.

I extend my hand out and hunt for my phone but then hear it clatter to the floor, hitting something on its way down.

"Ugh." My fucking head feels like someone flung a ton of bricks at it and my throat is as dry as the Sonoran Desert. *What the fuck did I do last night?*

While I'm still trying to work up the energy to pull myself out of bed, my annoying dog bounces on top of my back, nipping at the side of my face like I'm a damn chew toy.

"Damn it, Griz," I slur, hardly able to form the words on my tongue.

I start dozing off again, not wanting to be a human today, but the fucker is now humping my goddamn leg, apparently as sex deprived as I am. I can't really fault the furball.

"Fine. I'm up. Happy?" I look at him, waiting for a

response, and then remember that he's a damn dog. God, I feel like shit.

I walk to the bathroom and splash some cold water on my face before hooking Griz to his leash.

I have no idea what time it is, but I know he's not going to leave me alone until he's done his business.

As I'm walking toward the living room, I'm immediately assaulted with flashbacks from the night before. *Mystery girl.* She stayed all night? In my house? Not in my bed?

Holy shit. I need to get laid before this seductive stranger has me doing something I'm going to regret. Although, she probably thinks I'm an even bigger ass after the way I acted last night. How did she find me? And how do I know she's not deranged? I mean, this complete stranger stayed in my house with me while I was as drunk as they come. A sexy stranger, but still a stranger. I don't even know her damn name. *Mystery girl.*

Like the lunatic I am, I lift the pillow up from the couch and inhale her warm, sugared scent. God, the aroma is mouthwatering. I'd love nothing more than to drag my tongue down her neck, breathing in her syrupy fragrance. Okay, so I'd like to lick more than her neck, but I'm trying to be a gentleman. I'm never washing this thing again. *What the hell is wrong with me?* I'm being borderline stalkerish right now.

I LIVE near Greenwood Park which has a lake and walking trail. I try to take Griz here at least a couple times a week.

This morning, it's pleasant even before the sun is all the way up, the light, cool breeze causing my unruly hair to waft in the wind. The weather is one of the reasons I never left Phoenix. I'm too much of a pansy for frigid temperatures. It's peaceful being the only walker out this morning. Some mornings, I come out here and kids dash in front of us, trying to pet Griz, and I have to pretend to be thrilled about it.

Ahead, I see a woman running. Her dark hair is pulled back into a messy knot on the back of her head, her body gorgeous and curvy. All she wears are tight spandex shorts and a purple sports bra. *Hot damn.* I can't make out her face, but I'm sure it's stunning too. She gets closer and I see who she is. *Mystery girl. My brown-eyed stranger.*

"Hi," I say as she gets closer to me and my dog.

"Oh, hey, Ryker…" she says with hesitation in her voice.

"I don't think we've formally met," I say giving her an arrogant smirk.

She busies herself with fixing her messy updo, noticeably at unease.

"Yeah, I guess not." She wipes her sweaty palms on her pants, most likely doing nothing because her entire body seems to be covered in perspiration. *Holy shit.* My pants are growing excruciatingly stiff at just the idea of her wet body.

"Ryker Allen." I extend my free hand out to her, trying to divert my mind from the erotic images I'm now having of this beautiful goddess.

She surprisingly takes my hand in her small one and shakes it.

"Claire Davis." I suddenly feel like I owe this woman my life after she saved it.

"Uh, thanks for taking me home last night," I say as I look down at my dog, now sniffing some other dogs shit. *Fucking awesome*. I'm hit with shame at the thought of her seeing me plastered. "Sorry, if I acted like a douche." I tug on Griz's leash, trying to pull him away from the shit lying in the grass before he tries to eat it, which will then make me throw up *again* in front of this woman.

She waves me off. "No need to thank me, but you really should be more sensible. You could have really hurt yourself."

"Yes, ma'am." I salute her like a fucking prick. God, she probably thinks I'm the biggest asshole to ever walk the planet. "But, really, I appreciate your help. It had been a rough night and I suppose it could have been much worse had you not rescued me from my alcohol-induced stupidity."

"Trouble in paradise?" she bites. Wow, this gorgeous woman is more of a spitfire than I realized. She starts jogging in place as if she's planning on darting away from me any minute.

"I'm sorry, what?" I have no idea what she's talking about.

She saw you with Vanessa last night, dumb ass.

"Oh, you mean Vanessa?" I ask even though she has no idea who Vanessa is.

"Is that Malibu Barbie's name?"

I nearly choke out a laugh. "I'm sorry, what?" I'm now holding my stomach, hunched over in laughter.

"Oh, sorry, I meant Skanky Barbie. Or how 'bout Brainless Barbie?" *This girl is on a roll.*

Once I finally compose myself, I'm able to look at her without laughing.

"Yes, that would be Vanessa and I wouldn't really say there's trouble in paradise, but, yes, we broke up last night." She probably thinks I'm utterly callous for not even caring, but I feel nothing but a reprieve after getting rid of that bitch.

"I'm sorry to hear that," she says, but I'm mindful that she's undeniably *not* sorry.

"Don't apologize. She was just helping me keep my bed warm." I waggle my eyebrows at her.

"You're a pig. You know that?" She starts back toward the lake in a full-on sprint. She has an hour-glass physique and it's giving me exceedingly tactless thoughts.

"Wait!" I holler toward her retreating back. "I was only joking," I lie. For some reason though, I want this woman's approval.

She slowly comes to a stop, not turning toward me right away.

"I'm sorry, that wasn't funny. Honestly, we weren't serious and I decided to end things with her last night." I know I sound like an ass, but I'm really not disappointed.

"Why did you sing that song last night?" she asks, still staring out at the opaque, sapphire-colored water.

"What song?" I only played two songs and I know exactly what she's referring to, but I want to hear her say it.

She doesn't answer me but turns so I can see her chocolate eyes, their warmth wrapping around me like a blanket on a chilly night. I am such a fucking pussy.

"Those were just a couple of my favorites. I play them

every time we have live music." I'm so full of shit and I know she isn't buying my BS.

"Right." She slowly bobs her head, the knot on top gradually coming undone and causing loose hairs to drape around her heart-shaped face. She looks fucking adorable. She reminds me of Pebbles from *The Flintstones.* "Are you sure? Because you gawked at me the entire time you sang *Brown-eye Girl.*"

"I did not *gawk.*" She's making me sound like a prowler. *You did just sniff the pillow she slept with.*

"You *so* gawked." Now she's laughing that youthful, carefree, giggle. Once again, I'm becoming agonizingly tight down below.

I chuckle. "Okay, so what if I did sing that for you? What would you say?"

I hold my breath, having no idea what to expect from her. She probably thinks I'm a fucking whack job.

"You don't even know me," she whispers, driving my dick almost all the way through my damn shorts.

"You're right. I don't. But you caught my eye as soon as you walked into my bar. I can't really explain it."

She gives me a half smile, telling me she's not sure how to respond to my admission.

"Well, it was nice meeting you, Ryker, but I need to get home. Enjoy the rest of your walk." Before she strolls off, she bends down to stroke my dog on the head. And now I'm envious of the little fucker.

"Would you like to go for coffee over at the Espresso Bean?" I ask once she's already nearing the lake.

"Uh, I don't think that's a good idea," she says before continuing away from me. "Let me just make this clear, Ryker Allen, I'm not interested in your cocky-ass flirting.

It does *not* turn me on like I'm sure it does all your play-things." *Ouch.*

"Who said I was flirting? I just want a damn coffee."

"Right. Well, no, thank you." Without another word, Claire slowly descends from my sight, abandoning me and my raging hard-on.

❧ 15 ❧

CLAIRE

"I am fucking exhausted," Sierra says, blowing a fallen hair out of her face. She has sweet little Auggie strapped to her chest.

"Is he sleeping better for you?" I ask as I push Brady in the stroller, thankful he's sleeping after the epic tantrum he just threw as we were walking into the mall.

"Ugh, not really. And I get to hear all about how much I'm failing as a mother. My wonderful mother-in-law." She pauses. "Stupid bitch," she mumbles under her breath which has me chuckling.

"Just ignore her. She obviously has nothing better to do than bully you when she isn't having tea with the other country club bitches."

She starts shaking so hard in laughter that I'm concerned she's going to wake poor Auggie, but he just keeps snoozing away.

Since I met Sierra, I've learned that her mother-in-law is rather the socialite. I'm sure she'd keel over dead from

98

shock if she saw that we're both in yoga pants and flip flops right now. In a way, she reminds me of my own parents, but I never had to live up to standards like that, thank God. Although, Trevor would have preferred me to be more of a conformist but screw him. In all the years I was with him, not one of those people I met through him, ever became one of my friends. I don't care to be a part of that counterfeit bullshit.

We continue our stroll through the crowded stores, not finding a single thing we're looking for. I've been trying to find a bathing suit to wear in Evan's pool, but everything I've tried on has made me feel like a freaking bloated cow.

"Claire, you look gorgeous girl. Just pick a damn suit," Sierra whines, apparently over my indecisiveness. "Here, go try this one." She holds up a yellow and black floral-patterned two-piece. Typically, I'd tell her "hell, no", but this one is actually giving me some hope.

After trying the suit on, I head back to the rack to grab two more in the same style, one fuchsia and the other teal. If nothing else, I'll have another one for next summer.

"So, um," Sierra starts as we're heading out of the department store I found my suit in.

"What's wrong?" I ask hesitatingly.

"What do you think about moving in with me and Auggie? I mean until Miles comes home." Woah. That was definitely not what I was expecting her to ask. But hell, she's brilliant.

"Really?" I'm suddenly elated, as I've been dying to get out of Evan's house. They've been so helpful since we came to Phoenix, but I feel like I'm always in their way.

"Yeah. I mean, why not? You don't want to live with your brother and I'm lonely as hell in the house by myself."

"Okay, but we're going to clean that shit up before I start moving in." I tease her, but really, I refuse to live there if there's garbage overtaking the whole damn place.

"Yes, Cinderella." She bats her long lashes at me and then rolls her eyes. I don't know what I'd do without this girl. "When do you think you'd want to move in?" She asks as she stops at a shop filled with knick-knacks that I refuse to push the stroller through, knowing I'll most likely break something.

"Well, I don't exactly have a job yet, but I can dip into my inheritance to help with rent and groceries and whatever else we need."

She swats her hand at me in annoyance.

"Girl, I'm not worried about that shit at all. I always buy enough food to feed a small army anyway and we have to pay the rent, with or without you there." She has me tearing up now. Stupid woman hormones.

"You're the best, but I promise I'll pay you back as soon as I find a job. I wish one of those damn places would call me back."

"They will. Don't worry."

We head toward the food court so she can feed a now wailing Auggie.

When she got discharged from Ahwatukee, she decided to go back to school. She and Miles married right out of high school, so they both had to work full-time jobs, leaving no time for classes or homework.

"When do you want to move in?" She asks again as she

lifts Auggie over her shoulder. The kid wastes no time in giving his mama a good burp.

"Is Saturday too soon?" Brady sits beside me in the stroller, slapping my leg because, apparently, I'm not giving him his puffs quick enough. "Chill out, dude." I lean in and kiss his nose.

"Hell, no! I can't wait!" Poor Auggie startles in her arms because of his loud mother.

———

"So, are you going to tell me where the hell you went the other night when you didn't come back?" Sierra asks as she backs out of the parking lot, careful not to hit the car next to us.

"I told you I had to get home."

"You're full of shit and you know it." She gives me a pointed look as she drives out of the insanely busy parking lot.

"Yeah," I huff. "I wanted to stop at the store to get some snacks, but when I passed Ryke's, the dumb ass was outside, stumbling around like a flipping idiot."

"What?" She laughs. "He walked out of his own bar trashed?" She shakes her head amused.

"Yep." I pop the "p".

"Okay… so, what does this have to do with you?" She gazes at me out of the corner of her eye.

"I may have taken him home," I mumble, hoping she'll drop the topic.

"I knew it!" she shrieks, causing Brady to bellow from the backseat.

"Yay!" my son shouts as he slaps his chubby little hands together. "Mama!"

Sierra and I both laugh.

"You *totally* want to screw his brains out," she states straightforwardly.

I stare at her with my mouth agape, in total disbelief.

"I so hit the nail on the head." *Damn her.*

16

RYKER

It's Wednesday night, so this place is slow as hell. I think I've helped two customers in the three hours that I've been here. I should probably tell Austin to go home, but I'm using him as a distraction from a certain brunette.

"It's hump day, dude. Why the fuck isn't anyone out drinking tonight? Isn't that what everybody does before they get laid?" The logic in this guy's head often has me flabbergasted.

I chuckle. "Man, you're fucking insane." I grab a beer from under the counter, popping the tab off then taking a long ass swig. I don't normally drink while I'm working, but right now, I desperately need something to divert my attention.

"You never drink when you're here. What crawled up your asshole?" He seriously can't say anything without sounding like a crude fucker.

"Fuck you." I throw the bottle cap at his head and laugh at the red mark it leaves behind.

"Damn it!" he yells which causes us to get stares from the few customers we have, sitting in a corner booth.

"That's what you get."

The bell over the door chimes, alerting us to the crowd of college-aged girls who wander in.

I won't lie and say that a few of them aren't eye-catching, but they remind me way too much of Vanessa. Never will I deal with a chick like her again.

"Hot bitch at twelve o'clock," Austin says as he holds the neck of his beer bottle, tipping his head back to take a long pull from it.

"Why does Amanda put up with your stupid ass?" I shake my head at him.

"Whatever. At least I'm getting some." He slaps me on the back.

"Hey, sugar. Can I get a Guiness?" A young girl, probably just twenty-one, with a southern drawl asks. She has dishwater blonde hair and she's wearing a skintight, leather skirt. I'm pretty sure if I looked close enough, I'd see her ass cheeks. Definitely not from around here. I have a feeling this girl has never had beer before, much less a Guiness. I think it tastes like shit, so I can't imagine her being fond of it.

Along with an iced mug, I grab a bottle for her and pour her drink.

I feel like a total ass, but I stare at her as she takes her first pull and immediately spits it out onto the counter.

"You don't like?" I snigger at her and she shoots daggers at me with her cobalt eyes.

"That tastes like," she pauses as she spits some more and I hand her a glass of water. "Fucking hell." She gags and then grabs her nose. She obviously inhaled the offending beverage. I'm trying so hard not to laugh at this girl, but she's making a complete fool out of herself. I know she came up here by herself just to flirt with me and show off. The showing off part is biting her on her nearly bare ass.

"Would you like a different kind? That one's on the house." I have no doubt in my mind that she's going to turn me down, but I'm not done giving her hell for her reaction to the first glass.

"Uh, no," she says as she wipes her bright cherry-stained lips on the small napkin I gave her. "I'll stick with water, thanks." Her cheeks now the same color as her mouth, I feel kind of bad for giving her shit, but that's what happens when you try to act like a jezebel.

"Lyla, what the hell are you doing?" I turn at the demanding voice, immediately recognizing the black-haired girl as Claire's friend. My insides turn and I suddenly feel like there may be hope for me to see her again. I know she wants nothing to do with me, but I haven't been able to stop thinking about her since I saw her the other day.

"Just getting a drink." She leans into the other girl. "I think he might want to take me home." She winks and then turns back toward me. Does she really think I didn't just hear her? *Oh, my fucking God*. Why do I always attract broads like this?

"Lyla," Blackie hisses. "He does *not* want to take you home. He's trying to work, not get hit on by a floozy like you." She couldn't have said it better.

"That's not true, is it, sugar?" What am I, her fucking grandson?

I cough into my hand. "Uh, yeah, sorry. I'm just working." I turn away from them, pretending to look busy, hoping *sugar* will leave me the hell alone.

I'm in the middle of drying out a glass when I hear Blackie behind me. I don't mind talking to her because she's my only hope to getting to my brown-eyed girl again. *What the hell, Allen? She is NOT your girl.*

"Sorry about her. She's a bit straightforward with no filter whatsoever." She shakes her head in disgust.

"You think?" I chuckle. "Where's your friend?" Why bother beating around the bush?

"Who? Oh, you mean Claire?" I have a feeling she knew exactly who I was referring too. If that's the case, she's been talking about me. *Why do I fucking care?*

"Yeah, did she come back with you tonight?" I'm assuming that she has no desire to ever see me again after witnessing my alcohol-induced vomit session.

"No, I'm just out with some classmates tonight." I raise my eyebrows at her because I'm having a hard time believing that this girl is in school.

"You're only in college? How about Brown-Eyed Girl?" *Fuck.* Did I really just say that aloud?

She laughs. "Brown-Eyed Girl? Oh, my God. That's the song you sang to her!" She shrieks in excitement. I have a good feeling about this girl. I forget about my embarrassment, knowing that she'll most likely help me.

"She told you that?" I ask, probably looking like a blushing school girl.

"Uh, yeah! She totally did, but she also told me about how you lost your cookies the other night in front of her." She points at me. "Let me make one thing clear here, buddy." Man, she's feisty like her friend. "She is a no bullshit kind of girl. She's not looking for a skirt-chaser, so if that's what you want, you better look elsewhere."

"I'm not a skirt chaser," I lie. I have to wonder if this girl knows my reputation. I mean, I have seen her around here several times.

"Right," she sniggers, which tells me she knows I'm full of shit.

"No, I just wanted to apologize to her for acting like a douche the other night and thank her for saving my life." Blackie raises her brows at me. "What? Scouts honor." I raise two fingers up at her, not really knowing if I'm doing the sign correctly or not.

"You obviously were not a boy scout or you'd know. It's three fingers." She chuckles as she sips on her water.

The last time she was in here with Claire, I noticed they were both drinking waters. I'm not sure why you'd come to a bar and not drink, but, hey, I'm not complaining.

"Guilty." I shrug my shoulders. "But really, I just wanted to talk to her. She seems like she could use a friend." At this point, I'm just pulling shit out of my ass.

"She has me, asshole." She reaches across the counter and smacks me on the back of the head as if we're old pals.

"Fuck! What the hell?"

"Anyway," she starts. "I'm meeting her tomorrow at Martin's at noon if you want to meet us there. Come a little late, unless you want her running for the hills when she sees you.

"Yeah, sure." I agree.

"Alright, Romeo, I need to get home. But I'll see you tomorrow. And don't make a bigger ass out of yourself."

She glares at me, reminding me of a reprimanding mother.

"Promise." She heads toward the door. "Hold up, Blackie, what's your name?"

"Blackie, really? That's the best you could do?" She sniggers. "Sierra. And Romeo? Don't try hitting on me. I'm a married woman." She waves a hand in the air, making a dramatic exit.

I already knew she was married when I saw the ring on her finger, but it wasn't her I was interested in. What the hell is wrong with me? I could have any woman in this goddamn place I want and here I am chasing after one who is obviously appalled by me. It must just be the chase that has me going after her. Right. That's it.

🐚 17 🐚

CLAIRE

"What do you want, Trevor?" I answer after the first ring. This is the first time he's tried contacting me since Brady got back to Phoenix. Why now?

"Now come on, Claire Bear. We haven't spoken in weeks. Don't you miss me?" He has sarcasm in his voice, which really shouldn't surprise me since I know he's not that upset about us being here. If he were, he would have tried harder to get us to stay in Chicago. You know, maybe by not having sex with another woman. Just an idea.

"You never call to see how Brady and I are. Why now?" There's hatred in my voice. These days that's pretty much all I feel for this man.

When I started seeing Desiree, I told her about my weird feelings toward my husband. I explained to her that I couldn't be with someone who could hurt me so bad.

She told me that I was very brave for leaving him because many women don't leave their husbands after an affair. I honestly don't understand how you could stay with someone who would cheat on you, but I guess that's just me. I couldn't look at him without feeling disgusted. He had touched a woman that wasn't me and that alone was reason enough for me to leave.

"I want you and Brady to come home this weekend for his birthday," he says as if it's no fucking big deal. What the hell is he even thinking? But I have to admit that I'm surprised he remembered our son's birthday.

"Trevor, that's ludicrous! Tomorrow is the weekend and we cannot fly to Chicago on a day's notice." The truth is, I wouldn't fly to see him even if he told me a month in advance.

"What do you have going on that is more important than your husband?"

"Why are you doing this?" I whisper into the phone. "We're not getting back together and I need you to understand that."

"Oh, is that right?" he asks with malice in his tone. "We'll see about that."

He hangs up without another mention of us visiting this weekend. That made no fucking sense, but whatever. I don't know what Trevor Davis has up his sleeve, but I don't care to find out.

I am supposed to have lunch with Sierra this afternoon at Martin's, but suddenly I have no desire to do anything. *God damn it.* I've been doing so well in my recovery, hardly feeling depressed at all anymore, but then fucking Trevor calls and sets me back.

I'm half tempted to go get a new phone and number so he can't contact me anymore. I can ignore his calls all I want, but he won't stop.

"Claire, Sierra's here," Evan calls from the other room. He has Brady bouncing on his knee while they watch *Shrek*.

Ever since I told him and Avery that we'll be living with Sierra come this weekend, he's been acting a lot different. I don't think he's mad that we're leaving, but he's been spending every second he has free with Brady. He acts like we're moving across the country, instead of just across town. I'm sure we'll see them often, but now they'll have the privacy I'm sure they've missed.

"Hey, sister girl," Sierra greets me with a hug. Acting as if we haven't seen each other in weeks when it's only been a few days. She's been busy with classes and I know she went out with some of her college friends last night. Being only twenty-two, she doesn't mind being around all the college mayhem. She's told me stories of some of the shit her friends from the University of Phoenix have done. Honestly, it's kind of surprising how many friends she's made there, considering she lives off campus.

"Hey, you ready to go?" I ask as I bend down to kiss Brady on the head. "I'll see you in a bit, baby." He swats at my face, clearly annoyed that I'm interrupting his movie time with his uncle.

"Tell your mama to leave us guys alone," Evan says as he takes a drink from his Dr. Pepper.

"Awone!" Brady shrills at the top of his little earth-shattering lungs.

"Nice, bro." I roll my eyes, leaving the two goofballs to their movie.

As we climb into Sierra's gold Prius, I decide to tell her about my asshole of a husband.

"So, Trevor just called, right before you got here." I sigh, suddenly feeling stressed out again.

"What the hell for?" she asks as she whips out of Evan's driveway.

"Sierra! Please don't kill me. My son needs me." I chuckle, only half joking. Every time I get in the car with her, I feel like my life is on the line.

"Have I killed you yet? No. No, I haven't." Bitch.

"'Yet' being the key word." I roll my eyes.

"*Anywho,* what the hell did Trevor the Tool want?"

I laugh at her ridiculous name for my husband. But, yeah, he is a tool, so it totally fits.

"He wanted me and Brady to come home tomorrow for his birthday. Who the hell does that? Then when I told him we weren't getting back together, he acted like I was putting him up to some kind of challenge. Does he honestly think I'd take his cheating ass back?"

"If I ever meet the douche, I swear to God I'm going to wrap my hands around his throat and then shove my tits into his face."

"Uh, what the hell is the point of that?" I laugh at her insaneness.

"If I don't strangle him, I know he'll die from suffocation." She points down at her boobs. "With these bad boys in his face, there's no chance of survival."

❧ 18 ❧

CLAIRE

"I've never had lunch here before. What's good?" We just walked into Martin's, luckily scoring a table as this place is crazy town right now. I mean, I know we're in Phoenix and its noon. But damn, it's Thursday. Don't people ever eat at home?

"The chicken Caesar wrap is to die for."

Knowing I can't go wrong with that, we both place our orders. As the wickedly handsome waiter walks away, I scrub my hands down my face.

"Are you still stressing out about that douche? Because, girl, he is not worth it," she says as she tears at the napkin sitting in front of her, forming a pile of paper in the middle of the table.

"What are you doing to that poor napkin?" I ask, changing the subject unintentionally. But it gets her away from the topic of Trevor.

"Just a nervous habit." She leaves it at that, making me wonder what she has to be nervous about right now.

Not a minute later, I get my answer in the form of a six-foot drink of deliciousness whom I can't stand.

"Is this seat taken?" Ryke asks but then sits before we can answer.

"Yes," I say at the same time Sierra says "no." Fucking traitor.

Ryke laughs and I want to smack that smug look right off his damn face.

"How's it going, Claire?" He asks as he looks through the menu. Why the hell is he here and why do I feel like I've been set up?

"Uh, good," I say as I stir my sweet tea. I really should stop ordering this shit because nobody makes it as good as Gino's East at Navy Pier.

Okay, now I'm using damn tea as an excuse not to think about Mr. Arrogant across the table from me.

"How's the bar?" Sierra asks him, ignoring the fact that I'm uncomfortable with him being here.

This is flipping Phoenix. What are the chances of him just happening to choose the exact same restaurant as us? Not very good. Which means I'm going to have to suffocate *her* with *my* boobs when we leave.

"It's really good. Ya know," he starts and then looks at me before turning his attention back to my back-stabbing friend. "There was this attractive brunette that came in last week who kept making googly eyes at me while I was trying to sing and play my guitar. She was a total distraction, but I haven't been able to stop thinking about her."

What the hell? I know my cheeks are now crimson and I'm nauseated. I really need to run to the bathroom before I throw up all over the damn table. Although he deserves to be puked on after the shit he pulled the other night.

Sierra throws her head back in a laugh. "Good-looking, huh?" My fucking friend asks, encouraging him to go on. In the meantime, all I can do is sit and stare at the two of them while they talk about me like I'm not even here.

"Yeah." He slurps on his Coke. "She had these curly locks and stunning chocolate colored eyes. I don't think I could ever forget them."

What is going on here? Right now, I want to strangle them both.

"What the hell are you two talking about?" I don't know why I ask this, as I know without a doubt that they're talking about me. I'm not going to admit that I have a million damn little butterflies swarming inside my stomach. I feel like I'm in junior high all over again. But this time, I know that guys like this are trouble.

"You, sweetheart." At the sound of his voice, I turn my head and catch the wink he throws my way. *Damn it*. He's got me all tingly down south and I have to cross my legs under the table to relieve the pressure.

"For one," I hold up one finger. "I was *not* making any kind of eyes at you. And two," I hold up another. "I'm much too old to be playing games with a Casanova like yourself." I glare at him and at that he laughs.

"Claire, you're not *that* old," Sierra says in response, not helping me at all.

I eye the pile of paper made from her napkin and toss it in her face.

"Bitch!" she yells in the middle of the restaurant, which causes us to receive annoyed looks from other customers.

Ryke chuckles at our childishness. Okay, so I'm not doing a very good job at proving my point here.

"No, but really. How old are you?" he asks, bringing the spotlight back on me.

"Didn't your mother teach you that you should never ask a lady her age?" I bat my eyes at him, not meaning to flirt, but I know it's coming out that way. I sip on my tea, but then notice the melancholy look on his face. It's gone before I can think much about it, but it has me wondering if he doesn't have his mom either. I decide to brush the thought off.

"I guess she forgot to mention that," he laughs. "But don't you think it's a good idea for a guy to ask, you know, just in case the girl is underage?" He gives me that cocky grin again and I'm hating myself for liking it.

"You're disgusting," I say this with a smile.

Our playful banter is interrupted by the sound of Sierra's phone chirping with a text message. I know I'm a terrible friend, but I kind of forgot that she was sitting at the table with us. All my attention had zoned in on Ryke.

"Shit," she says as she quickly types out a response to whoever she's talking to. "I've gotta run. Auggie has a temp."

She stands and grabs her purse off the back of her chair and is out the door without another word. I know she has to be worried sick, as I'm sure this is the first time her baby has ever been ill. But now I'm also super annoyed because I'm stuck here with this sexy, egotistical man. Fuck. How am I getting home now?

Now that we're alone, neither of us speaks.

"So, uh. She was my ride." I point my thumb behind me toward the door, breaking the silence.

"I can take you home," he says sweetly. I have to admit I like this side of him. He's almost shy, unsure of himself now. I like a confident man, but a vulnerable man is nice too.

What the hell am I thinking? I could never be more than friends with this guy. I've got enough of my own shit going on right now. Plus, he's way too much of a woman-izer, even if I were looking.

As turned on as he's making me, I cann*ot* let my guard down.

19

RYKER

We sit in silence as I finish eating my burger and Claire picks at the shell of her chicken wrap. I can tell she's nervous to be here alone with me, so I'm trying to give her a little breathing room. I know I can't pursue anything with this girl. She's not like the other women I pick up for a night and then toss the next morning. No, she's different, and for that reason alone, this will never go further than this.

"Are you from around here?" She surprisingly breaks the ice.

"Born and raised." I nod and smile. "You're not though, right?"

She shakes her head as she looks up from her food. "No, I'm from Chicago. I just moved in with my brother and sister-in-law.

"Did you move here for a job?" I'm being fucking nosey, but for some reason, I want to know all about this girl.

"No, I wanted to be closer to my brother and his wife.

They've helped me a lot with my son, Brady." *She has a child?*

"How old is your son?"

She smiles. "He actually turns one tomorrow."

I cough into my hand. "What about his father?" I shouldn't be asking this because it shouldn't matter. I can tell I hit a sore subject.

"Things didn't end well with him." She's clearly over talking about her ex so I move on.

"You seem close to Blackie." It doesn't sound like Claire has been in Phoenix long, but somehow, she's already established a close-knit relationship with the other spitfire.

"Blackie?" She nearly spits out her tea which has me laughing in amusement. "Yeah, we are." She smiles and has me uncomfortable under the table. "I'm actually moving in with her this weekend."

"That should be interesting." I laugh.

"Uh, why?" She gives me a dirty look. Even the attitude and glares she shoots my way make me hard as a fucking rock.

"You both are something else." I shake my head. "I like that," I say as I give her a genuine smile, not wanting to come off as an ass anymore. I think I've already managed to do enough of that.

"She's a married woman, you know?" she says, but I know she realizes I'm not talking about her friend anymore.

"I know she is. I was talking about you." She blushes and, damn, if it doesn't make her ten times sexier. How is that even possible?

"Well, I think we've already established that I'm not

interested in bullshit." This girl is endearing. I'm used to women who do whatever the hell I say. Not her. She's the "take no shit" type.

"Fair enough. I don't date. I only fuck." I stare at her waiting for her response.

She cringes. "Yeah, you definitely will *not* be fucking me." She looks around in embarrassment, making sure no one else heard her.

"I wouldn't dream of it, sweetheart." *Lies.* But all I'll be doing is getting myself off at night to images of her.

"Good." She stands from the table, letting me know she's done with this conversation.

As we're walking out to my truck, I grab her by the arm, which causes goose bumps to appear on her soft, silky skin.

"Do you have to get home yet?" I know I shouldn't be doing this, but I really don't want my time with her to end yet.

She raises her brows at me in question. "I thought I made it pretty clear that I wasn't sleeping with you?"

"Yes, you made that *very* clear." I laugh. "Look, it's nice out and I was going to walk Griz at the park. Want to join us?" When she looks at me skeptically, I add, "Just an innocent walk. No funny business."

When she realizes that I'm serious, she nods her head in response. I silently let go of the breath I was holding, anticipating her answer.

We get to my truck and I'm itching to open her door for her but know that'll piss her off, so I go around to my side and climb in.

"Do you walk by the lake often?" she asks as she buckles her belt. Usually, when I have women in my truck, they scoot their annoying asses over to the middle seat and practically dry hump my leg the entire drive. I'd rather have her across the cabin from me than deal with any of those flakes, any day.

"I try to take Griz in the morning whenever it's nice out. It's a good place to clear your head, ya know?"

She nods her head without saying anything else. This woman really is a mystery and she has me wanting to crack her shell open.

She comes across as a bad ass, but I have a feeling she uses her hard exterior to hide something deep inside of her. I know all too well what that's like.

"I probably shouldn't stay out too late, but I could definitely use some fresh air." She stares out the front window.

I nod my head even though I'm sure she can't see me and we finish the rest of the drive in comfortable silence.

20

CLAIRE

I don't know what I'm getting myself into. Why the hell did I agree to hang out with this guy? Don't get me wrong. He's nice to look at and honestly fun to be around too, but I don't want him getting the wrong idea. I guess I shouldn't be worrying about that, though, after making it perfectly evident that I'm not interested in his bullshit.

"So, what do you do for fun, Claire Davis?" Ryke asks as we stroll along the lake. It's a beautiful night out, the only noise coming from the crickets in the distance.

"Not much. I'm not that fascinating." He doesn't need to know anything about my personal life.

"I find that extremely hard to believe. Come on, throw me a bone." He walks backward in front of me, somehow not falling over his dog's leash.

"Um, I like to read, but that's about it." There. I'm not being too bitchy, but I'm not giving too much away. After tonight, we'll probably never see each other again. Plus, I'd never dream of bringing him around my son. He is certainly not the family type. Perhaps he doesn't even like kids.

"Uh huh," he says as he nods. "Let me guess," he positions his pointer finger on his chin, feigning deep thought. "Romance?" He gives me his beautiful, panty-melting smile. Do men have beautiful smiles? This one does. What the hell has gotten into me? I can't let this guy get to me.

I shake my head as if that's actually going to get the wayward thoughts of this guy out of it.

"Why do you say that?" I feel like we're starting to walk on extremely hazardous ground here. Is he flirting with me?

"I'm right, aren't I?" he pushes. "Don't be embarrassed. Guys like when girls read filthy shit like that. It benefits us in the bedroom. If you know what I mean." He flashes that big, bright grin at me. *Damn him.*

"Well, I'll have you know, I'm not reading it to please anyone but myself." As soon as the words leave my mouth, I want to crawl in a hole and die.

"How does it please you, Ms. Davis?" The fucker can tell I'm mortified but doesn't seem to be giving up any time soon.

I know my cheeks most likely match the color of my pink lips.

Ryke pulls Griz closer to him and then walks back to where I'm standing on the sidewalk. He gets right up to my ear, causing the hair on the back of my neck to stand at attention. He smells like he just got out of the shower, the scent of coconut and wood wafting up to my nose. I'm guessing it's only his deodorant, as he doesn't seem like the cologne wearing type.

"Do those books make you wet, sweetheart?" he whispers in a sultry tone.

I shiver at his words.

"I'll take that as a yes." He starts to walk away with that stupid ass smirk on his face.

"Asshole," I mumble toward his retreating back, but then he turns around, obviously hearing what I said.

"I'd offer to take care of that problem for you, but I'm too much of a Casanova for you. Remember?"

"I can take care of myself, thank you very much!" I shout toward him.

"Oh, sweetheart, I'm sure you can."

A part of me wants to just screw this guy to get him out of my system, but I refuse to be another notch on his bedpost. I'm sure his bed has seen heaps of women over the years. And probably lots of diseases too.

Okay, now I'm just trying to talk myself out of this guy. But, damn it, it's not working. In the words of Shayna, he's giving me a lady boner.

❧ 21 ❧

RYKER

I've clearly got Claire flustered, and fuck, she's got me hard as steel. I would love more than anything to take this girl home and fuck her until the sun comes up, but there's something about her that tells me that she's worth so much more than that. She doesn't settle for losers like me.

"I should probably get Griz home for some water. Want to come by for a beer before I take you home?" I know I'm walking on thin ice, but I have to at least try. I really do just want to spend more time with her. Will I see her again after tonight?

"Uh, I don't drink, but I can stop by for a bit." She's hesitant, but her answer is good enough for me.

WE WALK into my two-bedroom house and Claire looks around, taking in her surroundings. It's nothing special, but it's decent enough for me.

"Would you like a bottle of water?" I ask as I poke my head in the fridge. Which is empty, other than two things of beer and a few covered dishes.

"I'd love one." She pulls a stool out from under the bar and makes herself at home. I could tell she was nervous at first, but now she's seeming to warm up a bit.

I desperately need to get laid to get this damn woman off my mind. Why did I invite her over?

"So, how long have you owned your bar?" she asks, interrupting my inappropriate thoughts.

"I got it about two and a half years ago. I always wanted to open a bar, but my ex always tried talking me out of it. She didn't want me to settle when I could do bigger things in life." I do air quotes and shrug.

"How ridiculous! It's great you finally went for it. It sucks when others try to get in your way of doing something you want." She puts her head in her hands. Once again, making me curious. What's got her looking so troubled? Most of the time I see her hard exterior, but times like this, she becomes more transparent. Just not transparent enough to where I can get answers from her. I have no business wanting to know more about her, but this woman captivates me.

"Did you go to college?" It's a stupid ass question and always makes me look like a dumb fuck, but I want to keep hearing her talk.

"Yeah, I went to Illinois State University to be a teacher." She halfheartedly laughs. "That was a waste of time and money."

"Why didn't you become a teacher?" I imagine her being great with children and I'm sure she's an exceptional mother. *Unlike mine.* I have got to stop having thoughts of her like this.

"I decided to work at a daycare instead. It wasn't what I wanted, but I met my best friend there and could take Brady with me every day."

"Well, I bet those kids loved you."

She smiles. "So, what about you, Casanova? Where did you go?" I can tell she's trying to take the spotlight off her. If it'll make her more comfortable, I don't mind if she finds out that I don't have a college degree.

"Well," I take a pull from my Corona. "Owning a bar doesn't require having a degree," I say, only half joking. "I had wanted to go to Phoenix College with some of my friends from high school, but, at the last minute, I decided to take a break. That break ended with me never going and here we are now.

She gives me a genuine smile. "I think that's great. Like you said, not every job requires a degree and all that matters is that you're doing what you like."

"So, are you doing what you enjoy, Claire?" I know I'm being pushy, but I have a feeling something has happened to her, resulting in her not doing the things she wants.

She thankfully doesn't look pissed at my question. "Actually, right now I'm still trying to find a job here. Hopefully, I'll hear back from one of the daycares I applied to. I also applied for a couple reception jobs, although I'd rather work with kids if I can."

"There are tons of schools around here. Why don't you look for a teaching job?" I take another swig from my beer, but when I look at her again, this time I can tell I'm starting to make her feel unnerved.

"It's just not in the cards right now."

At that, I can tell she's ready to move on from this conversation.

"Want to go sit in the other room? The couch is comfier than these hard stools."

She nods in agreement, so we walk toward the living room. She takes in the walls that are painted a masculine gray color. A black leather sectional fills most of the room, along with two end tables and a coffee table. My sister was given strict orders of making sure this looked like a man cave. I didn't want any girly shit in here.

"You have a nice bachelor pad here." She waves her hand in the air as she looks at all the decorations around the room.

"Thanks. My sister helped me decorate before she got busy with her own life."

We both walk to the couch. She sits on one end and I sit on the other.

"Where does she live?" she asks, seeming to take interest in my personal life.

"She and her husband live in Scottsdale. They're expecting their first child this summer. A boy." I smile, letting her know I'm excited about being an uncle. I'll most likely never have kids of my own, but I can be happy for my sister.

"How exciting! You'll be an uncle." She claps her hands in elation, which is fucking adorable. I love seeing her like this.

I chuckle in response. "Yeah, he'll be the first baby in our family in years. Honestly, my sister is the last person I'd ever expect to have a kid. She's kind of self-centered and I'm sure she's in for a rude awakening."

"She'll come around, I'm sure."

We visit for the next hour and I have to confess that I love having her here in my space. She pulls her phone out of her pocket, most likely checking the time.

"I should probably get going so my brother doesn't worry." For some reason, it puts me at ease, knowing someone is looking out for her.

We both rise from the couch and I take her empty water bottle from her hands. I take it and my beer bottle to the kitchen and we make our way towards the front door.

When we get to my truck she gives me her brother's address and I start the brief drive to their house.

She opens the door and starts to get out but then turns back toward me. "Hey, Ryke? I'll be at the park tomorrow night at eight. I'd love to see you again." She doesn't linger for my response but instead darts out of the truck and up the front porch, closing the front door before I even think about pulling out.

Holy Fuck.

I wasn't expecting her to be so straightforward, but damn. I really shouldn't even entertain the idea, but how could I possibly turn her down? I mean, I don't even have her number to let her know I can't be there. *Well, shit, guess I'm going to have to see her again. What a shame.*

22

RYKER

I wake once again with an infuriating little bastard scratching at my face.

"I'm up. I'm up." I push Griz off me and roll over to look at the time. My alarm is about to go off in four minutes, so I switch it off.

I didn't sleep well last night because I couldn't get *her* off my mind. I loved having Claire here. She quickly became comfortable and she looked damn good sitting on my couch while we talked. It was as if we had done it a thousand times before. I don't know what it is about Claire Davis, but she's doing something to me.

She told me she hoped to see me tonight again at the park. I really shouldn't go because I've already done more than I should have, but what kind of man would I be if I let a beautiful woman walk in the park by herself after dark?

I do have to remind myself that I can't get close. Not that she'd let me anyway, but I'm going to die a single man before I let another woman crush my damn heart. I know I sound like a fucking chick, but a man can only handle so much in one lifetime. I took a huge risk when I let Monica in all those years ago. I should have known better after everything my mother did to me, Becca, and my dad.

Today, I'm off, so I take my time getting up and ready for the day.

As I step into the shower, I let the sweltering water hit my back. I lean one hand up against the tiled wall while the other finds my dick on its own accord. It's been weeks since I've let a woman touch me. Honestly, it hasn't bothered me, but thoughts of my brown-eyed girl always drive me fucking crazy.

I slowly run my hand up and down my shaft, wishing it weren't my own hand. Thoughts of coffee-colored locks bouncing up and down while taking me into her wet mouth have me painfully stiff. The water behind me becomes even warmer which has my hand moving faster.

"Fuck!" I groan as I throw my head back.

Once I finally come down from my high, I rub my hands over my face in frustration. I've never wanted a woman as bad as I want Claire Davis. What the hell is wrong with me? There are women all over the streets of Phoenix who would willingly have me in their beds, but I want the one who is absolutely appalled by my lifestyle. I'd love nothing more than to change my ways for her, but I know that can only end in disaster.

After I'm dressed, I decide to take Griz for a walk. I'll take him to the park this morning because I don't plan on taking him with me tonight when I meet Claire.

After tonight, I can't see her again.

I quickly tie my shoes as Griz jumps up and down at my feet, pleading to go out.

"Calm down, boy. We're going." I walk to the kitchen and grab his leash and hook it to his collar.

We finally make it to the park after Griz sniffed every single tree on our way. It's pleasant out this morning because it's early enough that it's not too warm. Soon, it'll get to where it doesn't even cool off at night, so I'm going to enjoy this while it lasts.

We have to stop every few feet so that my slow as hell dog can sniff around. He jerks away from me and his leash bolts out of my hand. *Damn it.*

"Damn it, Griz, get back here," I holler but then see who he's headed toward. *Fuck my life.*

As I get closer to Griz and the bitch that ruined my life, she says, "Hey, baby, I didn't know you have a dog." She giggles her infuriating little giggle that has always grated on my damn nerves. Fuck, it still does. She bends down and starts rubbing behind his ears. She needs to get her damn hands off him.

I finally notice the little tyke in the stroller behind her. She isn't paying any attention to the little girl and, if it were busy, someone could swipe her in a heartbeat. She starts jumping up and down in her seat in enthusiasm. I have to admit her kid is cute.

I don't say anything to her but grab for Griz's leash. She's still touching him, so I pull him away from her.

"Come on, Griz. Let's go."

I spin around with my dog to walk away, but she clutches my arm. "Come on, baby, talk to me. Want to go have coffee at Martin's?" Fuck, no, I'm not going somewhere with her I've been with Claire. Monica would ruin it, keeping me from ever taking her again. *You are not going anywhere with her after tonight.*

"Monica, don't call me that and I'm not having coffee with you." I try moving away from her, but she continues to be fucking maddening.

"Why not?" Is she being serious right now?

"Why would I do anything with you after the shit you pulled?" I growl, completely pissed. Has she lost her damn mind?

"It was one time, Ryke. I'm so sorry I hurt you." She starts sobbing and I almost feel sorry for her because she's making a fool out of herself in the middle of the park. Almost.

"Fine, let's go talk somewhere, but not at Martin's. Let's go to Stella's Corner up on North Street. But I have to take Griz home first." She smiles her phony smile like I just proposed to her. *Sorry, babe, you lost that chance.*

I HEAD home to drop my dog off and I'm kicking myself for agreeing to meet with Monica. But a part of me knows that she won't leave me alone if I don't. I'll give her this one chance to talk, but then I want her to fucking leave me alone.

Once I make it to Stella's Corner, I immediately spot Monica because she's flapping her arms in the air like a damn idiot. I know I'm being cruel, but I really don't know what I ever saw in her. I know I have trust issues with women and I'm still pretty bitter, but I don't have any feelings for her. Not a damn one.

"I'm so glad you're here, baby." Why the hell does she

insist on calling me that? "My mom is watching Kayla, so we can have some alone time."

"I can't be long. I have things I need to do," I lie. But if it gets me away from her quicker, I don't care.

"Can Kayla and I stay with you? My mom is making me crazy."

"Monica, you cannot stay with me." I look away from her as I sit across the table. I can't bear looking at her. I know I'm behaving like a child, but why the hell does she think I would let her stay in my house with me?

"Please, baby. We don't have anywhere else to go."

"It's not a good idea. You have plenty of friends. Ask one of them."

I raise from my chair, but she grasps my hand and says "I love you, baby. Please?"

I look across the café because I'm sure that the whole place is looking at us. That's when I see *her.* She's staring right at me. *Damn it.* She's waiting in line for her order with a redheaded woman around the same age as her. Monica still has my hand and I really don't want Claire to think I'm with someone. She'll probably assume I'm with another one of my hook-ups. Not that I should worry about what she thinks. We're only friends.

She looks pissed. But why?

Once I pull away from Monica, I tell her again that she can't stay with me and head for the door. Thank God, she didn't keep pleading because I was about to go mad.

"Hey, Claire." I look toward the other woman. "Ryker Allen." I hold out my hand to the redhead and she nearly breaks it. Damn, I wouldn't want to get on her bad side.

"Avery," The redhead says looking between me and Claire.

"Hey, Ryke. What brings you out today? Who's your lady friend?" Claire asks, with sarcasm in her tone.

"Just a friend." I look at her to make sure she understands what I'm saying, but now she won't look at me. "See you tonight, Claire." I turn toward the door and I'm pretty sure I won't be seeing her tonight. *Fuck.*

🦢 23 🦢

CLAIRE

I feel like a total bitch, but I honestly don't care. Why am I letting Ryke get to me like this? I have a feeling that woman was more than a fuck buddy, if he was bringing her for coffee. But why the hell do I even care?

"Hey, you okay?" Avery asks as we grab our iced coffees from the barista.

"Why wouldn't I be?" She's no moron, so I don't know why I'm even trying to play dumb.

"Claire, you were obviously uncomfortable around that guy. What's going on?" I turn away from her to find a booth, but I know she's going to question me as soon as we sit down.

We have to walk by the skank to get to an open table and I hear her on her phone, "I'm headed to Ryke's now, but I'll call you later." I want to pull her stringy, bleached blonde hair out.

Avery gasps. "You like him, don't you?"

I sit down at a corner booth. "What? No." I pretend to

be searching through my purse because I don't want to look at her. "Avery, I just left my husband."

"Okay, whatever you say."

"Also, he's a freaking playboy. Why the hell would I even entertain that idea?"

She shrugs. "Could be fun to take care of that obvious lady boner you have." She wags her eyebrows at me.

"You are insane. You should really move to Chicago to be Shayna's bestie." I smirk at her as I slurp my drink.

"Whatever, biatch. You'd miss me." She winks.

She thankfully drops it and we enjoy our coffee while we chat about her interior design business.

"Once I finally get my own place, you're going to decorate for me, right? I don't care what it costs because I'll need all the help I can get."

"Of course." She claps her hands. "And you've lost your mind if you think I'd make you pay. I'd do anything for you and Brady." She reaches across the table and grabs my hand. "Seriously, Claire, I hate what Trevor did to you and it's the least I could do to help." She gives me an almost sad look. "We're really going to miss you guys when you leave tomorrow."

I now have tears in my eyes that I'm trying desperately to keep from falling. "That means a lot, Av, but you guys have done so much for me already. I know you and Evan will be glad to have your house back once we leave."

"You're crazy. We love having you two with us." I can see the sincerity on her face. "But now we'll be able to have all the wild monkey sex we want. I've been dying to do it on our new kitchen counters." And…sweet moment over.

"Gross!" I throw my napkin at her.

She gives me a wicked smile and winks.

We finish our coffees and then head back to Avery's car. We're just down the street from their house, but it's enough time to think about whether or not I'm going to meet Ryke tonight. Chances are he won't be at the park anyway after the way I acted. Screw it, I'll stay home and maybe go to bed early. I'll probably be tired after Brady's party anyway.

Today is my baby's birthday. While he napped, Evan offered to watch him while Avery and I finished getting the last few things we needed before everyone comes tonight. It'll be nice to spend some time with all the important people in my life. Minus Shay. *God, I miss her.*

Avery and I spend the next few hours making Mickey Mouse cupcakes while Evan has Brady in the pool.

"How's Mommy's boy?" I ask as I sit down on a lounge chair in the backyard.

"Hey, sis," Evan says from the pool as he lifts Brady into the air, while I internally smack him for being careless with my child.

"Evan Daniel, put my baby down. Now!"

"Dayum. Ev, you better listen. She busted out the middle name." Avery chuckles in the seat next to me as she lowers her sunglasses over her nose. She's wearing a skimpy little white bikini. The girl totally has the body for it, but I'd be worried about showing my nipples to everyone. Avery doesn't care though. That's why I love her.

"Seriously, Claire? It's not like I tossed him. He's fine." He holds Brady in his arms as the little guy splashes around in the water. This is the first time he's been swimming. "Your mama is an overprotective bitch. Yes, she is."

Evan coos at him and I jump from my chair, ready to jump in the water to strangle him.

"Evan! Do not talk like that in front of him! He repeats everything," I huff and then throw myself back in my chair.

"Mama bit!" Brady squeals. I'm going to kill my brother.

He's laughing his ass off. I'm glad he is amusing himself.

"I know where you sleep, big bro." I point my finger at him.

"Yeah, yeah. Someone's gotta teach this kid how to be cool. Obviously won't be his mom." He chuckles.

"HAPPY BIRTHDAY, SWEET BOY!" Sierra screeches when she walks to the backyard.

My baby boy claps his hands, excited to see her. She's quickly become a big part of both our lives.

"Hey," I say as I stand up, adjusting my swimsuit top.

"Hey, you gonna swim or just sit there looking hot." She looks me up and down and then whistles. "You, my friend, are one sexy mama."

"You're ridiculous." I chuckle. "No, I'm gonna swim. It's hot as hell out here. I'm just waiting for Avery's parents to get here so I can say hi."

Once everyone is here, we all congregate in the back-yard. Evan and Avery have picnic tables set up away from the pool. My brother even went as far as gating the pool off for the day to make sure Brady didn't go near it when we weren't with him. I hate to admit it, but I'm going to miss my brother once I leave tomorrow. I know I bitch about him, but I couldn't have made it through these last few months without him and Avery.

Brady has had a fun day, but I can tell he's completely beat as he rubs his eyes while trying to help me unwrap his gifts. He gets spoiled with every Micky Mouse toy under the damn sun. I hope Sierra doesn't mind us taking over her house.

We say goodbye to everyone and I hug Sierra, promising to see her bright and early.

"See you tomorrow, roomie!" she hollers as she gets into her car.

I head towards my room to get Brady ready for his bath, but my phone rings from inside my swimsuit cover-up.

"Hey Shay," I answer after the first ring.

"Hey, mama. Can I talk to the birthday boy?" I look down at my baby who is starting to doze off in my arms, but I don't have the heart to tell Shay no.

I sit him on my bed and put my phone on speaker so he can hear Shay while I strip him of his clothes.

"Alright, Shay, you're on speaker now."

"Happy birthday, buddy!" she squeals, which now has my son wide-awake.

He claps his hands. "Say hi to Aunt Shay," I prompt him.

"Hi, Say!" I seriously can't believe how much he's talking. Working in a daycare for so many years, I know it's not common for a child his age to be talking like this. What can I say? I have a smart kid.

"Hi, baby. Aunt Shay loves you." She makes a kissy noise into the phone which has Brady leaning down on my phone, slobbering all over it as he gives her kisses in return. Damn, he's adorable.

I pick the phone up to talk to her.

"How's it going?" I ask wrapping Brady in a towel before carrying him to the tub.

"Girl, I'm going crazy with this wedding. I *really* wish you were here," she whines.

My heart cracks, wishing I were closer to her. I'm thankful to have Sierra here, but this girl is my ride-or-die, as she always calls me.

"Maybe we can work something out so I can come up for a week or so. I'm not working yet, so I have plenty of time."

"Yes!" she shouts in excitement. "Let me know when and I'll clean the spare room."

At that, we hang up. I put Brady in the tub, trying to get him clean while barely being able to keep my eyes open. It's been a long day.

❧ 24 ❧

CLAIRE

I'm sitting in Brady's and my room, trying to rock him to sleep after he had his bedtime bottle. I have a feeling he's going to want a sippy cup soon because he mostly just chews at them.

I finally get him to sleep and my phone alerts me to a new text message. It's only seven o'clock, so it's not like its late or anything, but I'm freaking out that whoever it is just woke my son. I look down at him and, thankfully, he's still resting peacefully in my arms.

I lay him in his bed and check to see who the message is from.

Unknown: Hey, Claire, it's Ryke. We still on for eight?

Damn it. How the hell did he get my number? And I'm still pissed about earlier. I honestly have no reason to be because he can be around whatever women he wants to. I guess I'm jealous. I can at least admit that. But I'd never tell him that because he can never be more than a friend. I'm not sure why he's such a player, but he's more of the "love 'em and leave 'em" type. He seems to be around my age, so it's time for him to grow up. But I don't see that happening any time soon.

Me: How did you get my number?
Casanova: I got it from your phone the other
night when you went to the bathroom ;)

Sneaky son-of-a-bitch. And did he just send me a winky face?

Me: I'm too tired tonight, but thanks.

I know he's not going to buy my bullshit and that's proven with his next text.

Casanova: Did I do something to upset you?
Because if I did, I'm really sorry.
Me: Nope, I'm fine. Goodnight.

I throw my phone on the bedside table and get up to wash my face and put on some pajamas. I've been hurt by one man and I really don't care to put my heart in another's hands.

I walk back into the room and see that Brady is still sleeping soundly. I then notice I have yet another message from Ryke.

Casanova: Please meet me if only for a couple

minutes. I have something I need to talk to you about.

This guy is not going to give up until I agree to meet him. I really do want to see him, but I know that he only looks at me as a friend. I have to admit I'm surprised he would want to spend all this time with me, knowing that I'm not going to put out. I find it hard to believe that he has many friends with vaginas.

I get into bed and lay there for a few minutes trying to decide what I'm going to say back to him.

Casanova: Please?

He knows I'm ignoring his last text, but if I'm going to be his friend, I should try to be civil, right? Damn it.

Me: Okay, but I can't stay out long. Can we meet now instead?

I don't have to wait but thirty seconds before his next text comes through.

Casanova: Perfect. See you in 10?
Me: See you in 10.

I'm in my pajama shorts, but I don't care. I don't feel like changing again and when I get home, I'm going straight to bed anyway. My ass is practically falling out of them, but it'll be dark, so nobody will notice. I quickly tie my hair up on the top of my head and tell Evan and Avery I'm leaving, asking them to check on Brady in a bit.

"Ow Ow! Where are you going in those hoochy mama shorts?" *Dear Lord.* Did she really need to say that right in front of my brother?

"What are you talking about?" I hear my brother ask.

Before he sees me, I quickly scoot out the front door. I'm not that skanky-looking, but he probably wouldn't approve of my attire.

I make it to the park a couple minutes early but see Ryke sitting on the bench, waiting for me right inside the entrance.

"Hey," I say because he hasn't yet noticed me.

"Hey." He stands and his face lights up with a smile. This man is making my ovaries flip just from looking at him. Right now, he looks so youthful, care-free. He's not trying to be a bad ass like he typically is.

"So, uh, do you want to go for a walk or something?" I'm a bit uncomfortable, but I should at least let him say what he needs to.

"Sounds good."

We head toward the sidewalk that runs along the lake. There are a few lights on, but other than that, it's dark. We can see the ducks wading in the water and it's such a peaceful sight. I can also hear a few birds chirping in the distance.

We walk in silence for the first few minutes until Ryke finally speaks.

"So, that was my ex-girlfriend you saw me with earlier," he says as he turns to look at me. I'm still looking straight ahead but then stop walking.

"You don't owe me an explanation, Ryke. We're friends, remember?" I really do hope it wasn't anything serious with his ex, but, in all fairness, we are only just friends.

"Okay, but then why did you look mad at me when I was trying to talk to you?" *He can read me like a freaking book.* Not that I wasn't obvious or anything.

"I was just tired is all."

I'm sure he doesn't believe me, but he goes on. "I caught her cheating on me three years ago." He turns away from me as if he's embarrassed by his confession. I had no idea we had so much in common. Apparently, there's a lot to him that I don't know.

"I'm so sorry." This would probably be a good time to tell him that I understand what he's going through, but Trevor's cheating is still pretty fresh on my mind. I don't love him anymore, but I did not long ago.

He changes the subject. "How was your son's birthday?"

"It was good. We had a few friends over for a cookout. He got way more toys than any child needs and surprisingly fell asleep after eating way too much sugar." I chuckle.

"I bet you're an amazing mother, Claire." He looks at me and smiles.

"Thanks," I whisper.

"So, you move in with Sierra tomorrow?" He asks.

"Yeah." I smile. "I'm really excited."

"I can only imagine how much trouble you two will get in to." He chuckles.

We continue to walk in silence for the next few moments.

"So, what do you like to do for fun, Mr. Allen?" We stop on the bridge to look out at the water.

He throws his head back in laughter. God, I love that sound. "Well, Ms. Davis, I enjoy playing my guitar when I'm not busy with the bar."

"Do you play often?"

"Only when beautiful brunettes come into my bar." He smiles and I get all tingly. Why do I let him get to me like this? *This is dangerous ground, Claire.*

"You're full of shit." I swat at his arm, pretending like his words aren't affecting me.

"Think what you want, sweetheart." God, I love when he calls me that. But I wonder how many other women he has pet names for?

"You're crazy." I half smile at him as I turn away from the water.

"What do you like to do for fun? You know, besides read porn?" He gives me a playful wink before we continue on our walk. *My God, I need to go home to change these panties.* Does he have any idea what he's doing to me?

"Oh, my God!" I shake my head at him. "It's called erotica." I grin.

"Right." He chuckles.

"I like to write," I confess, a little embarrassed.

"Like poetry?" There's no way in hell this guy thinks I write poetry.

"No, like books." I put my head down because I know what he's going to ask next.

"Why are you embarrassed? What kind of books do you like to write, Claire?" He has now stopped walking and takes me by the arm so I'll look at him. When I don't answer him, he continues to stare at me, starting to make this awkward. He knows I'm embarrassed, but he won't let up. Why is he making a big deal about this?

"Romance. There, I said it. Are you happy now?" I give him a half smile to let him know that I'm only joking with him. He doesn't know me well enough to be able to tell if I'm pissed or not. *But* he knew I was pissed this morning.

"Yes, I am. That's sexy as fuck." He once again gives me that goddamn panty-destroying smile. "But really, that's incredible. Have you published anything?" I can't believe he isn't appalled by my confession. Trevor hated that I wrote, so it mostly stopped once we got married. When he did see me sitting at our computer typing away, he always had something smart to say about it, telling me that I needed to get a life. Not even kidding. Those were his exact words.

"No, I haven't really written in a couple years." I'm constantly thinking of different stories I could write, but I'm not sure I'm capable of it anymore.

"Why not?"

"Honestly, I just haven't had time lately." Well, it's not a lie.

We continue our walk and I'm thankful he's dropped the subject of my writing. For some reason, it makes me feel guilty because I haven't told him everything about me. I don't know him that well, though, and I'm sure there's a lot he hasn't yet revealed.

❧ 25 ❧

RYKER

Damn, she looks good tonight. Not that she hasn't every other time I've been around her, but tonight she's wearing short ass shorts. I mean *short.* Honestly, I'm glad she's with me and not someone else because any pig would be undressing her with their eyes right now. I'm trying to not be a perv, but it's difficult when she's got legs that go on for miles. Legs that would fit perfectly around my body as I fuck her into oblivion. *Shut the fuck up, Allen.*

Her body is very toned and it's obvious that she takes good care of herself. Maybe she'd want to go to the gym with me sometime. Nope, not happening.

We're now by the park's exit.

"Thanks for meeting me, Claire." I'm a few feet away from her, but I can smell her warm vanilla-sugar scent. It's subtle, unlike the strong ass shit all the women I've been with wear. Why do they think guys like that? It is not a turn on if I can taste your damn perfume.

"Of course." She starts to walk away from me, but I grab her arm.

"Do you want to meet again tomorrow night? I'm off at seven and could meet you around the same time." I can tell she's unsure and the last thing I want to do is make her uncomfortable. "If you're busy, no problem."

"No, no, I'm not busy. Seven-thirty?" I'm fucking ecstatic but don't let her know that. *She's just a friend. She's just a friend.* Why does this feel so different then?

I walk home from the park with a damn spring in my step even though I know I will never have Claire Davis as my own. She and her child deserve so much better than me. All she sees me as is a dirtbag. But I'm still anxious to see her again tomorrow night. Even if only as a friend.

I slide through my front door after unlocking it, careful not to let Griz escape. He's freaking fast and I don't feel like chasing his ass tonight.

"Down, boy." I scratch his ears and then he rolls over for me to rub his stomach. He thinks he's a cat.

I go to the kitchen and grab a beer out of the fridge. *Damn, I need to go shopping.* I currently have two boxes of beer along with a lasagna and a meatloaf my stepmom Gail sent me home with. My dad married her about five years after my mom left us. She has two boys who are younger than me and Becca that live in Wyoming near their dad. I think they're assholes for never visiting her, but it's not my business.

I pop the cap off my beer and head back into the living room where my lazy dog is sprawled out on the couch. I grab my phone off of the coffee table and push Griz over so I can sit.

I turn on the TV and watch a rerun of *Game of Thrones* but quickly fall asleep on the couch. I can't remember the last time I fell asleep before midnight. I dream of a curly-haired brunette and her breathtaking chocolate eyes.

❦ 26 ❦

CLAIRE

"**R**oomie!" Sierra yells as Brady and I walk through the front door of her house. *Our house.*

"Hey," I say as I set a bag of groceries down on the kitchen table. Against her wishes, I went shopping before coming so I could fill the fridge and cabinets. I also have a check in my back pocket that I'm going to make her take so I can help pay part of the rent.

"What the hell did you buy?" she asks, trying to sound irritated. But I can tell she's excited as she eyeballs the chocolate donuts I bought.

"Just some food." I start unloading the bags to get all the cold things put away.

"I told you not to worry about it." She's now sitting at the table, devouring a bag of Dorito's. Obviously, not that upset that I went shopping.

"I just want to do my part, ya know?"

Once I'm finished in the kitchen, I take our bags to the guest room, to start unpacking. I can't stand living out of a suitcase, so the sooner I get this done, the sooner I can relax.

After I unpack the few things we have, we decide to relax while both boys are napping.

"Are you sure you don't mind watching Brady for a bit? I mean, we literally just moved in. I don't want you to think I'm trying to take advantage of you." I lift my tea from the coffee table and take a drink, knowing she's going to reprimand me for having such thoughts.

Avery had wanted to pick me up for lunch this afternoon. I was going to tell her no until Sierra insisted that I go. I feel bad for all the breaks I'm always taking, but it's not often I ask. Usually, Avery or Sierra offer.

"Why the hell would I think you're taking advantage of me? I just wanted to help and you know I love spending time with sweet Brady. You'll be watching Auggie some, so it's only fair."

Because I still haven't found a job yet, I told Sierra it made sense for me to watch Auggie for as long as I can, so he doesn't have to be left with her mother-in-law. Glenna wasn't thrilled because I'm sure she thinks that I'm not capable of watching her grandson, but I know Sierra would rather have my help.

"Well, I appreciate it." I once again get all teary eyed at the thought of all the support I have here. As much as I miss Shay, I can't imagine leaving Phoenix. Surprisingly, it has quickly become my home.

"Love you, sister." She winks at me. "But anyway..." She sips on her water, seeming to be contemplating her next words.

"Yes?" I reach for the bowl of Skinny Pop sitting on the

table. Why the hell didn't I buy some real popcorn while I was out this morning?

"How are things going with Ryke?" She knows that we've hung out some, but I haven't said much to her about it.

"Uh, good. I guess." I know she isn't going to take my bullshit answer.

"Are you guys like a thing now?" She crunches obnoxiously on her popcorn, smacking her lips like a child. She's insane but has me cracking up.

"What? No!" I'm hoping beyond hope that she'll leave this alone. She knows that the last thing I can be thinking about is jumping into another relationship.

"Why the hell not? Is he as enormous under those pants as he looks?" Oh, my fucking God.

"What? Sierra, I have *not* slept with him, so I wouldn't know." I stare at her like she has two damn heads. "I'm not going to, either. You know I refuse to get mixed up in something like that."

"It could be totally fun. I've always wanted to know what it would be like to have a one-night stand. That's the shitty part about marrying your high school sweetheart. I didn't get to try out all the flavors before I chose one."

She is way too damn much.

"For one, you're ridiculous. Two, you have a sexy husband who loves you and your child more than anything. You have nothing to be jealous of. My husband cheated on me, did you forget that?" I don't mean to sound like a bitch, but she's acting like that fact is exciting.

She grabs my hand. "I was kidding, Claire."

Now I feel bad. "I know. I just can't let myself get hurt again. Plus, even if I did sleep with him, which I'm sure he has no desire to do, it would totally ruin what we have now. I don't think I'd be willing to risk that.

"Have you asked him what he wants? I'm not just talking about sex. Do you think he wants a relationship?"

"What?" I shake my head as my eyes go wide. "No way. He told me his ex-girlfriend cheated on him a few years ago and that he hasn't dated ever since. Well, unless you count the tramp he was with when I met him."

"Well, I just think it's odd that he hasn't even mentioned sleeping with you when that's all he seems to do with the chicks he hangs around with."

"Uh, I made it pretty clear that I wasn't interested." *Just keep lying to yourself, Claire.*

"Okay, well, then why hasn't he moved on to someone else?" I don't know why he wants to spend time with me, but what's it hurt to have another friend?

"Who fucking knows?"

I lay my head on the back of the couch, thinking about what Sierra just said. Maybe he considers me a challenge, so he hasn't given up yet.

❦ 27 ❦

CLAIRE

"Hey, mama," Avery says as I climb into her car.

"Hey, did you miss me already?" I bat my eyes at her.

"Hell, yes. I'm going to miss having you and Brady around." She pulls out of Sierra's driveway, thankfully a better driver than my maniac friend.

"Well, we're not far from you. I'm sure we'll see you all the time. Plus, Sierra doesn't have a pool, so I'll have to use yours."

"Uh, definitely. Us hot bitches gotta keep our sexy asses looking good." I turn toward her.

"Av, my ass will not be sunbathing." She's insane.

"Why not? Who the hell wants a pale ass?" Are we seriously having this conversation?

"Uh…"

When I don't answer, she goes on. "You need to get laid, but that's not going to happen if you have a white caboose." Wow. That wasn't as crude as I was expecting.

I slap my forehead in exasperation and then chuckle.

"Why did I agree to hang out with you today?"

"Because you love me." She winks.

"Will we be back by seven? I, uh, kind of have some-where to be at seven thirty." *Shit.* Now she's going to question me.

"Claire Davis, have you been sneaking around?" She has a Cheshire grin on her face.

"I'm not sneaking around. Ryke and I have just been hanging out."

"Yay!" She claps while she jumps up and down like a fool. "I knew it!"

"Calm down. We're only friends."

"Mmm hmm, sure."

"Whatever." I roll my eyes dramatically, even though she can't see me. "That guy is bad news, Av. I don't have time for that shit. Anyway, where are we going?" I urgently want to change the subject.

"So, I might have lied to you." She stares ahead at the road while I look at her with my mouth wide open.

"What are you talking about?"

"Um, well."

"Avery Porter, what did you do?" I'm nervous as hell because it's just like my sister-in-law to do something I want to strangle her for.

"So, we're meeting Evan and Ryke at Don's." She doesn't look away from the road as she says this, surely knowing I'm having a heart attack in the passenger seat.

"I'm sorry. Come again? Evan doesn't even know Ryke." *What the actual fuck?*

"No, but I do." What the hell did she do now?

"I have a feeling I don't want to know what you did."

She throws her head back and snorts and I worry for a

second that she's going to get us killed because she's not watching the road.

"All I did was go to his bar last night for an innocent drink with Carly after work and I may have invited him to join us today." What the hell is up with people doing this shit to me?

"What? Why the hell would you do that? Avery, we're not together, no matter what you and Sierra think. This is the kind of shit couples do, not people who occasionally hang out as friends."

"Oh, stop being so dramatic." I'm about to reach over the console and pull her damn hair out.

I love spending time with Ryke, but we're only supposed to be friends. This seems like a double date, if you ask me.

"Please don't tell me you have Evan thinking I'm with this guy." Good Lord. It's only noon, but I'm already desperate for a damn drink.

"Evan is going to think whatever he wants. You know this."

She's right. Evan is as stubborn as they come. But Avery is the only one who can occasionally get him to do what she wants. It doesn't happen often though.

"Oh, God." I rub my face up and down with my hands. "What if he embarrasses the hell out of me?"

"I may have threatened him with no sex for a month." She chuckles. *Oh, my God, she's crazy. And eww, I don't want to hear about their sex life!*

"Avery, gross! I love you like my sister and we can talk about anything. Except that. You will not tell me about your sex life, got it? Like I've got it in my head that you haven't done it since I moved in."

She is cackling hysterically like a witch and, once again, I'm worried for our lives.

"Think whatever you want."

We spend the next few moments in silence and I'm trying to work up the courage to have lunch with Ryke and my brother. I wonder what Ryke must think about having lunch with Evan. I'll be lucky if I don't scare the poor guy away after this.

When we finally make it to Don's, Avery turns in her seat to face me.

"Do you like him?" She blurts out, as if it would be no big deal if I did.

"What? No, Av, you're insane." I look out my window to avoid eye contact with her.

"Yes, you do. I've known you for a long time and you can't get anything past me."

After a minute of ignoring her, I finally give in to get her off my back.

"Fine. Yes, I do. Are you happy? I know it makes me a huge slut to be pining over a man who isn't my husband. You don't have to tell me." I'm kicking myself at my confession, but I know she wouldn't say anything to Evan because he's so overprotective. Although, I have a feeling he already knows.

"Claire Davis, you are the furthest thing from a slut. Now, let's go get your man." I roll my eyes. *Easy for her to say.*

❧ 28 ❧

RYKER

What the hell am I doing here, having lunch with Claire's brother? But I guess if I'm going to be friends with his sister, it would be nice to get on his good side. I don't want to worry that he'll kick my ass every time I'm around her. Not that I couldn't take him. But he seems like a nice enough guy. Super overprotective of her, but I'm glad she has him looking out for her.

"Look, I know you're a good guy, just don't hurt her," Evan says matter-of-factly.

"Um, you do know we're only friends, right?" I'd love to be more than friends with Claire, but she deserves someone that has their shit together and that isn't me.

"Yeah, okay." He chuckles as he drinks the soda in front of him, not believing me.

Claire's sister-in-law came into the bar last night and said Claire wanted me to join them all for lunch today. I'm not a dumb ass and knew that she was obviously oblivious to all this or she would have invited me herself.

"I would never hurt her, but I promise we're only friends."

I tell Evan about Monica and how she screwed me over. I think he finally believes that I'm not looking for more with his sister. But why the hell does it feel like I'm lying? *Because, of course, I want more with Claire.* She gives me this peace I've never found with anyone else, but I also know that she has the power to destroy me. Worse than Monica ever did.

"Shit, sorry."

"Nah, man, don't apologize. I'm glad I found out before I married her."

We talk for the next few minutes and then we see Claire and Avery walk into Don's. *My God, she's beautiful.* I've found her attractive since the first time I laid eyes on her, but today she looks amazing. The dark jeans she's wearing make her legs look sexy as hell along with the purple, sparkly top. I think purple is my new favorite color on her. *Okay, am I growing a vagina or something?*

"Hey, guys," Avery says as she leans in to kiss Evan on the cheek and they both sit down. We're at a table for four and I'm between Evan and Claire. Can't say that I mind.

I look over at Claire and have a feeling that Avery didn't tell her I was going to be here. I've enjoyed getting to know her and she seems to feel the same way. So why is she so uncomfortable?

"Hey." I nudge her with my knee while Evan and Avery are whispering about something. I swear they are like teenagers.

"Hey, yourself." She gives me a half smile, which starts to make me feel better.

"Are we still on for tonight?" I'm hoping to God that she hasn't changed her mind about seeing me again.

"Sure, but do you really want to see me twice in one day?" She asks, half joking, but I can tell she's really unsure about me wanting to spend time with her again.

"Why wouldn't I?" She turns toward me.

"I don't know, but I'm sure I'm keeping you from some kind of social life, aren't I? I mean, how are you going to meet your next girlfriend when I'm around?" She has got to be fucking kidding me right now. I say the only thing I can think of.

"You know I don't date, so no."

I turn back in my seat, but I can see that she's looking at me out of the corner of my eye. She doesn't get a chance to respond because the waitress interrupts to get their drink orders.

The four of us visit for the next hour and I have to admit that Evan is pretty friendly. He comes across as a macho ass, much like myself, but he's really a pretty nice guy.

Claire has been joking with all of us the whole time. The sound of her happiness is music to my ears. Evan and Avery have to take off before we're done eating and when Claire jumps up to leave with them, Avery stops her.

"You're still eating, so stay. I'm sure Ryke doesn't mind giving you a ride home." She winks at me. I knew I liked this girl.

"Avery, I need to get back to Sierra's anyway." She looks at Avery with pleading eyes. Why is she acting like this?

"No, it's fine. I really don't mind taking you home. We'll both finish eating and then I'll get you home." I'm really trying here, but I'm not sure she's going to take the bait.

"Okay." She sits back down as she tells them both goodbye. *Thank fuck.* I'll take any time with her that I can get. I don't want to wait until tonight to see her again.

Keep it together, man.

We both get back to our meals and neither of us speaks for the next few minutes. She's clearly avoiding me, so I decide to let her be for a bit.

"Hey, you doing alright?" I grab her arm. I can't read her very well today.

She pulls away from me. "Yeah, I'm fine." She goes back to eating, but hell if I'm going to let her off the hook.

"Talk to me, Claire." I grab her chair and turn it so she has to face me. She looks pissed, but I don't care.

"What do you want to talk about?"

"How about you start off by telling me why you're acting so uncomfortable around me? Did I do something to upset you?" I look at her, but she doesn't give me anything so I go on. "I thought you wanted to hang out? Did you change your mind?"

She just sits there looking at her lap for several seconds and then finally speaks. Not answering my questions, but at least she says something.

"Was this a date, Ryke?" *Oh, shit.* She's probably freaking the hell out right now.

"What? No. Avery asked me to have lunch with you guys. That's it."

"Okay, because I feel like I was just set up. You made it very clear that you don't date after what Monica did to you, and anyway, we seem to want different things in life. You and I are nothing alike."

Is she upset I don't date?

"You weren't set up. Evan and Avery both know that we're friends, so they thought it would be fun. Now, let's get you home." I'd rather spend the rest of my afternoon with her, but she doesn't want that, so I'll take her home.

29

CLAIRE

"Claire, if you don't want to meet at the park tonight, we don't have to." Ryke grips the steering wheel and I'm afraid he's going to hurt himself with how white his knuckles are turning.

"That's okay. We can meet unless you're busy." I prop my head against the passenger window and pray for the next few minutes to go quickly because I urgently want to get out of his truck, away from him.

"I'll see you at seven thirty, then." When he pulls into Sierra's drive, I reach for the handle to get out. "Claire, wait."

I slowly turn around to look at him, afraid of what he's going to say next. "You have nothing to worry about with me. I'm just fine with being your friend. I've been hurt badly by every woman I've let get close to me and I'm not looking to do that again.

Damn, that hurt.

"Okay, bye, Ryke." I get out of his truck as fast as I can and sprint up to the house. I'm sure I look like an idiot, but I need to get away from him. Why did his words hurt so much? I'm in no position to be dating anyone, but to hear him say he can't trust me hurt like hell.

"Hi, Buddy!" I exclaim when I walk in the door and see Brady playing with his toys on the floor. I have to at least pretend that I'm alright. I still have my son to take care of.

He reaches his arms up to me, so I snatch him off the floor. I sniff his little head. There's nothing better than the smell of a baby. I kiss his face and then he slobbers all over mine. I don't need anyone in my life besides this little guy. With him, everything will be fine.

Sierra already fed Brady, so that's one less thing I have to worry about. I put him in his little bath seat in the tub and he starts splashing water all over the place and has me soaked.

"Brady!" I laugh. "You're getting Mama all wet." He just giggles in return.

I hope that I can give this little boy the best life possible. It's just me and him, but I think we'll make it just fine.

After I'm done washing him, I grab his hooded puppy dog towel and dry him off. I carry my wet baby to our room and dress him in his Micky Mouse outfit that Evan and Avery got him for his birthday.

"HEY, you going to take off soon?" Sierra peeks her head into my room.

"What are you talking about?" I continue changing Brady's diaper.

"You said you were meeting Ryke tonight. It's seven-fifteen."

"No, I decided to stay in tonight," I say, not looking at her.

"Does Ryke know that?"

"We had a weird argument this afternoon. I doubt he even wants to see me." I button Brady's pajamas up. "I guess I'm not sure if I'd call it an argument. It was strange, though."

"He likes you," she says, like her statement doesn't mean anything. *Fuck, it means everything.* But that doesn't matter. We'll never be more than friends.

"What? No, he doesn't. You're on drugs." I hand Brady his sippy cup, avoiding eye contact with my insane friend.

"Yes, he does. He cares a lot about you. You two may not be able to do anything about it, but what's wrong with spending time with him?"

I look at her like she's out of her freaking mind. Because she is.

"Sier, he made it very clear that he doesn't trust women. Why would I spend time with him, even as a friend, if he can't trust me?"

"Claire, he was cheated on, just like you were. Of course, his guard is up, like I'm sure yours is."

Of course, my guard is up, but I know that Ryke would never hurt me. I'm more concerned about my child and everything else I have going on in my life. I still have a divorce I have to worry about. I don't want to burden someone else with my problems.

"I just really can't deal with anymore heartache right now. I do want to be his friend, but what if I start to feel more but can't do anything about it?" *Too late for that.*

"Why don't you worry about that if and when it

happens? Go have some fun. You deserve it. Besides, you deserve to have friends."

"I have you." I shrug my shoulders.

"Well, I don't have a penis, so I can't help you out there."

"You are so crude." I shake my head at her.

I have no idea what I'm going to do. I kind of doubt that Ryke is expecting me to show up tonight after the way I acted earlier.

Brady is now snoozing in his bed, so I quickly put on yoga pants and a t-shirt and then grab my tennis shoes. If nothing else, I'll get a nice jog in and it won't be a complete waste of my time if he doesn't show up.

30

RYKER

S even forty-five. She's fifteen minutes late. Why the hell did I even bother coming here tonight? I know I keep telling her and myself that I only want to be her friend, but she still has the capability to crush my damn heart.

I felt like an asshole earlier when I basically told her I didn't trust her, but I didn't know what else to say. She looked scared to death with just the thought of us possibly on a date. Would it really be that bad? The truth is, I can already tell she's different from the rest. But I still can't let my guard down completely. For now, I'll be her friend. If she proves me wrong, I'm not sure I'll bounce back from this.

I've already done two laps around the lake, so decide it's time to head home. Once I'm almost to the exit of the park, I hear her.

"Ryke!" *She came.*

I turn toward the sound of her voice. "I didn't think

you were coming." I don't mean to sound like a douche, but that's how it comes out.

"I'm really sorry. If you need to get home, I understand, but I'd love to walk with you." I can tell she's worried what my response will be.

"No, let's walk." We walk side by side in silence back toward the lake. "You doing alright? You seemed upset earlier." I hope I'm not being too straightforward, but I really do want to make sure I didn't upset her.

She sighs. "Yeah, I'm fine. Honestly, I'm just mentally exhausted. Sorry for the way I acted."

"Claire, you never have to apologize to me. I just wanted to make sure I didn't upset you. I'm sorry you're feeling that way, but just know that I'm here whenever you need a friend."

"Thanks, Ryke. That means a lot."

The rest of our walk is a lot less depressing. I even get her to laugh a few times and, damn, do I love the sound.

"Did you get settled into Sierra's alright?"

"Yeah." She smiles. "I don't have much here besides a suitcase, so it wasn't too big of a deal."

After doing a few laps around the lake, we start making our way back so I can get to work.

"Thanks for hanging out."

She laughs. "No, thank *you* for wanting to see me again even after I was a bitch to you earlier"

This woman is the furthest thing from a bitch.

I grab her elbow. "Claire, you're not a bitch." I grab her chin and she tenses a little but then quickly relaxes in my grip. I want her to know that I'm serious.

"Thanks," she whispers and I know that I'm done for.

In this moment, I realize that I'm done fighting whatever this is between us. I just have to figure out a way to tell her, without freaking her the hell out.

I GET to the bar an hour early so Austin can leave to go somewhere with his girlfriend.

"Dude, she's got you by the balls." I punch him in the shoulder.

"Fuck you." He laughs. "You're just jealous that you don't have a woman." Fuck, he's right, but I won't admit that. I'm not lonely because of what Monica did to me, but I'm realizing more and more every day that I really do want to settle down someday. But it scares the shit out of me.

Once Austin leaves, we get swamped. Brian, one of my bartenders, is thankfully quick, so we get through our orders pretty fast.

Two hours before closing time, we finally slow down and we only have a couple customers left. I turn toward the front of the building at the sound of the door swinging open. It's quiet in here now, so I notice that someone's walking in.

Her. God, she's beautiful.

I finish wiping the counter off that's covered in beer and then head over to the table they're sitting at.

"Hey, guys. What brings you out so late?" It is after eleven o'clock.

"This girl needed a night out." Avery points her thumb toward Claire.

"Yeah, it was like pulling teeth to get her out, but we finally swayed her," Evan says.

"I'm glad you did," I say in response as I look Claire straight in the eyes. She doesn't respond, but then I get a half smile. That's good enough for me. "I just need to close out my last couple tabs, but then I'll grab some beers and join you."

Once I'm done with my customers and they've all left, I grab a couple beers and quickly get Claire's water. We visit a while and then the girls decide to get up and put some music on my jukebox. Austin's dad donated it to us when we opened. It doesn't get used often, but I love having it. I'd rather listen to music on there over the radio any day.

They have me and Evan cracking up as they dance to Beyoncé's *Single Ladies.* They are putting on quite the show for us. Thank God, there's a table over me, so I can hide my reaction to the sight of Claire dancing.

Tonight, she's wearing a navy blue, knee-length dress along with a pair of brown boots that only go to her ankles. She looks sexy as hell.

Beyoncé finishes singing about being single and Avery puts another song on. Garth Brook's *To Make You Feel My Love* comes on and Evan gets out of his chair to dance with his wife. I'm not usually a country fan, but I can't leave Claire standing in the middle of the dance floor by herself.

I scoot myself out of my chair and make my way towards her.

"Milady, can I have this dance?"

She giggles and then takes my outstretched hand. "Well, yes, kind sir, you can." *Damn, she's making this really hard on me, in more ways than one.*

I have her right hand in mine and I hold our hands

close to my heart so she's forced to be close to me. My right hand snakes around her hip. I have to be careful about how I touch her because her brother is only ten feet away from us. I'm not sure why, but, tonight, she is very carefree and I'm loving it.

She wraps her free arm around me. I'm sure she can feel what she's doing to me, but, frankly, I don't fucking care. It's time she realizes how much she affects me.

🦋 31 🦋

RYKER

The next day, I'm sitting in my truck at the park. I'm nervous as hell and my palms are sweating like crazy. I need to man up and get this off my chest. This will either work in my favor or crush me. I'm not sure if I'm ready to find out, but then I see Claire walking toward our bench, probably wondering why the hell I'm in my truck.

I turn the truck off and work up the courage to face the woman that has changed my life.

"What are you doing?" She gives me a confused look as I shut the door.

"Just wanted to see you. Is that alright?" She's standing next to the bench but then runs to where I'm standing in the parking lot. She leans in and gives me a tight hug and then kisses me on the cheek. *Oh, my God. She smells incredible.* I think I need to get some of this vanilla shit she always wears, so I can spray my pillow with it. I'd love to smell her all night. *Allen, you're fucking nuts.* Once I snap out of it, I hug her back.

"What was that for?" I don't let go of her as I stare down into her awe-inspiring eyes.

"Nothing." She starts to back away, the apples of her cheeks turning pink. I wonder what the rest of her looks like when she's flustered. *Stop being an asshole.*

"Claire?" I catch her by her arm.

"Yeah?"

"Don't ever be embarrassed around me, alright?" The last thing I meant to do was make her feel uncomfortable.

"Okay." She nods and gives me that smile that always has my dick coming to attention.

Without another word, we walk toward the lake.

"Do you want to, uh, go for some coffee?" I'm acting like a fucking dumb ass.

"Uh. You asked me to come to the park so we could go for coffee?" She looks at me like I'm insane. I *am* fucking insane. I don't even know what I'm saying to her at this point.

"No." I shake my head.

"You okay? You're acting strange." I've only known this woman for a short time, but she already seems to be able to read me well. I'm good at putting on a front, but she sees right through my bullshit.

"Yeah, I'm fine." I look straight ahead, trying to figure out what I'm going to say to her. I feel like a damn high school girl.

"But, seriously, why did you ask me to come? Not that I mind, but I have a feeling you need to talk about something."

I grab her hand and take her to the nearest bench. Not *our* bench, but I really need to sit down before I say anything else.

I let go of her hand and run my fingers through my too long hair. *Damn, I need a haircut.* She's now completely facing me, waiting for me to say something. I stand back up. She gives me a questioning look but doesn't say anything as I squat between her legs. When I look up at her, she looks nervous. *Here goes nothing.*

"Ryke, what are you doing?" Her voice is shaky.

"Do you want to know why I was sitting in my truck like a pussy?" When she nods, I go on. "I want more with you, Claire. I know there's a good chance you don't want the same, but I needed to tell you."

She gasps. "You mean like you want a relationship? With me?"

"Yes, Claire Davis, I do." I smile up at her.

"You said you don't do relationships."

"You're right, I did say that. But you've changed me."

"I think there's something I need to tell you first." She looks around at everything but me.

"What is it, sweetheart?" Suddenly I'm terrified to know her answer.

"I'm..." She hesitates.

"You're what?" I'm trying fucking hard to be patient, but she's got me freaking the hell out.

"Married," she whispers and I feel like I've been socked in the damn stomach.

I stand to my feet. "You're what?" I growl.

"Hear me out, alright?" I look down at her and see that her eyes are glossed over with tears. I hate seeing her like this, but I can't bring myself to comfort her right now. How could she do this?

"Hear you out? You want me to fucking hear you out?"

I'm sure that if there are any other walkers out, they can hear how pissed I am.

She stands from the bench.

"Yes! Would you fucking hear me out?"

She looks at me as I tug at my hair with both my hands.

I shake my head. "No. No, I can't do this."

Without taking another glance at her, I'm sprinting toward the parking lot, not able to get to my truck fast enough. How the fuck could she do this to me? I told her that Monica cheated on me and now this.

I sound like a goddamned caveman because it's not like she waited until we got serious to tell me. But how could she spend all this time with me and never mention her fucking husband? I should have known when she was vague about her son's father.

32

RYKER

It's been two days. Two, long, grueling days. After I caught Monica cheating on me, I was hurt, a lot. But this is different. I could actually see myself settling down one day with Claire. I should have known she didn't feel the same way when she wouldn't even bring her child around me. I know I don't have a very good history when it comes to women, but damn.

I don't think I've ever drunk so much in my fucking life. My head hurts as I turn to look at the bright blue numbers on the clock next to me, reminding me of the night before.

Claire hasn't stopped texting me since Friday, asking me to call her or to at least respond to her messages. What the hell would I even say to her? *It's okay. I understand you have a fucking husband. No big deal.* No, I have absolutely nothing to say to her. As much as I miss her beautiful smile and contagious laugh, I won't allow myself to talk to her.

Once again, my phone goes off. Fuck. I've considered

running to the cellular store to get a new phone number so she can't contact me, but what the hell good will that do if she shows up on my doorstep, wanting to explain herself? Not that there's anything to explain. She's married. Plain and simple.

Brown-eyed Girl: Please call me. I think you'll want to hear what I have to say.

Pretty sure I don't want to hear anything she has to say. I know that she had said she didn't want a relationship with me, but she hinted at it several times. Why the hell else were we spending so much time together? Friends don't do that. At least, I don't do that with friends.

When I left her at the park the other night, I went to an old bar that my dad used to frequent when we were kids, Maverick's. I knew she wouldn't think to look there because I had never told her about the place. I drank too much, completely forgetting I was supposed to close the bar. Austin left Brian in charge and ended up rescuing my ass before I got the police called on me for acting like a shit head. Why am I letting this woman get to me like this? Maybe I'm the dumb ass for letting her get close to me. We weren't even fucking together. Hell, we never even fucked, but this still stings like a bitch.

I finally decide to drag my ass out of bed to take a shower. Since I met Claire, most of my showers have consisted of me getting off with thoughts of her in my head. Not today, though. My dick is the last thing I'm concerned about right now. Call me a pussy, but the ache in my chest is much more domineering.

Tonight's my night off, but I decide I don't care and go

in anyway. If nothing else, I'll get piss drunk again. And I don't have to worry about the authorities coming because it's my fucking bar.

I've been sitting at the bar for what feels like hours now. I'm four or five drinks in, I think. I've started to lose count. I'm in my own world, thinking about a certain brunette who led me on, when I feel an ice-cold hand on my arm.

"Hey, stud. This seat taken?" the skinny blonde asks me. I used to find broads like her attractive until I found my brown-eyed girl. My chest tightens at the thought of her. *She was never my girl. She fucking belongs to someone else.*

"No, you can have it." I look over at her but then quickly go back to watching the game that's playing above our heads. I'm really not interested in it and I'm not even sure which teams are playing, but at least it's keeping my mind busy. For now.

"I'm Cynthia." The girl giggles and it makes me fucking nuts. She reminds me of a mixture of Monica and Vanessa. Both of whom drove me up a damn wall.

"Ryker." I turn in my seat and offer her my hand. I decide I have nothing to lose by flirting with this girl. I say girl because I'm pretty sure she's hardly legal. I hope Austin fucking carded her before giving her the beer sitting in front of her. I'm too exhausted to care, but I really don't want to deal with the law because one of my employees gave this underaged girl a drink.

"Nice to meet you, Ryker. What's got you so down, handsome?" She tilts her head back, taking a long pull from the drink.

"Oh, you know. Typical shit," I chuckle. "Found out the woman I was starting to fall for was married. No big deal."

I toss back the rest of my Corona and then slam the bottle down, letting Austin know to bring me another one. He shoots me daggers from across the counter. He's helping other customers but he better hurry his ass up or I'm going to fire him. *Fuck, I need to go home and sleep.*

"Well, I know just the thing that'll help take your mind off that." Her suggestive words do nothing for me, but I decide to entertain her anyway.

"Oh, yeah? What's that?" I grin at her, knowing exactly what she's talking about.

She leans in to whisper into my ear. "I'll fuck you all night long. I won't even give you the chance to think about that bitch while you're with me." Still nothing. What the hell is wrong with me? Have I consumed so many of these beers that I can't even get a fucking hard-on?

I grab her hand, deciding that I'm going to try like hell to get my mind off Claire. Losing her has got me slipping right back into my old habits. Tonight, I'm going to try not to care.

33

CLAIRE

I wish I could erase the image in my head, of how hurt Ryke looked when I told him I'm married.

"Trevor, watch Brady," I holler and then grab Sierra's keys, hoping she doesn't have somewhere she has to be because I have to find him.

Trevor flew in this morning to take Brady back to Chicago for a couple days. He wanted to spend some time with him since he didn't get to see him for his birthday. His mom is also desperate to see him. It pissed me off, but I agreed. I don't want to keep Brady from his father. He shouldn't be punished for our problems.

It's been three incredibly long days since I've seen him. I texted him several times but, of course, got no response. Even if he refuses to have anything to do with me, I at least need to explain myself to him. Okay, so I should have told him about Trevor before, but I didn't think he'd actually want something serious with me. He hasn't had a relationship in several years and he pretty much vowed to never again entertain that idea.

When I get to his house, the only response I get is Griz barking from the other side of the door.

How did I possibly think that he wouldn't get hurt in all this? I should have known better with how differently he treated me from the other women he's been with. Hell, I didn't even sleep with him and he still stuck around.

I try calling him, but it automatically goes to voicemail. I shoot him another text.

Me: Do you think we could meet somewhere?

Who the hell am I trying to kid? Why would he listen to me? He just found out that I'm married. Of course, he isn't going to hear me out.

Not surprisingly, I get no response, so I head to the bar.

"Austin, is Ryke here?" I say in a rush, looking around to make sure I didn't miss him when I walked in.

"No, he doesn't come in until seven. What's wrong, Claire?" He gives me a concerned look.

"Can you just have him call me when he comes in?" I rush toward the door.

"Yeah, sure."

There's one last place I can think of that he might be. I pull into the park, but I'm immediately disappointed when I don't see him here either. I don't know where else he'd be.

My phone goes off in my hand and my heart stops in my chest. I'm soon disappointed again when I see that it's not Ryke.

Trevor: Where are you? Me and Brady need to

head to the airport soon if you want to see him before we leave.

"HEY, MAMA!" Shay greets after one ring.

I plop myself onto Sierra's leather couch.

"Hey, Shay." She's one of the only people who can calm me down when I'm upset like this. I miss Ryke like crazy, but also it was hard for me to tell Brady goodbye. I detest being away from him this long.

"Hey, you doing alright?"

"Yeah, I just wish I could see you." I had thought about going to Chicago with Trevor, but I really didn't want to deal with him more than I had to.

"Me too, girlie. Are Trevor and Brady on their way now?"

"Yeah. Are you going to be able to see him while he's there?"

"For sure. As long as fucktard lets me see him." I chuckle at her. "Koda has been asking about him. He wants to take him to the park or something." Shay's son adores Brady. And I love Koda like he's my own. *Damn, I miss those two.*

"Just have K ask Trevor. He'd have to be completely heartless to tell that sweet boy no."

I imagine Shay throwing her head back as her laugh bellows through the phone. But the next second, it ends and I can tell she's concerned about me.

"Have you talked to Ryke?" I hear the reluctance in her voice.

I sigh. "No. He won't return my calls or texts. I think I really blew it, Shay."

"I really doubt it, babe. I think he was just shocked. Maybe he'll let you explain."

I chuckle. "If he won't even pick up his damn phone, there's no way he'll hear me out. He probably won't be able to trust me again after this." I wipe my eyes, trying to rid the few tears that have begun to fall. My fucking husband cheated on me, but that didn't feel as cruel as Ryke's silence.

"Just give him time. If he's as crazy about you as I think he is, he won't let this get in his way of being with you." I know she's right. I mean, I know I was wrong not to tell him sooner about Trevor. I honestly just didn't want to talk about him and I didn't think he could possibly want to be with me more than friends. How foolish am I?

"Maybe you're right."

"I know I am. But, hey, Koda is yelling at me from the other room to put another Sponge Bob on. These damn spoiled kids today have no idea how shitty it was to have to wait an entire week to watch another episode of a show."

"How did we ever survive?" I joke.

"Right? We were so deprived. Anyway, call me later this week, okay? I want to know how you're doing."

"Okay, I will. Love you, Shay."

"Love you too, babe."

34

CLAIRE

"Honey, I'm home!" I startle at the sound of Sierra's booming voice. Damn, I've got a headache and she's so boisterous. And I sound like a fucking bitch, but I'm in a terrible mood.

"Hey, Sier." I rub my eyes as I sit up on the couch. I dozed off after talking to Shay earlier. Now that Brady isn't here, I'm not sure what to do with myself.

"Did the douche bag and Brady already leave?" She's never even met Trevor but probably hates him as much as I do.

I huff, "Yeah." I look over at the clock on her TV. "A couple hours ago."

"You doing okay?" She eyes me doubtfully.

"Honestly?" There's no reason to lie to her. Besides my brother and Avery, she's all I have here.

"Honestly." She waits patiently as I gather my thoughts.

I thought I was done crying, but here I go again. I'm

186

pretty sure Seattle hasn't seen the amount of moisture that has come from my eyes over the last week.

She lays Auggie on the floor with some of his toys.

"Come here." She sits next to me on the couch and reaches her arm out to me for a side hug. "It's going to be okay, I promise."

I sniff and I'm pretty sure I just got snot on her new shirt.

"I miss him so much. I didn't realize how much he meant to me until it was too late. Why did I have to go and fuck everything up?"

"Girl, stop being so hard on yourself. He's being a dick by not hearing you out. I know it would change things for him."

I nod. "I hope you're right, but I don't think he's going to be doing that any time soon."

"Don't lose hope. He'll come around." She squeezes me. "But let's forget about asshole men for the night, okay?"

I stare at her in disbelief. She never talks about Miles like this, so now I have to ask.

"Uh, what happened?"

She groans. "Nothing really. I just miss Miles like hell and sometimes it causes us to argue when we finally get to talk to each other. It's like I'm so fucking good at ruining the short amount of time I get. He got mad at me this afternoon and hung up without a goodbye. Claire, what if something happened to him over there and that's how our last conversation ended?" Now she's the one weeping. We both desperately need alcohol. I'm cursing my therapist right now for telling me I shouldn't drink.

"Damn, I'm sorry. Is there anything I can do?" I feel

like the biggest bitch for complaining about my nonexistent relationship while her husband is currently in the line of fire and she doesn't know when she'll see him next.

"I just need chocolate and a good non-chick flick. Let's watch a comedy." She wipes her nose on the back of her hand. It's totally disgusting, but she gets a pass tonight.

"I just got some rocky road. Want a bowl?" She nods and grabs the blanket off the back of the couch.

I head to the kitchen and hear my phone go off with a text message alert. I keep getting my hopes up that it's Ryke, but I'm always sorely mistaken.

Trevor: We made it home. Brady is sleeping.

Wow. At least he had the decency to let me know they made it safely to Chicago. I honestly thought I'd have to call to make sure.

I quickly text him back and then grab two bowls from the cabinet and overflow each with the chocolatey goodness.

"I come bearing gifts." I hand her ice cream over and then throw myself onto the couch next to her. I grab the blanket she's already covered with and snuggle close to her. It's hard to believe that we've only known each other for such a short time. It feels like I've known her a lifetime. I guess that's what happens when you practically live in a prison cell together for two months.

"What'd you decide on?" I mumble over a bite. Damn, this stuff is heavenly.

"*Dumb and Dumber*" She presses play with the remote and puts her feet up on her cluttered coffee table. This place is much cleaner now that Brady and I are here. But Sierra still lives here, so it's still messy.

"Seriously, Sier?" I roll my eyes. "This movie is dumb as shit."

"Claire. It's called *Dumb and Dumber*. Of course, it's dumb." She does a valley girl sigh and rolls her eyes at me in return.

I shove at her playfully and then settle in for the most ridiculous movie ever made. At least, it takes my mind of Ryke for a bit.

———

AFTER MY NIGHT WITH SIERRA, I decide to visit Ryke's bar again. If he wants to be a stubborn ass, that's fine, but I'm not giving up yet.

I climb out of the car and slowly make my way through the gravel parking lot, careful not to trip on a rock in my heeled sandals. Tonight, I'm wearing jean shorts with a red tank top. The collar sparkles in the light. My hair is down, even though it's hot as hell out.

I pull the wood door open and instantly feel a headache coming because the music is at an ungodly level. Why the hell they keep it this loud is beyond me. I can hardly hear myself think.

I scan the bar nervously, not knowing if Ryke is even here or not. I don't see him but still decide to take the empty stool at the end of the bar.

"Hey, Claire," Austin greets as he brings me a water. They don't know why, but everyone here knows I don't drink.

"Hey, Austin." I sip at the water, buying myself a few seconds to gather the nerves to ask about Ryke.

"He's not here tonight." Well, damn. I got worked up for nothing.

"Oh." I'm obvious about my disappointment. I miss him like crazy and just wish he'd talk to me.

"He's not doing good."

"What do you mean?" I slowly look up from my drink.

Before he can answer, a blonde bimbo sits next to me. There are four other empty stools so this irritates the hell out of me. I don't need everyone hearing my business.

I scoot closer to the end of the bar because I'm uncomfortable sitting next to this stranger.

"Ryke hasn't been himself."

"Austin, I'm married, but it's not what he thinks."

"I know, and I think he does too. But he's scared of getting hurt again."

I nod. I know he's been put through the ringer before, so I can't really say I blame him.

"He was a good lay," I hear from the seat next to me and my head darts toward the annoying girl.

"Excuse me?" I'm assuming she was talking to me, but I have to make sure.

"Ryker. He was fabulous in bed." She smirks. "Honey, he's over you. It's time to move on."

My heart once again cracks in my chest. I didn't know it was possible to be more crushed than I was before.

He already moved on.

The girl gets up and walks toward a large group. They are loud as hell, clearly drunk off their asses.

I take one last drink and then stand to leave.

"Thanks, Austin." I wave behind me.

"Claire, don't believe her," he begs. I don't know if he honestly believes Ryke didn't sleep with the bitch or if he's just trying to make me feel better. It doesn't matter anyway. Either way, he doesn't want anything to do with me anymore.

"It's okay. I'm fine." I give him a half smile as I push the door open to leave. I need to get out of here as fast as I can. Before I was desperate to see him. Now, I can't stomach the thought.

When I get back to Sierra's, I decide to do something I hadn't thought of before. I grab my phone out of my purse, open my Facebook app, and hesitantly type in Ryke's name. I immediately recognize him from his picture and click on his profile. The picture is of him and an older woman. I'm guessing his stepmother. He has his profile set to private, so I'm only able to see a few things that are recent. Like me, he doesn't post anything but pictures. I see who I assume are his family and also a few girls, but those are from before I knew him. That makes me feel a little bit better. He's free to do whatever he wants, but the thought of him with someone else makes me queasy.

Not wanting to torment myself any further, I click out of the app and carry my phone across the room to the dresser. If it's out of reach, I won't be tempted to look anymore. I crawl back in bed and that's when the tears start. It doesn't look like I'll be getting any sleep tonight. It's time to move on. I'm just not sure how to do that yet.

35

RYKER

After I ignored her calls and texts for an entire week, Claire gave up. A part of me wishes she was still trying to reach out to me, as shitty as that sounds. I miss her like crazy, but I still can't get over her confession. Was she ever planning on telling me she was married? She had told me that things didn't end well with Brady's father, but I had no idea that they were still together. I wouldn't have been spending time with her if I did.

Of course, Claire and I never slept together, thank God. But I have always made sure that I didn't get involved with a married woman. After the shit Monica did to me and the hurt I saw on my dad's face after my mother left us, I pledged never to do that, ever.

"Dude, are you ever going to grow a fucking pair and go see her?" Austin asks as he restocks the bar. The asshole has some nerve.

"Shut the hell up," I mumble at him before punching him in the shoulder.

"I'm tired of dealing with your mopey ass." He

chuckles at me and I want to ram my fist through his shiny white teeth. "Did you ever see her after she came in looking for you?"

What the hell is he talking about? "What? She came in here?" From what I knew, she had only tried calling and texting me. She hadn't tried coming to see me here or at home.

"Uh, yeah, dude. The first time, she was ecstatic. But the second time, she got to meet one of your bunnies."

"What the hell are you talking about?" *Shit.* Did someone say something to her?

He shrugs his shoulders. "Some blonde skank came in here, staking her claim on you."

Fuck.

"What the fuck?" I roar. I honestly don't know why this makes a difference to me, but the thought of her being that upset over me has me feeling wanted. I know I'm a shitty person.

"Dude, calm your tits. Go see her." He throws a dish towel at me and smirks. "I'll close."

I shake my head. "Nah, man. There's no way she'd want to see me now. I ignored her for the last couple weeks and she finally gave up on trying to get me to talk to her."

He shakes his head in annoyance. "Man, seriously. Listen to me. This same shit happened between me and Amanda. If I hadn't pulled my head out of my ass, I would have lost her for good."

I fly out of the parking lot, having no fucking clue what I'm going to say to her. I don't even know if she'll listen to me anyway.

It still bothers me that she's married, but I have to

believe that there's more going on than I realize. This all could have been avoided, if she had just been honest with me in the first place.

I hope to God I didn't just fuck all this up because I wasn't willing to hear her out. This visit could go one of two ways. Either she'll forgive me for being a douche or she'll slam the door in my face, making it clear she never wants to see me again.

"What the hell do you want?" Sierra hisses at me when she opens the door. "You've ruined her and if you think I'm going to let you in this damn house, you're greatly mistaken."

"Sier, who is it?" I hear her beautiful, intoxicating voice for the first time in weeks.

"Nobody." Sierra tries shutting me out with the door, but luckily for me, I'm twice her size and can block her.

When she comes into view, my whole world tilts on its axis. My heart stops as we stare at each other without saying a word. She's expressionless, so I have no idea what's running through that gorgeous head of hers.

"Hi," I whisper, loud enough for her to hear me.

"Sier, I'm fine. Let him in." Sierra hesitates, but then slowly walks away, leaving us alone.

"What are you doing here?" She has a mixture of hurt and anger in her tone and I hate that I'm the reason for it.

"I wanted to see you," I tell her honestly.

"Why?" she asks as a tear trails down her face. I want nothing more than to swipe it away for her but refrain from walking toward her. Right now, she looks like a scared animal who will run if I make the slightest move.

"Do you think we could go somewhere to talk?"

"Uh, yeah, sure. I'll meet you out on the porch in a minute." I want to run outside like a damn fool, shouting to the world, because I feel like she just handed me the moon. I know I can't get my hopes up, but after not seeing her for so long, this is a huge deal.

I walk back out to the front porch and sit on the swing. I listen to the birds chirping in the distance and the cars roaring up the busy road.

I lay my head back and sigh in relief. I really can't believe that she agreed to talk to me.

The front door creaks open as Claire walks out in an Illinois State University tank top along with short as hell spandex shorts. My dick twitches on its own accord. Waking after being away from Claire for so long.

"Hey," she says as she walks toward the swing and then surprisingly takes the seat next to me. We're not touching, but the swing isn't big so we're close in proximity.

"Hey. How's everything going?" I ask, acting like this isn't uncomfortable as shit.

"Okay." She nods. "Brady is in Chicago with Trevor so I'm just trying to stay busy." She smiles at the mention of his name, but I can tell she misses him.

I've never met the little guy and she's only spoken briefly about him, but I can tell that she's a wonderful mother.

"So, uh." I drag my hands through my hair.

"I need to explain," she interrupts me. When I try to cut her off, she stops me. "No, Ryke. I need to say this to you, okay?" I nod and she goes on. "I'm really sorry for never telling you about Trevor. I left him a few months back after catching him cheating on me. It messed me up something bad. I had just gotten out of a psychiatric hospital right before I met you." She puts her head down in embarrassment.

What? Oh, my fucking God. What have I done? I was a complete dick for not letting her explain this sooner.

"I know I had plenty of opportunities to tell you. I just never wanted him to taint my time with you. I'm planning to divorce him soon. It'll just be more difficult since I'm here and he's in Chicago."

"Claire, why didn't you tell me this? I would have done everything I could to help you."

"I'm sorry," she whispers as she reaches across the swing to my hand. At her touch, my body is set on fire. I have missed this woman so damn much. "Ha-have you moved on?" This woman has no idea how hard she'd be to move on from.

"No way." I smile at her.

"What about that blonde?" she asks with a quiet, pained tone.

Shit.

"Cynthia?" What the fuck did she say to her?

She shrugs. "I don't know her name, but she told me that you were a good lay and that I needed to move on because you were over me."

I slide closer to her and grab her face. "That night I got completely trashed and I thought being with her, or anyone, would make me feel better, but I swear to you I didn't sleep with her. I didn't even kiss her. I turned her down and she left me in the parking lot."

I can see the relief in her eyes.

"Come on." I stand from the swing and reach my hand out to her.

"Where are we going?"

"I'll show you."

I lead her off the porch and down the street to our favorite spot. I don't want the park to be tainted by our last memory here. I'm ready to make a new one with this beautiful, brown-eyed woman.

Once we get to our bench, I guide her to sit and then squat between her legs.

"What are you doing?" she whispers with a smile on her face.

"Sweetheart, I am so sorry for not listening to you. I'll admit that I was taken back, finding out that you were married, but I should have known that you'd never do anything to hurt me."

She sniffs and now has tears rolling down her gorgeous face. No matter what, this woman is always breathtaking.

"I'm so sorry."

"Shh." I hold a finger up to her lips. "No more apologizing, alright?"

She nods. "Okay."

"I know you've worried that we couldn't make this work, but, baby, let me prove you wrong."

She stands on the bench and in the next instant is in my arms, her legs wrapped around my waist. God, I've missed this woman.

"Is that a yes?" I muffle into her hair.

"Yes!" She giggles and it's fucking music to my ears.

"Can I kiss you now, sweetheart?" I look down at her.

"I'd be upset if you didn't."

With that, I sit us both on the bench and she straddles my lap. I know she can feel what she's doing to me through my pants. I hold her face in my hands, staring deep into her soul. My lips connect with hers and I've never felt so on top of the world in all my life.

My girl.

❦ 36 ❦

CLAIRE

R yke and I have been together for three glorious weeks now. I have to admit that when we first got together, I was a bit hesitant. Don't get me wrong. Of course, I wanted to be with him, but I was worried because he hadn't been in a relationship in a long time. I voiced my concerns to him and he reassured me that he was done living the playboy life. I totally trust him, but my insecurities seem to get the best of me at times. He's been a complete gentleman, but I have to admit it's making me fucking crazy. I mean, we've had plenty of make-out sessions, but nothing beyond that.

I open the door to his house.

"Hey, sweetheart. I'm in the kitchen," Ryke hollers from the other side of the house. He informed me that tonight he's cooking me dinner. It smells delicious in here and I have to admit that the fact he cooks has my lady bits going crazy. He probably shouldn't have invited me here, near his bed, after doing something like this for me. Damn, I need to get laid.

"Whatcha makin'?" I wrap my arms around him from behind as he stirs a red sauce at the stove.

"Chicken parmesan. Is that alright?" He turns and kisses me on the cheek. I've never been affected by a man like this before. For God's sake, I was married to one, *am* married to one, but he never made me feel like this.

I have yet to bring him around Brady. I guess I'm just hesitant to bring another man into his life, to take the risk of him leaving like Trevor did. Okay, so technically I left Trevor, but I worry Brady will get close to him, only for him to leave us.

"Sounds amazing," I answer after realizing I had been in a trance, thinking of things I shouldn't be while I'm with him. I'll let myself off the hook for now.

"Hey, you okay?" Ryke asks as he plates our food. I realize that I haven't said much in the last few minutes.

"Yeah." I smile at him as I take my seat at his small table.

He has a candle burning in the middle, setting the mood perfectly. Ryker Allen isn't the type to woo women, so I know that he really does feel something for me. At least, for now.

We enjoy our dinner and then I help him clean up when we're finished.

I dry my hands on the dish towel and make my way to the gorgeous guy across the room.

"What are you doing?" he asks as I stand on my tip toes to kiss him. My hand making its way toward the zipper on his pants.

"Can't a girl seduce her man?" I wiggle my eyebrows at him.

He halts my hand. "Claire, stop."

I back up, hurt by his tone. I wasn't expecting that from lover boy.

When he sees that he's upset me, he tries to grab me, but I keep retreating from him. I make it to the front door and start to put my shoes on. I need to get away from him. I've embarrassed the hell out of myself and I really don't care to be around this asshole right now.

"Where are you going?" he asks with confusion in his voice.

"Home." I try to open the door, but he stops me.

"Why are you doing this? Can't we talk before you just take off mad at me?" I guess I do at least owe him that, but I'm too pissed to reason with him right now.

"Come here." He pulls me away from the door and into his arms.

"What?" I know I'm acting worse than my toddler right now, but he really hurt my feelings.

"Sweetheart, I want to take my time with you. We don't have to rush into anything."

That's when I push away from him, pissed off even more now.

"Seriously?" I gasp "Before you were with me, you hopped in bed with anyone who had a fucking vagina. And now me, your *girlfriend*, you won't even fucking entertain the idea with!" I'm fuming and worried there might actually be steam coming from my ears.

"Claire, you know those women meant nothing to me. Baby, come here." He slowly walks toward me, hesitantly. "None of that is true."

"Now you're calling me a fucking liar? How long did you know any of those bimbos you picked up before me?" He doesn't answer. "Exactly. You've known me for months but have yet to touch me." I wipe at the tears that have started falling down my face. Pissed at myself for letting this upset me this much.

Refusing to let me object again, he grabs my face between his hands. Not harshly but letting me know that what he's about to say is important for me to hear. I decide I can at least give him that.

"Sweetheart, you are right. In the past, I did sleep with anyone who was interested, but I don't want that anymore. I want you now and you deserve more than to be treated like one of them." He looks me in the eyes. "You mean too much to me to risk our relationship because I was stupid and rushed this. What we have," he points his finger, waving it between the two of us. "Is special, and I'm not about to fuck it up."

I lean into him, now feeling like a bitch, tears still falling.

"I'm sorry," I sniff.

"Baby, you have nothing to apologize for. I promise you that one day soon I'm going to take you to bed and it'll be the best fucking night of your life. But until then, I think we should keep getting to know each other better."

I nod. "Okay. I don't like it, but I'll let you have this one."

He leans down and kisses the top of my nose.

"Good. Now, since you have your shoes on already, let's go somewhere."

He grabs his keys off the entertainment center.

"Where we going?" I ask. Now feeling better but feeling like an idiot for a completely different reason. I should have known better than to assume that he didn't want to sleep with me.

"The fair." He sits on the couch to lace his shoes up.

"I'm sorry. Come again?" He has got to be kidding.

"You heard me, sweetheart." He smirks. "We're going to the damn fair."

He stands and wraps his arms around me.

"Ryke, I'm twenty-six years old. I've never been to a fucking fair and I don't plan on changing that."

He gasps. "What? You've never been to a fair? Are you even American?" He holds his chest, feigning shock. Although, I think I really did just surprise the hell out of him.

"Yep, just never been before. My parents didn't have time to take us to things like that. Although, I'm not sure they would have anyway."

"You, my lady, have not lived until you've had a funnel cake and lemon shake-up from the fair."

Well, then. I guess we're going to the damn fair.

❧ 37 ❧
CLAIRE

We arrive at the insanely crowded fairgrounds, smells of fried foods waft through the air. I have to confess it makes my damn stomach rumble. I won't admit that to Ryke, though. I protested the entire drive here, not stopping until realizing I wasn't going to win.

"What do you want to do first?" he asks as we walk through the entrance. Small children run aimlessly through the park. I know Brady would enjoy something like this once he's a bit older.

"What do you suggest? I have no idea what you do at a fair." I know I sound like an idiot and I'm beginning to realize how deprived I was as a child. Don't get me wrong. We had more than enough entertainment growing up in Chicago, but this would have been considered very improper in my parents' eyes. Looking back, it doesn't make sense at all, but it is what it is.

Ryke tugs on my hand, leading me toward a food truck that reads "Frankie's Funnel Cakes."

"You *have* to try one of these fantastic things." He pulls

the fried food from the truck window, sprinkling an absurd amount of powdered sugar all over it.

"How do you eat this thing?" I ask, eyeballing the plate in front of us as we sit at a picnic table, side-by-side. "I need a fork."

"Nope, they don't have forks." He begins pulling the funnel cake apart, acting like a damn kid, as he shovels it into his mouth. His face covered in white.

"You're a slob!" I laugh at him, loving how carefree he is. I've been kind of uptight tonight and he deserves for me to have some fun with him.

He flicks powdered sugar at my nose. "Ryker Allen!" I shout. I grab a small piece of the cake and have to admit that it tastes heavenly. Damn, how have I never tried one of these before?

"Good, huh?" He continues devouring the food and now I'm worried he's going to eat it all before I can have another bite.

I take the plate from him, sliding it in front of me. "The rest is mine." I wink at him as I take bite after bite. This may just be my new favorite food.

He doesn't even try stealing it back but throws his head back in laughter. The funnel cake is almost forgotten over the fact that my panties are now damp from arousal.

We finish eating and then Ryke walks me toward the Ferris wheel.

I've never really been a fan of rides like this, but I don't have the heart to argue with him about anything else tonight. He's obviously put a lot of thought into our date.

After getting our tickets, we find an empty cart and slide into one corner together. He wraps his arm around me and we both look around the park. I, of course, don't see anyone I know, but he recognizes a few from the bar.

Soon, we're starting to go up into the air and I scoot closer to him, yearning for his nearness.

He stares down at me as if I hold the entire world in my hands. He grabs my hand and, the next thing I know, I'm caressing him through his pants. I'm a little confused after he stopped me from doing this very thing earlier but decide not to ruin the moment by questioning him.

"Oh, God, sweetheart. Don't stop." We're far enough away from the next cart that nobody can see what's going on between us. I know it's frowned on, but I lift from the seat and straddle him. He grabs my face and instantly devours my mouth as if his life depends on it.

I start moving up and down on his jean-covered shaft, wanting, no, *needing* the friction between us.

"Ryke, you're making me so fucking horny. You have got to stop teasing me," I mumble into his shoulder.

He slides his hand down my side and, the next thing I know, his fingers are teasing me through my pants. God, I want to rip the damn things off, but don't want to go to jail tonight for indecent exposure. Then I definitely won't be getting any later.

Once we're back on the ground, Ryke grabs my hand and tugs me through the park at lightning speed.

"Babe, what are you doing? Slow down!" He doesn't answer, clearly on a mission.

We get a couple dirty looks thrown our way as we run into a few other fairgoers. I silently apologize, but Ryke doesn't seem to notice them. If he does, he doesn't care.

We finally make it to his truck in the parking lot and

before I climb up into my seat, he stares down at me with hooded eyes.

"Hi," I whisper as I run my hand through his unruly hair. Since we've been together, he's been letting it grow out a bit and I find it extremely sexy. It's a good look on him.

Without responding, he devours my mouth as he lifts me from the ground. If I wasn't already about to lose my freaking mind, I am now.

When we pull apart, we're both gasping for air.

"What was that for?"

His chest rises and falls intensely, causing him not to be able to answer right away.

"Claire, I know that I said I wanted to take my time with you, but fuck baby. I need to be inside of you right now."

Holy. Shit.

"Okay."

When he pulls out of the parking lot, he drives without saying another word.

"Where are we going?" His house is a good thirty minutes from the fairgrounds and I have a feeling he isn't willing to wait that long.

The next thing I know, we're pulling onto an extremely bumpy gravel road.

"Uh, are you going to tell me where we're going?" I look out the windshield, noticing we're in the middle of nowhere.

He pulls into a driveway that sits in front of an old, red barn.

"Baby?" I say as I take in our surroundings, still not having a clue why we're out here.

"Stay put." His tone is demanding as he opens his door, coming around to open mine for me.

"What are you…?" Before I can finish my question, I'm being lifted from my seat, the door slamming behind me.

"I'm sorry I couldn't wait to get you home. I know this isn't how you imagined our first time together, but I really, *really* need to be inside you.

Well, damn. How can I argue with that?

❧ 38 ❧

CLAIRE

He's still carrying me as he walks us toward the barn. He pulls at the iron knob and the door swings open. His mouth hasn't left mine since we got out of his truck, so I'm not sure how he hasn't stumbled into anything.

Once we're inside, I pull my lips away from his, looking around at the empty space. There's literally nothing in here besides a couple stacks of hay laying in the corner. That's where he lies me down, not pulling his eyes away from me.

"What if someone catches us out here?" I croak.

"Sweetheart, nobody is going to come out here. This used to be my dad's land before they tore the house down. They left the barn. I promise, we're all alone."

At his assurance, I start working at the buttons on his shirt. Once they're all open, I slide it down his arms before he raises them so I can lift his white t-shirt over his head. This guy is a fucking god. My breath hitches as I take in his perfect form. A small amount of hair spatters his chest, showing that he's all man. His shoulders appear even more broad now that he's not covered. I've seen the beautiful tattoos that adorn both his arms, but his chest is overwhelmingly gorgeous. Over his left pec, where his heart is, sits a Chinese symbol with a date beneath it. On his ribcage, he has an open heart that reads "bruised, not broken." My heart leaps into my throat, thinking about this man ever being in any kind of pain.

He pulls his form-fitting jeans down his legs. He is now completely exposed to me, besides wearing his emerald boxers. They leave nothing to my imagination, making my mouth salivate.

"Come here," I whisper up at him and he immediately leans down, once again taking my mouth into his."

"You're wearing a bit too much clothing, Ms. Davis," he says as he begins to unbutton my jeans. The sound of his voice alone makes me wet all over again. I need him to hurry the hell up or I'm going to lose my damn mind if he's not inside of me soon.

After my pants are completely off, he stares down at my crimson-colored panties. What he doesn't know is that the bra matches. It seems to be affecting him, if the bulge in his underwear is any indication.

"Sit up, sweetheart." He lifts me from the hay into a sitting position and pulls my shirt over my head, now showing him the upper half of my body. "My God," he gasps. "You're fucking gorgeous."

He lays me back down as he gently places kiss after kiss on my exposed chest and then works his way down my stomach. At first, I'm a little hesitant at the thought of being on display because my body has been through so much lately, but he quickly distracts me of any negative thoughts towards myself.

"Ryke," I say his name in a moan as I throw my head back, desperate to have more of him.

He rubs his fingers over my panties and I nearly jump out of my skin.

"You're so wet, sweetheart. How did you get so wet?" he asks as he looks up at me, longing in his eyes. I desperately want to grab my phone, so I can take a picture of him in this moment. Not that I could ever forget this. No man has ever worshipped my body like this before.

"You," I groan, incapable of saying much else.

He drags his thumb along the top of my panties, slowly pulling them past my wetness. I hear him inhale a heavy breath, apparently liking what he sees.

"I knew you'd be gorgeous under all these clothes, but, fuck, sweetheart. I'm going to combust if I don't have you now." *Oh, my God.* His words are about to make me come undone.

"Then have me," I whisper up at him as I run my hands through his dark hair. I can't get enough of this man.

Without further invitation, he finishes pulling my panties off and tosses them onto the ground behind him. He then helps me back up so he can release my breasts from my bra. That soon joins my panties.

I start to grab for his boxers, but he beats me to it, yanking them off. I know my eyes must be bulging out of my head at the sight of his *very* large dick. I'm a little nervous it isn't going to fit, but the thought leaves my mind as soon as I feel his fingers on my heat.

He slowly inserts one finger and then soon another one joins it. He's straddling me but my ass flies off the hay at the intense contact. It's been too damn long since I've been touched. I don't know how much more of this I can take.

"Baby, I really need you inside of me. *Now*." Without responding, he slowly enters me and the space around us begins to spin. He pulls out, leaving only an inch of himself inside of me, but then rams his dick back in and I swear I start to see stars.

"Ryke!" I yell, knowing that if anyone drives by the barn, they'll hear me from the road.

"Fuck, sweetheart. You feel incredible." He kisses down my neck and then nips at my earlobe. He then finds my right breast and takes the erect nipple into his mouth, driving me further to my release. He twists the twin nipple and immediately fireworks erupt inside of me.

I'm gifted with the most intense orgasm I've ever had, his following soon after.

"Claire," he grunts into my shoulder as he releases himself into me.

Once we're both dressed, I start toward the barn door, but he grabs my arm.

"What's wrong?" I ask, noticing the worry in his eyes.

"We didn't use a condom." This sweet man who often acts like a badass is completely vulnerable in my hands.

I lift up on my toes to kiss him on the nose. "It's okay, I'm on the pill." I stare at him, hoping he's okay with the fact that we didn't use protection. We're completely exclusive, so I don't see why it would be a problem.

He nods his head. "Okay." For some reason, he still looks upset. "I just don't want you to think that I was careless with you. I swear to you, I'm clean. When we got together, I went to the doctor to make sure and everything came back good." This man.

"Babe, I know you'd never do anything that would hurt me. I completely trust you." I hug his middle, letting him know that I don't think he was being thoughtless.

"Good. You mean way too much to me to ever risk ruining this." He looks me in the eyes, seeming to have more to say to me. "I love you, Claire."

My heart explodes. I've known I loved him for some time now, but I didn't realize he felt the same.

"You do?" I hate the way my voice sounds when I ask, but I didn't realize how serious he was about me.

He grabs my head so I'm forced to look at him. "Yes, baby. I've never loved anyone like this before. I don't know what's going to happen down the road, but I promise I'll give you everything I can.

And…my ovaries are erupting. Again.

"I didn't want to say it while we were having sex because I didn't want you to think I was just saying it in the heat of the moment, but I really do, Claire." He looks at me, trying to read my reaction. "You don't have to say it back, but I wanted you to know."

He swipes at the lone tear I didn't realize had slipped from my eyes.

I sniff. "I love you too, Ryker Allen." I wrap my arms around his neck, taking charge of our kiss this time.

When we break apart, I can see the light shining in his eyes. Neither of us has ever felt this way before and I'm going to do everything I can not to blemish our love.

🦋 39 🦋

RYKER

"Hello?" I answer without looking to see who it is, trying to keep the phone to my ear with my shoulder while I quickly put my groceries away. I invited Claire over tonight for dinner. She always says that it turns her on that I cook, so damn. Of course, I'm going to fucking cook for her. I'm guessing I'll be rewarded for my efforts afterward.

"Hey, son." Dad.

"Hey, is everything alright? Is Becca okay? Gail?" There has to be something wrong if he's calling. We rarely talk. Not that we don't have a good relationship, because we do. It's just that neither of us care to talk on the phone. Most of our communication is when I visit him and Gail, which hasn't been for a while.

"Did you forget your sister is pregnant?" He chuckles.

"What? No, of course not. She's not due yet though." I have concern in my voice. I know it can't be good if she's going into labor this early.

"She's not due for another three weeks, but she's gone

into labor." I can't believe how fucking calm he is. This is his baby girl after all. She never could do any wrong in his eyes. I love my sister, but this always pissed me off growing up. I got in trouble for dumb shit while he always turned a blind eye on her.

"Is-is that alright?" I choke out. His tone should reassure me, but it doesn't.

"Yeah, it's fine. They might have to stay in the hospital a little longer than expected, but they are both fine. The little booger is just anxious to get out is all." He laughs and I know he's proud to become a grandfather soon. Damn. I'm going to be an uncle, too.

"Okay, well, I should be there in the next hour or so."

"It's okay. Take your time. Hey, why don't you bring that girl you've been seeing. What's her name? Candice?"

"Claire," I grumble. "Uh, yeah, sure. I'll ask her." I don't know if I'm ready for her to meet my family, but why the hell not?

"HEY, SWEETHEART," I say when I hear her pick up on the other end.

"Hey. Are we still on for tonight? I got a new bra and panties today that I can't wait to show you.

Well, fuck.

"Shit. You can't say stuff like that over the phone. I can't fucking touch you right now."

She giggles, which makes me even harder than I already am.

"Sorry." She's totally not sorry.

"Anyway, my dad just called and my sister is in labor."

"Oh, how exciting!" She exclaims. "Are you on your way to Scottsdale now?"

"No, not yet. My father wanted me to invite you to come with me."

The line goes silent and I'm worried I've freaked her the hell out.

"You there, sweetheart?"

"Yeah." She clears her throat, obviously buying herself some time before answering me. "You want me to meet your family?"

"Of course, I do. Why don't you bring Brady too?" I've asked her to bring him several times to hang out with us, but she always has someone lined up to watch him. I'm not sure when she plans on letting me meet him.

"No, that's okay. Evan and Avery were already watching him tonight anyway. I'm sure they won't mind if I'm gone a little longer than planned." I'm not sure what she's afraid of. I've shown her time after time that I've changed. I've changed for her. I'm no longer the player that I used to be. I don't sleep around with random women. No, she's it for me.

"Okay." I sigh, positive she can hear the annoyance in my voice. "I'll be there in a bit."

"Hey, sweetheart." I lean over to her side of the truck to steal a kiss once she's settled into her seat.

"Hey, Uncle Ryke." She smiles. "Are you excited?" It's fucking adorable how thrilled she is for me.

"Yeah, but I'm more excited to see that bra and panties

you're wearing under there." I wave my finger up and down toward her body as I raise my eyebrows at her.

"You, Mr. Allen, need to be good." She winks at me and props her feet up on the dashboard. If anyone else did this, I'd smack them, but she can do whatever she wants in my damn truck.

I squeeze her thigh. "Ms. Davis, how can I be good when you're always teasing me?"

She shrugs her shoulders. "I wasn't teasing. I really was going to show you them tonight." She giggles.

"Was? I don't get to see them now?" I ask, trying my best to sound offended.

"Maybe next time, mister." She bends down to the floorboard and digs through her large purse and then pulls out her Kindle. This woman is always reading something. Not that I can blame her. I'm sure after everything Trevor put her through, she needed some way to escape.

"Do you and Brady want to stay at my house tonight?"

I'm still facing the road, but I can see out of the corner of my eye when she slowly turns her head towards me. I have a feeling I already know what the answer will be, but damn it, I'm not giving up. I'd never hurt her or her son.

"Maybe another night. I'm sure Evan and Avery will already have him in bed by the time we get back."

"Okay." I know I sound irritated because I fucking am. But I decide to let it go. She spends the rest of the drive reading and I try not to let this upset me. I guess she'll bring me around her son when she's ready.

❧ 40 ❧

CLAIRE

W e spent most of the drive to Scottsdale in uncomfortable silence. I could tell Ryke was getting annoyed at my lack of enthusiasm of him meeting Brady. Deep down, I think I know that he wouldn't hurt us, but I just can't let my guard down. Ryke is not the settling down type and, honestly, the last thing I should be thinking about right now is remarrying. Hell, I'm not even divorced yet.

Ryke pulls into the busy parking lot and has to drive around for several minutes before he finds a spot. Once he does, he parks the truck and then turns to me.

"Ready, sweetheart?" I can tell by his tone that I upset him earlier, but I don't want him to worry about that right now. I want him to enjoy seeing his family and his new nephew.

I reach over and squeeze his hand. "Yeah, let's go."

We both climb down from the truck and he meets me behind it.

"You, Ms. Davis, need to stop opening the door for

yourself." He leans in to kiss my cheek which makes me sigh with relief. I'm glad to know he's not completely pissed off at me.

"I'm a big girl." I wink at him.

He leans into my ear and breathes down my neck. "When you're with me, I take care of you. Understand?"

"Yes, sir." I swat his ass as he starts to walk away, not caring who sees.

"Claire, I really want to go into that hospital and see my family, but if you keep that shit up, I'll be forced to find a bathroom and have my way with you in it."

He goes back to walking and I shout behind him. "Is that a threat?"

He stops and turns back toward me. "No, it's a promise. Now get your sexy ass up here with me."

I decide to stop goading him and grab his hand.

"Are you sure you're ready for me to meet your family?" I wasn't surprised when he invited me because he wanted me to go to his family's Sunday dinner last week. I had turned him down, telling him that I had plans with Sierra. I wasn't lying, but I really was a nervous wreck, thinking about meeting them, especially in such an intimate atmosphere. I figured the hospital wasn't a big deal, but I'm still anxious about meeting them.

Once we finally make it to the labor and delivery unit, Ryke immediately spots his family.

"They're going to love you," he whispers in my ear when he feels me tense beside him.

I first see a man who looks identical to Ryke, aside from a head full of salt-and-pepper hair and proof on his face that he's up there in age. He's really a good-looking man. I bet he looked just like Ryke when he was his age.

Beside him sits a petite woman with short, red, curly hair. She seems to be a bit younger than his dad, but she's beautiful.

"Hey, Dad. Gail." He greets them both and then leans in to hug his stepmother.

"This is my girlfriend, Claire."

His dad stands from his seat and grabs me into a bear hug. At first, I'm shocked but then relax. I shouldn't be surprised his family is so friendly.

Next, Gail stands and gives me a hug and kisses me on the cheek. My family has never been like this, but I find it endearing.

"Nice to meet you, Mr. and Mrs. Allen."

"Oh, please. Call us Gail and Rodney," his father says.

I nod my head, feeling shy all of a sudden. They're very welcoming, though, so I shouldn't be.

Ryke grabs my hand again and sits next to his dad, so I take the empty chair to his right.

"How's Becca? Has anything changed since I talked to you?"

"She's dilated to a five now, so she's about halfway there," Gail says as she knits what appears to be a scarf. Why someone would need a scarf in Arizona is beyond me.

"Uh, what the hell does that mean?" he asks, genuinely clueless as to what happens to a woman's body during labor.

"Watch your mouth, boy." Gail reaches over Rodney and smacks Ryke in the side of the head which has me chuckling beside him. I already like this woman.

"Oww!" he hollers and causes others to turn their

heads towards us. "And are you laughing at me?" he asks as he looks at me.

"Nope." I pop the 'p' and shrug my shoulders.

"Do you know what that means?" he asks and I could seriously strangle him about now.

"Uh." I start to bite at my nails, a nervous habit I've had since I was young.

"Leave that poor girl alone," Rodney says, coming to my rescue. "Gail will explain it to you." He says, clearly uncomfortable about talking about his daughter's womanly parts. I can't exactly blame him.

"It's when…" Gail starts but is cut off when Ryke waves his hand at her.

"No. I want her to tell me." Gail grabs his hand and smacks it.

"Boy, don't you wave your hand at me."

"Sorry," he mumbles and I'm hoping to God that he's now too distracted to remember what he asked me.

No such luck though.

"So?" He's talking loud enough for both his parents to hear our conversation.

"Google it." I bite my lip, knowing that he's not going to let this go. *Damn him.*

"No." Stubborn asshole.

I huff. "A woman's cervix has to stretch ten centimeters before she can deliver a baby." I say the words as quickly and quietly as possible.

"Why the hell did you tell me that?" He stands up and yanks at his hair. He's acting like a freaking dramatic woman right now.

"Uh, because you told me to."

"Ryker Allen, sit your ass down." This time Gail

smacks Rodney on the back of the head for cursing. I imagine Ryke has gotten smacked a number of times for cursing in front of her over the years.

Before either of them can respond, a good-looking, tall, blond man who appears to be in his mid-thirties sits next to Gail.

"Hey, Justin. Any news?" Rodney asks and the four of us stare in his direction.

"Benjamin is here." He's now wearing a huge grin on his face.

"That's wonderful!" Gail shrieks.

"Congratulations, Dad." Rodney stands to hug Justin.

Then Ryke follows. "Congrats, man," he says as he gives him a dude hug. You know, where they slap each other on the back with their fists.

"Can we see him?" This comes from Gail. I can tell she's anxious about seeing her new grandson.

"The nurses are helping her nurse right now, but they said once they're done, she can have visitors."

"Great! How big is he?"

"Six pounds, six ounces." He's a tiny little guy. Brady was nine pounds even. I wasn't surprised because Trevor was also a big baby.

"Is Bec doing alright?" Rodney asks with concern etched on his face. I know that, for several years, he played both parents to Ryke and his sister.

"She's doing great. Just tired."

At that, Rodney sits back in his seat and now seems more relaxed.

Ryke leans into me. "Is six pounds little for a baby?"

"He's little, but he's perfectly fine at six pounds." I smile at him and squeeze his knee.

"How big was Brady?" His interest in my son makes me feel even worse about not taking him to meet Brady yet.

"He was nine pounds."

His eyes go wide. "You pushed a nine-pound bowling ball out of your hoo-ha?" He has a look of shock on his face which has me holding my stomach with laughter. "Why are you laughing? That's not normal."

"Baby, that's why a woman's cervix has to be at ten centimeters before she can deliver."

He shakes his head. "That's just not right." I can just imagine him in the labor and delivery room. He'd probably pass out and need more medical attention than the mother and baby.

The thought of him having a baby makes my heart hurt. I don't know if I could ever give him, or anyone else that, again.

Justin leaves the room to be with his wife and baby and the rest of us continue to visit. The longer we sit with his parents, the more I realize that I had nothing to be worried about. Both his father and stepmom are great people.

❧ 41 ❧

RYKER

Being at the hospital has me desperately wanting to have this with Claire one day. Although, after she told me about what happens to a woman when they have a baby, I don't think I could make her go through that again. But if she's willing…

Justin comes back out and tells us we can go see Becca and Benjamin.

"Come on, sweetheart," I say when I stand to leave the waiting room. She looks at me with apprehension in her eyes. "What's wrong?"

"You go. I'll be right here when you get back." She gives me a half smile.

"What? Why?" I look at her, surely with confusion laced in my expression.

"That's your family. I don't want to intrude." Damn it. I don't know what she's so scared of, but I thought she had been comfortable around my parents. Why is she acting this way now?

"They want you back there. Come on." She finally agrees and takes my hand.

I knock on the door before we enter. My sister is laying on the hospital bed with a little bundle in her arms. A smile graces my face when she sees me. We didn't always get along growing up, but today I'm fucking proud of her. I can't believe my sister is a mom.

"Hey, bro," Becca says as I lean in to kiss her on the cheek. "Meet your nephew." All I can see of the little guy is his face, but he has a cute little button nose and round chubby cheeks. Yep, he's an Allen. "Want to hold him?"

"Uh, no. He looks comfy with you."

She rolls her eyes at me. "Ryke, he won't break." I know this but I've only held a few babies in my life, the last being a long time ago.

"Okay, but I want to sit down first." At least, I know this way I won't drop him.

Justin takes Benjamin from Becca and places him in my arms. Tears immediately come to my eyes and I feel like a damn pussy. This is so not me. I don't get emotional like this, but this little guy is amazing.

"Hey, buddy," I whisper as I take in all his little features. His hands peek out from the blue blanket and I can't get over how tiny they are. He's only a couple hours old, but he squints his eyes open at me and, damn, it's adorable.

I don't know if I'll ever have this. But, damn, do I hope so. With the brown-eyed girl staring at me from across the room with an enormous smile on her face. I wink at her.

I try to imagine what she looked like when she had her

son. I know she was beautiful as always, but I can see her in my mind cradling Brady and perhaps nursing him. Why that turns me on is beyond me. Those tits are only for me.

I hand the baby back over to Justin and then stand to be with Claire. We visit for a bit longer, but Becca looks extremely exhausted, so we decide it's time to leave.

I grab Claire's hand as we walk through the hallways of the hospital.

"He is so cute."

"I know." I smile. "What did you expect though? He's my nephew." I smirk at her and she rolls her eyes.

"You are so full of yourself."

"But you love it." I lean in to kiss her.

"Yeah," she sighs. "I do." God, this woman causes me to feel things I've never felt before. I fucking love it.

We both climb into my truck and start our way back to Phoenix. Some country song plays softly, but other than that, it's quiet.

After a few minutes, I grab her hand and bring it to my lips. They linger on her soft, delicate skin. I can't get enough of this woman.

"I love you." I quickly turn my head toward her, not wanting to get us in an accident from being careless.

"Love you, too," she sighs as she gives me a heart-warming smile. She leans her head against the seat.

"Do you want to have more kids someday?" I don't know why the words tumble from my mouth, but they just felt right. I never imagined myself having a family before her. Not even with Monica. We never talked about having children.

She doesn't answer me right away, so I chance another look at her.

It's dark in the truck, but I can still see the tear that trickles down her cheek.

"Hey, what's wrong?" I'm on the interstate, so I can't pull over to gather her into my arms.

"Nothing." She wipes at her face. "Just that time of month." She waves her hand in the air trying to dismiss the conversation. I know she's lying.

I decide to let it go until we get closer to home. She's upset and obviously needs to talk about whatever caused the pained look on her face. I know just the perfect place to take her.

❧ 42 ❧

CLAIRE

Ryke's question completely threw me for a loop. And not in a good way. Being with him has always felt like an escape from all the bullshit in my life. That was why I never mentioned Trevor to him when we met. Only Shay and Sierra know about my miscarriage. I never even told Evan. I know I'm a shit sister, but I just couldn't bring myself to tell him. He'd kill Trevor if he found out that he caused the loss of my child. Not that he pushed me down the stairs on purpose. He'd never hurt me physically. Just emotionally.

"Where are we going?" I ask in confusion as I realize that we're not headed to his house or Sierra's. It's nearing eleven o'clock, so nothing is open this late besides a few bars.

Finally, it dawns on me where we're at. I usually walk here a different route, so it looks different.

Ryke pulls into a parking spot and then undoes his buckle and turns towards me.

"You need to clear your head and this is a good place for that."

I don't respond but nod my head still looking out the front window. I undo my own buckle and then open the door to the truck and leave without waiting for him. I head for the lake where it's peaceful with only the sounds of the ducks splashing in the water.

I throw my head back and breathe in the fresh air. I've always enjoyed the outdoors, but since moving here, I've found solace being at Greenwood Park. I'm not sure if it's because of the beautiful scenery or the simple fact that it's a piece of mine and Ryke's story. I like to think the latter.

I'm so lost in my thoughts that I didn't realize Ryke was behind me this whole time. I startle at his touch.

"Sorry, sweetheart." He doesn't touch me again but continues to silently walk beside me, letting me get lost in my thoughts. There's an ache in my chest, but he makes it feel a little less intense.

After several minutes, he grabs hold of my hand. "Are you ready to talk?"

"Why?" I croak out. My face is damp with tears, I thought I could hold back.

"Come here." He wraps me in his arms, but I rapidly pull away from him. I'm being unreasonable, but I don't know if I can talk about this. He stops walking, hopefully to give me space and not because he's pissed at me. I wonder what's going through his mind.

I reach our bench. Once I sit, I rest my elbows on my knees and bury my face in my hands. I try to take relaxing breaths to calm my nerves.

I'm unaware of where Ryke is but then feel the bench shake as he sits down.

"I'm sorry," I whisper as I slowly look up at him afraid to know what his response will be.

"You have nothing to be sorry for." He smiles at me, but I can tell he's still worried about me.

I know he's scared to touch me after my reaction earlier, so I whisper, "Please hold me, Ryke."

In a heartbeat, he's standing again, lifting me into his arms as if I'm light as air. My legs wrap around his strong, steely frame and he sits us both back down.

"It's okay, I'm here," he whispers into my hair as he rubs my back. He does this a lot, and it always comforts me.

"I've ruined our night." I wipe at my nose with the back of my hand. This should embarrass me, but he doesn't seem to mind. "You're a new uncle and here I am sulking about something that happened months ago."

He pushes me back, just far enough that he can look me in the eyes. "You haven't ruined anything. If we're going to be together, we support each other no matter what. You're just going to have to get used to that." He smirks at me and I nod. "We don't have to talk about it, but if you want to, I'm here to listen. Even if that's not tonight.

I rest my hands on his shoulders as I close my eyes to take a few deep breaths.

"No, I need to talk about it." I feel the pad of his thumb wipe at my tear-stained face. It sends butterflies wafting through my stomach.

I push off of him to take the seat next to him again. He patiently waits for me to speak.

"The night I caught Trevor cheating on me, I had a

miscarriage," I say this in a whisper as I stare in front of me at the trees that bluster in the wind.

"Sweetheart," he whispers as he grabs my hand. "I'm so sorry."

I still can't look at him, but I go on. "After I confronted him, he accidentally pushed me backward down the stairs." I have no idea why I felt the need to tell him that, but now I'm regretting my decision.

"What?" he roars as he stands from the bench. "He fucking caused this?" I should have known he'd go off the deep end at my confession.

"Ryke, sit down," I cry.

"Shit." He blows out a breath. "I'm sorry, Claire," he whispers. "It's just the thought of him hurting you makes my fucking blood boil." He once again joins me and gathers me into his arms, nuzzling his face into my hair. I'm not sure if he's trying to comfort me or himself.

"He didn't purposely hurt me, I swear. We just got into an argument and he grabbed my shoulders and I tripped. Honestly, it doesn't even matter what happened, though. The fact is, I don't have my baby now and I don't think I could ever go through something like that again."

He doesn't say anything else but lets me cry into his shoulder until I've run out of tears and energy to weep any longer.

He grabs my hand and pulls my wearied body from the bench.

Once we're back at Sierra's, he takes me to my room and lovingly strips me of my clothes and tucks me into bed.

"Go to sleep. I'll call you in the morning." He leaves a kiss on my cheek and then exits the room.

43

RYKER

I t's rare I get a night off from the bar, so when my buddy Eric invited me over to his house, I couldn't decline.

I recognize a few guys from school and a few others who work out at the gym, but most I don't know. It's a nice night, so I decide to find a chair out in Eric's backyard. I grab a beer from his outdoor bar and find a lawn chair. I thought Claire would be here already, but I don't see her yet.

"Hey, stud, is this seat taken?" I turn toward the familiar and sweet voice. Chills immediately run through my spine.

"Hey, beautiful." It's dark out here, but it doesn't stop me from noticing the red creep up her neck and cheeks. It's a damn turn on and I love that I do that to her. I pull her chair towards me so our knees touch. I lean in and grab her face and run my hands through her hair.

She chuckles. "I know I sound like a super creepy girl-friend, but I missed you today."

"Maybe I like my girlfriend super creepy." I wink at her and then kiss her nose. "I missed you too." I only slept for six hours today, but I know I would have slept better with her next to me. I hope that one day she's in my bed every night. "Want a bottle of water?" She nods, so I grab one from the cooler. The night we first got together, she told me that she's on antidepressants, so she can't have alcohol. That explained why I never saw her drink at my bar.

We sit outside away from everyone else as we talk. I have to say that it's been one of the best nights of my life. She opens up more about her parents and I can tell she really misses them. I know what it's like to not have a mother, but I can't imagine not having either of my parents.

We walk around talking to a few people we run into. Being with her is natural. It doesn't seem like we only met a couple months ago, but more like we've known each other a lifetime.

"So, what's going on with you and Claire?" Eric asks when I walk over to the bar to grab a couple drinks.

"We're together, if that's what you're asking." I smile. I'm proud to call her mine.

"Dude, isn't she married?" *Jesus Christ, can't anyone mind their own damn business?*

"Yes, but she'll be divorced soon."

"Whatever. You'll be the one dealing with him when he gets a hold of her."

I immediately see red. I know Eric doesn't mean anything by it, but the fact that she could go back to Trevor at any time makes me fucking enraged. I know I should trust her, but she does legally belong to another man still.

"Everything alright over here, boys?" Elise, Eric's fiancé asks as she hooks her arm through his.

"Sure is, but Claire and I need to take off. Thanks for having us, guys." I grab Claire's hand. I know she's giving me a questioning look behind me because of my sudden change in behavior.

We walk through their big house and I just want to get into my truck and get the hell out of here.

"Ryke, what's going on? You're scaring me." My heart thuds in my chest. "Are you alright, baby?" She asks with a concerned look on her face. God, I love when she calls me that.

"Yeah, I'm fine. I need to head home to let Griz out," I lie. I don't want to tell her what has me upset, but she's making it hard for me to keep the truth from her.

"I don't believe you for one second." She pokes me in the chest to get my attention and I can tell she's losing her patience with me. "Come on. Tell me what's got you upset."

"Claire," I pause and make sure I have her full attention. "You know how you said you sounded like a creepy girlfriend earlier?" She nods. "Well, if that's the case, I'm a super fucking overprotective boyfriend."

"What's this about?" she asks on a whisper.

I grab her by the arm forcefully, but not strong enough to hurt her. I pull her through the hallway until I find an empty bathroom. After I shut the door behind us, I have her against the door and grab her face and look deep into her eyes. She's panting while she holds onto me for dear life. I don't even ask her if it's alright because I can tell by her reaction she wants this as bad as I do. I smash my lips into hers and she doesn't hesitate to kiss me back. It's the most frantic, yet passionate, kiss I've ever experienced. My arms wrap around her waist, trying to pull her as close to me as I can. Her hands run through my hair and pain shoots through my head, but it's the best pain I have ever endured. After several minutes, we pull apart for air, still panting.

"What was that for?" She's out of breath. She takes my breath away too, so I understand.

"Tell me you're mine," I say in a hard tone.

"I'm yours, Ryke. Only yours."

"Good. Brady is with Evan tonight, right?" She nods.

"Let's go." I pull her out of the bathroom and out of Eric's house. This is going to be the longest drive of my life.

If I'm ever forced to let this woman go, surely, she'll take half my damn heart with her.

❧ 44 ❧
CLAIRE

As soon as we get to Ryke's house, we waste no time. We haven't been together intimately since last weekend after the fair. But right now, he's got me wanting nothing more than to climb his body like a freaking spider monkey.

He lifts me off the floor and carries me to the couch. We start kissing like we haven't seen each other in years.

He starts working his way up my shirt, tickling my stomach. We're quickly interrupted when Griz starts barking at us.

"Damn it, Griz." Ryke continues to kiss my neck, trying to ignore him. Griz isn't having it, though.

"Go let him out. I'll be waiting right here for you."

Not a minute later he's lifting me from the couch.

"Ryke!" I squeal. "What are you doing?"

"I'm going to make love to my girlfriend." He continues his way toward his bedroom, not realizing how flustered he has me. At the mention of *making love* to me, I feel a tear slip from my eye but rush to wipe it away, not wanting to ruin the moment.

He guides me to the bed and my head lands on a down pillow that smells deliciously like him. All man. He grabs the sides of my pants and pulls them down my body, bringing my panties with them. I think he's trying to torture me because he's taking his sweet time. Once I'm fully naked, he steps back from the bed and admires my naked form. He then climbs up my body.

I look up at this handsome man, noticing the concerned look on his face.

"What's wrong?"

He stares down into my eyes before responding. "Promise me, you're mine." If this sweet man thinks he has anyone to compete with, he's out of his mind.

"I promise all I want is you." I rub the sides of his face, trying to reassure him. I hate that he thinks he has anything to worry about.

"Okay." He nuzzles into my neck, but I can tell that he still doesn't completely believe me. I decide to show him instead.

"Mr. Allen, I do believe it's your turn to get naked," I whisper into his neck.

"Ms. Davis, every time you call me that, you give me a fucking hard-on."

"Well, then, I guess it's good that I can take care of you tonight." I gently shove at his shoulders until he's on his back. I start by unzipping his pants and he has to help me with his belt buckle. I slide them slowly down his body, just like he did to me. When they are completely off, I slide both his socks off. I decide to leave his boxers on until last. He sits up for me so I can pull his navy shirt over his head. This man is beautiful with clothes on, but without, he is perfection.

I run my long nails along both of his nipples and then lean in to suck on one of them. I lay completely on top of him and run my soaking wet pussy along his throbbing dick, still covered by his boxers.

He gets impatient and pulls them off himself, then flips me to my back. The heat of his body is so overwhelming and I can't wait to have this man inside of me.

"Hi." He stares me in the eyes.

"Hi, back," I whisper.

"Tonight, I'm going to take my time with you, so I can savor every moment of this."

I nod at him, not having the words to say to this amazing man.

He smiles down at me and gives my lips a soft kiss in response. He rubs along my slit with his fingers and he's making me so damn wet I can hardly handle it.

He slides down my body and, at first, I'm unsure of what he's doing. But then he slowly inserts a finger into my core.

"Does that feel good?" he asks as he looks at me with desire in his eyes.

"Yes, so good," I pant.

He inserts a second finger and I don't think I can handle the intensity of it. I have my eyes closed as I'm lost in ecstasy, so I don't notice him bending down to take me in his mouth. He's not just licking me. He's devouring my core. I'm about to explode in his mouth.

I lift myself off the bed, so I'm pressed up against his face. Just the sight of him working my body is going to make me shatter into a million pieces. I'm starting to see stars as my body vibrates from his tongue. It's the longest, most desirable orgasm I've ever experienced. And from a mouth, nonetheless.

My toes curl around him as I come down from my high. He crawls back up my body and devours my lips the same way he did my pussy just a moment ago. I can taste myself on him.

I push at his shoulders for him to get off of me. "My turn now." I give him a half smile as he looks at me questioningly. I want to return the favor, but I'm also still too numb from the earth-shattering orgasm he just gave me. I need a minute to calm down before he's inside me.

"What are you doing?" he asks with a raspy voice even though he knows exactly what I'm doing.

"Lay back and I'll show you." He listens and puts his hands behind his head. I really suck at having a seductive voice, but it seems to be working on him.

Once he's completely on his back, I straddle him just above his cock and then kiss along his neck as I rub on his right nipple. His hands are immediately on my ass and I know he's turned on by my touch. While I'm still rubbing him, I suck on his other nipple and he nearly jumps off the bed. *Well done, Claire.*

I work my way down his beautiful six-pack and kiss along his stomach.

"I need your mouth on me."

"So impatient." I smirk at him.

"You're teasing me, Claire." He smiles, but I can tell that he's about to lose his mind.

I decide to skip the teasing and go straight to my final destination. I grasp his large cock in my hand and rub him up and down. My hand caresses him in slow strokes. He continues to pant as he runs his fingers through my hair.

"Claire, please. I need your mouth." He pushes my head toward his cock and I give in.

He's big, so I have to be careful not to gag myself, but he helps me by guiding my mouth down his shaft.

"So good, baby," he whispers.

He's almost completely in my mouth as I run my tongue along both sides of him. I release him with a pop and lick at the pre-cum that is seeping from him.

I look up at him and he has his eyes closed. It's such a turn on to see how much I'm affecting him.

"I'm going to come, baby, if you don't stop and I really want to be inside of you first."

I'm desperate to have him inside of me, so I don't argue. I'm on my hands and knees as I slowly crawl up his body, but then he lightly pushes me until he is on top. I want to give him the control that I can tell he needs right now. I wrap my legs around him so my heels are digging into his perfect ass. He grabs my head and brings his lips down to mine to consume me in a panty-melting kiss, if I were wearing any. He slowly drags his right hand down my body, stopping to massage my left nipple as he leans down to suck on the right. The next thing I know, he's inserting a finger inside of me. It feels so wonderful, but if he doesn't get inside of me in the next two seconds, I'm going to lose my damn mind. This is too much stimulation at once.

He releases my nipple and brings his hand back up to our faces. Slowly he sucks on his finger that is covered with my juices as he eases into me. *Oh, my God.*

"It feels fucking amazing. You're fucking amazing." He

kisses me harder as he rocks into me. I can taste and smell myself on his lips and it's a damn turn-on. The smell of sex mixed with his woodsy outdoor scent is my new favorite.

Sex for me has never been so mind-blowing and I'm not sure how much more my body can handle.

I let him take the control he wants. He grabs my hands and places them above my head. He uses his other hand to flick at my warmth while he's still pushing into me.

He leans down and whispers in my ear. "I love you, Claire."

"Ryke!" I yell. Between his rough, sexy voice and the desire he is causing, I come undone. I throw my head back as my eyes close. Once again, my toes curl around him as I come down from my high.

"Fuck!" He grunts as he fills me and it feels amazing.

Apparently, I was missing out all these years.

"I feel the same way." I smile at him.

He leans in and kisses me hard, letting himself soften inside of me.

"I'll go get a cloth to clean you up." He kisses me one last time and then pulls himself off me. I miss him already and it's a feeling I love. I don't know what I'll do if I ever lose this man.

———

I WAKE up from a persistent knocking on Ryke's front door. I roll over and the spot next to me is empty, but then I see a note lying on his pillow.

Sweetheart,
Went to get breakfast and coffee be back soon.

~Ryke

P.S. You're sexy as hell in my bed.

I smile, but then I hear that damn pounding again. I quickly grab a pair of Ryke's shorts and a t-shirt. Whoever is on the other side of the door is going to be strangled. I swing the door open fast and see that it's my frantic brother.

"Evan, what the hell is wrong?" I know I'm standing at Ryke's door in his clothes, but Evan doesn't seem to notice.

"Claire, Brady is in the ER. He fell and hit his head on our coffee table. He's alright, but he's going to need stitches." The room starts spinning. He's still talking, but I have no idea what about. My son, my world, got hurt and I wasn't there to take care of him.

"It's okay, but we need to go. Get dressed and I'll drive you to the hospital."

I run back to Ryke's room and quickly throw my clothes on from the night before, then tie my hair up so it's out of my face. I can't get to my son fast enough.

I'm pretty sure Evan breaks every traffic law on our way to the hospital, but I don't care. Brady needs me right now.

"I'm Claire Davis, Brady Davis's mother." The kind nurse takes me and Evan back to the room Brady and Avery are in.

"My baby," I cry. The sight of his little head bandaged, has my heart splitting in two.

"Are you his mother?" A middle-aged doctor in a white lab coat asks.

"Yes."

"The little guy is going to need some stitches, but then he'll be good as new.

I sigh in relief. "Thank you."

I carefully lift Brady off Avery's lap and kiss him on the cheek.

I tell them to leave because I know they both need to get to work.

"Claire, I am so sorry. I stepped out of the room for just a second to grab his cup." Avery has tears in her eyes, matching mine.

"Come here, Av." I wrap my free arm around her. "It's not your fault. I should have been there." I let out a hiccup from my crying.

"Text me later to let me know how he's doing." She pulls the door closed behind her.

"I'm so sorry, baby," I say into his hair. I can't believe I was so careless. How could I let something like this happen to my child?

In the midst of my panic earlier, I forgot to let Ryke know that I was headed to the hospital. If I hadn't been with him last night, this wouldn't have happened. How could I have been so stupid?

45

RYKER

When I get back from The Espresso Bean with bagels and coffee, Claire is nowhere to be found. *Where the hell is she?*

I quickly dial her but get no response and the same with my texts. Things have been going great over the last month. I can honestly say I've never been happier.

I try calling Sierra and of course don't get an answer from her either.

"Come on, Griz." I put him in his bed and then slide my shoes back on before walking out the door. I have no idea where the hell she is, but I'm freaking the hell out. Why would she just leave without telling me? She was sound asleep just thirty minutes ago when I left.

I pull into Sierra's driveway but don't see her car that is usually parked out front. I run up the steps and pound on the door. If she's sleeping, she's going to be pissed at me for waking her, but right now I just need to know where the hell my girlfriend is.

244

After waiting for several minutes, I come to terms with the fact that no one is home.

Next, I drive across town to Evan and Avery's house. Avery's car is parked in the drive, but once again, I get no answer when I beat on the door. It's early enough that they most likely wouldn't be at work yet. I have a sinking feeling in my stomach.

I climb back in my truck, checking my phone again, but see that I still have no response from Claire.

I try calling Evan, but, yet again, get no answer. What the fuck is going on?

I decide to head home to see if she came back, but I couldn't be so lucky. I'm hoping that she and Brady are alright, but if they are, she'll be getting an earful from me. She had to have known how goddamned worried I'd be when she just took off.

It's now been three hours since Claire left my house. My phone finally goes off and I'm quick to grab it off the coffee table, but accidentally drop it in my haste to answer it.

"Fuck."

Once I finally have it in my hands, I see that Sierra is calling.

"Sierra, what the hell is going on?" I'm sure she can hear the anger in my voice, but right now I don't give a fuck.

"Calm down. Claire is fine." I breathe a sigh of relief.

"Good, but where the hell is she?" I sound like a fucking control freak.

"She had to go to the hospital. Brady needed stitches."

"Is he okay?" I don't even know the little guy, but the thought of him being hurt crushes me. He's a part of Claire and that makes him important to me.

"Yeah, he's fine."

I feel like I'm being left in the pitch black with how unwilling she is to tell me anything. I could have been there for them, but she doesn't fucking want me around her child.

I hang up and throw myself back on the couch. I'm so pissed off, but I'm relieved at the same time that she's alright.

I doze off on the couch, but when I wake, I see that it's 5:00 in the evening. This entire day has been shit. Deciding not to call Claire or Sierra again, I hop in my truck and start my way back over to Sierra's. I know she has to eventually go back there.

I knock on the door, hurting my hand in the process but not giving a fuck. My beautiful girl swings the door open.

"Ryke, what are you doing here?" What the hell? I can't see straight.

"Why haven't you answered any of my texts or calls all day?" I'm trying not to take my anger out on her, but after the shit she's put me through today, I'm finding it hard to care.

"Mama!" I hear a little voice behind her. Once the boy comes in sight, he reaches for Claire.

"Mama, up!" The boy is freaking adorable. Looks just like his mother.

She kisses Brady on the top of his head and then sets him back on the floor. He toddles off down the hallway.

She steps onto the porch with me.

"Why didn't you call me? I would have been at the hospital in a heartbeat." I hate that she closes this part of her life up to me. I've tried time and time again to prove to her what she means to me.

"Babe, you don't even know Brady. Plus, I knew Trevor was coming, so I didn't think it was a good idea."

I yank at my hair and turn toward the stairs.

I spin back around. "Why the fuck is that, Claire?" When she doesn't answer, I start to leave. But before I do, I stop again. "I don't give a shit about Trevor. I just wanted to be there for you and your son." I shake my head. "I told you I loved you."

"Don't go." She has worry etched on her face.

"I can't do this right now."

"Do what?" She has got to be fucking kidding me.

I slowly turn back toward her. "Claire, you know I love you more than the fucking air I breathe, but the fact that you feel the need to keep your child from me hurts like hell."

"Well, well, well. Who do we have here?" I turn at the sound of the deep, malicious voice and the hairs on the back of my neck stand at attention. This is her fucking husband.

I walk to the front door and reach my hand out to him. He looks familiar but I know I haven't seen him before.

"Ryker Allen."

He doesn't extend his hand to mine, which is probably for the best. Instead, I grab him by the collar as I'm up in his face.

"You fucking touch her and I'll end you," I seethe.

When I let him go, he chuckles at me.

"I'd never hurt *my wife*."

I head toward the stairs but first catch a glimpse of Claire. Her expression is pained.

"I'm not him, Claire."

Without letting her get another word in, I leave.

✿ 46 ✿

RYKER

I decide I need a drink so I head over to the bar. It's Austin's night to work, but I'm wishing I would have gone in instead. Last night, I had the sudden fear that, one day, Claire was going to take her stupid husband's ass back and now this shit. I just can't handle it. I should have known better.

"Dude, you look like shit," Austin laughs. If I didn't have a damn headache, I would punch him in the face.

"Fuck you, man. Get me a Corona." I slouch on the stool at the end of the bar and put my head in my hands. There's no way I'm going to get a wink of sleep tonight.

Austin sets my beer in front of me and goes back to wiping the already clean bar. I'm thankful for his silence because all I want is to drink my beer, go home, and throw myself a pity party.

One beer turns in to eight. I want more but Austin cuts me off. *Asshole.* I leave my truck at the bar and walk the few short blocks back home. I'll get it tomorrow when I come in to work. I'll most likely be worth shit though.

When I get to my driveway, I notice someone sitting on my porch. Claire? No, this woman's hair is shorter, but there's a child sitting on her lap. *Damn it.*

"Hey, baby, are you alright? I've been waiting for you to get home." I don't want to deal with this bitch tonight. Or ever.

"Monica, what the hell are you doing here?" I'm seething. I made it pretty clear she wasn't welcome at my house, but apparently, she didn't get the hint.

"Aww, come on. I missed you and wanted to see you." She stands up from the bench and walks towards me with her child in her arms.

"Monica, I'm sorry, but I've had a shitty night and I need to go to sleep. Please leave." I unlock the door and her arms wrap around my waist. I've never been one to touch a woman, but I'm two seconds away from throwing her off of me. She is the last person I want to see right now.

"Baby, please let me and Kayla come in. We need somewhere to stay." Now I'm getting pissed.

"Go home to your parents. You're not welcome here." I'm being a major ass, but I can't stand to be around her. Does she seriously believe I'd welcome her with open arms?

"We've been staying with them, but I got into it with my mom and she kicked us out. Please." *Damn it.* She isn't going to stop until I let her in my house.

"You can sleep on the couch, but in the morning, you're gone. Understood?" I turn around to look at her and if looks could kill, she'd be dead. Her child is the only reason I let her in.

"I promise." I could tell she was going to be a pain in

my ass when I told her to leave, but tonight I want to go to bed and not deal with her.

When we get inside, I go to the hall closet and pull out a few blankets for them. I grab Monica a pillow and set everything in the living room. I can't even look at her because I'm so pissed about her being in my house. I'm drunk and need to go to sleep to clear my head. I'll hate myself tomorrow for the way I've acted.

I walk back to my room and slip my jeans and shirt off. I know that as soon as my head hits my pillow, I'll be out. Sleep doesn't happen because as soon as I get comfortable, I hear a pounding from the other room. My head hurts too damn much and I don't want to deal with any more shit tonight. I reluctantly walk out of my room to see what the hell is going on.

When I first see the front door all I can see is Monica in a shirt and no pants, answering whoever was banging from outside.

"Who the hell are you?" Claire. *Fuck!* I don't know what to do and I'm freaking the hell out knowing she'll assume the worst after seeing Monica here.

"I'm Monica. And who are you?" I hear the hatred in Monica's voice.

I finish walking the rest of the way to the front door, not knowing what to expect when I see her.

Once I finally get to the door and pull it further open, I watch as Claire's mouth hits the floor. And the next words out of mine are the worst I could possibly say.

"Claire, what are you doing here?"

"I was coming to see if you were alright, but clearly I was interrupting something." She looks me up and down and I soon remember that I'm in my fucking underwear.

She tries to run off my front porch, but I grab her arm. As soon as I touch her, she flinches as if I burned her.

"I can explain," I say, hoping she'll listen to me.

"You were so fucking worried about me going back to Trevor, but you were just looking for a reason to screw your ex. Go inside before you make more of a fool of yourself than you already have." I turn around and, sure enough, we have an audience consisting of my neighbors.

"Claire, listen to me!" I sound like an ass, but I don't know how else to get her attention. She's pissed at me and I need her to understand that I did not sleep with Monica. How could she think I would, after everything I told her about our past? *Dumb fuck, you're in your underwear.*

"Baby, leave the bitch outside and come back in with me," Monica yells from the front door. *Oh, hell.* She's sleeping outside tonight for all I care.

"You're obviously needed inside. I should have known you were no different than him." She turns around and walks toward her car.

"What the hell does that mean?" I'm fuming.

"You hurt me," she whispers and nearly crushes my heart inside my chest.

She gets to her car and turns around to look at me one last time.

"Goodbye, Ryker. I hope you find your happiness."

She walks right out of my life with my damn heart in the palm of her hand.

🐝 47 🐝

CLAIRE

I only got out of bed this morning because I heard Brady babbling next to me, telling me he was hungry. If it weren't for his persistence, I would have slept all day. But life still has to go on. I'm still a mother. I'm trying my hardest to focus on him and nothing else. He continues to make me smile throughout the day with his giggling and bubble blowing.

I made a huge mistake being with Ryke. How could I possibly put my heart on the line again for someone else to crush?

I give Brady his sippy cup and a snack of sliced bananas when I hear a knock on the front door. I'm sure it's Trevor. My stupid ass brother insisted on calling him yesterday when Brady was at the hospital. He flew in last night to see him even though he was fine. Why all the sudden, after all this time, is he interested in spending time with his son?

"Damn, took you long enough." Trevor smirks as he walks through the door.

"I was getting Brady settled. What's up?" We walk toward the kitchen, back to Brady.

"What the hell is this?" He slams an envelope down on the table. I didn't realize it was in his hand until now.

"Seriously, Trevor?" I rub my temples and look up at the ceiling in frustration. "Do we really have to do this?"

"You want a fucking divorce?" I cringe at his tone, suddenly a bit terrified.

"Did you seriously think this wouldn't happen after you cheated on me?" I yell. "Yes, Trevor. I want a goddamned divorce."

"I want custody of Brady." He says this like it's no fucking deal and I want to claw his damn eyes out.

"You're fucking ridiculous!" I'm about to come unglued. How did I put up with this asshole for so long?

He gets up in my face and points his finger at me.

"No, Claire. I'm not ridiculous. You're the one who took him away from me. If you want to fight this, Claire Bear, I promise you, you won't win."

I try to push past him.

"You're an unfit mother and I'll be sure to prove that to the court system."

Now I'm seconds away from killing him. How dare he say this shit about me?

"An unfit mother?" I yell. "How the hell can you even say something like that?"

He laughs evilly, which has my skin crawling. "Did you forget you were just in a psych ward?" He shakes his head in disgust. "No sane judge is going to let you have him after all that shit."

"I was in a fucking psych ward because of you, Trevor. God!"

"That's stupid, Claire. Nobody will believe that shit."

I just want him to leave and go back to Chicago. My life is a lot less stressful without him in it. I lift Brady from his high chair and he toddles down the hallway toward our bedroom. Clearly, ready for bed.

"Our plane leaves in two hours, so get him ready." What the hell is he talking about?

"I'm sorry. Come again?" Surely, I couldn't have heard him right.

"He's coming back to Chicago until the divorce is finalized. He should just get used to being with me anyway." The veins on my neck are about to burst from my anger and frustration.

"You're fucking insane if you think you're taking my child away from me."

"You can come too if you don't want to be away from him."

I shake my head. "No. Trevor, we are staying right here. This is our home now."

He cackles. "Right. And let me guess. You've been warming the bed of that white trash that showed up here last night."

I'm now up in his face. I have nothing on his six-foot stature, but I don't care.

"Shut the hell up."

He laughs at me in response.

"Get your fucking bags packed if you're coming with me. The Uber will be here in a half hour."

With that, my good-for-nothing husband goes to the other room, flipping Sierra's TV on. Tonight, she's out with some friends while Glenna watches Auggie. I had offered to help her, but now I'm glad I didn't since it looks like I'll be making an unplanned trip to Chicago.

I'm fuming as I throw random articles of clothing in a large suitcase for me and Brady. As much as I don't want to do this, I'm worried that he'll really try to fight me for custody. Why? I have no idea. Will the judge really find me to be an unfit mother?

I wipe at my tears as I grab my sleeping son, who is curled up on my bed. I'll do anything for him.

I quickly shoot off a text to Sierra and Evan. Then we're headed to the airport. Hopefully, we'll be back in Phoenix soon.

"CLAIRE, Brady! I've missed you both so much," my mother-in-law Lynn says as she opens the door and gathers us both into a hug.

"Hi, Lynn." I kiss her on the cheek and follow her inside. Of course, Brady is already in her arms. It seems like it's been forever since I saw her last. I can see tears glistening in her eyes and suddenly feel guilty for keeping her grandson away for so long.

"Claire, I've known you for a long time and you know you can't fool me, right? What's going on?"

"Trevor threatened to fight for custody of Brady." I start to cry after keeping it together for so long.

I've always been close to Trevor's mom. Honestly, closer than I ever was to my own. This morning, I wanted nothing more than to get away from him, so I called Lynn so she could see Brady. I've missed her since we left.

Lynn gasps. "What has happened to my son? You know

I'm nothing like Peter or Trevor. And you know I wanted to leave Peter years ago but chose not to because of Trevor. It was the worst mistake of my life and I wasn't happy because of it. I believed in the vows we said to each other many years ago, but I was miserable because of him. I loved him because he was Trevor's father, but I hadn't been in love with him for a long time."

Wow. I knew there were problems, but I've never heard her talk this way about Peter.

"So, please tell me what's going on. I love my son, but I won't stand for him treating his wife wrong. Hear me?" She points a finger at me jokingly, but I know she's serious.

"Yes," I sigh. "I left him because I caught him cheating on me with his assistant," I say in a rush because I want to get it out before I change my mind.

"Nicole?" She asks loudly "She's a tramp!" I can't help but smile at her words. This lady, who always comes across as being proper, is always surprising me.

"He's been acting like I'm in the wrong for wanting a divorce. I just can't be with someone who would do that to me. Lynn, I was in the damn hospital for two months because of all the stress. I hope you don't hate me." I put my head down at my confession.

"Claire, look at me." I do as she says. "I could never hate you. You've dealt with him way longer than you should have. You loved him as much as you could and you made me a grandmother. For that, I love you dearly."

"I love you too and thank you for everything." I give her a half smile.

After my visit with Lynn, she offered to keep Brady overnight. I know she had been wanting to spend time with him and I could use the break, so I really couldn't argue.

I'm now on my way home to grab my suitcase before I have a girl's night with Shay. Koda and Dennis are on a camping trip for the weekend, so we'll have the house to ourselves. Last night, I stayed at our house since we got in so late. But the rest of the time we're here, we'll be staying with Shay. Thank God. I really can't put up with Trevor any longer.

As I'm crossing the intersection before our street, I notice a car coming at me, but it's too late for me to stop. I quickly try to get out of the way, but then everything turns black.

✵ 48 ✵
RYKER

"Hello?" I answer, barely awake.

"Ryke, it's Sierra. There's been an accident." My heart stops in my chest. "Are you still there?" she asks when I don't respond.

"What kind of accident?" I choke out. I have no idea what's going on, but I'm suddenly fully awake, worried something terrible has happened to Claire or Brady.

"Claire was in a bad car accident." I can hear her crying on the other end.

I fly off the bed and slip my pants on.

"What hospital is she at?" I drag my hands down my scruffy face.

"She's in Chicago." My stomach drops. "It's not what you think, but you need to get there as soon as you can. I'm trying to get a ticket out there now."

After I talk to Sierra, I quickly dial Evan. I need to get to Claire and make sure she's going to be alright. I have no idea how bad it is.

Evan books our flights and I drop Griz off with Austin

before meeting him at the airport. It's a miracle I didn't get in an accident on my way because I wasn't paying attention to the road the entire drive. All I could think about was Claire and how I can't lose her.

I didn't sleep a wink last night after not being able to get a hold of her all day.

"Man, you have got to chill the hell out," Evan says when he notices my bouncing knee as we sit in the Uber. I can't keep calm. I'm not sure what kind of shape Claire will be in when we finally get to her.

"Why aren't you freaking out right now?" I snap.

"It's not going to do her any good if we're both acting like stupid asses." God, this guy is driving me crazy, but he's right.

I finally relax a little once we get to the hospital. We run to the front desk and Evan tells them he's Claire's family. They immediately let us back to see her. As soon as we walk through the hall, we see who I assume is Shayna, sitting on the hallway floor talking on her phone. Makeup runs down her face. She's obviously been crying.

"Hey, guys. She's in bad shape," she croaks out. She kisses Evan on the cheek as he hugs her.

We walk through the door and I see her helpless body lying on the bed. I'm completely numb. I've visited family in the hospital in the past when they were sick, but that was nothing like this. This is the woman I love and want to spend the rest of my life with.

As much as I want to see her, I stand off to the side while Evan has a moment with her. She's sleeping, but he whispers in her ear and kisses her forehead. He's mindful not to hurt her, as her entire body is beat up. Bruises and cuts cover her face and her shoulder is in some kind of wrap to keep it still. I feel like I'm going to be sick. How could I have been so fucking stupid to run from this woman?

"I'm gonna go get something to drink. I'll be back in a bit," Evan says as he leaves the room.

"Hey, sweetheart." I kiss her cheek. It crushes me seeing her like this. I still have no idea what's going on with her.

I'm not much for crying, especially after everything I went through with my mother and Monica. But this woman does things to me I'm not used to. I have tears in the corners of my eyes and I know if anyone comes into her room, they'll see what a damn softie I am. But fuck them. I don't care. I just want her back in my arms, where she belongs.

The room remains silent, aside from the occasional beeping of the machines she's hooked up to. I'm extremely uncomfortable slouched over her bed but refuse to leave her side. I want to be holding her hand when she wakes. Besides Evan and Shayna, there is no one else here to be with her.

I finally convince a young nurse to tell me what's going on. I find out that the other car T-boned her car, killing the other driver instantly. It makes me sick to think that could have been her. *God, please let her be alright.*

AFTER SITTING with Claire for a while, the staff made me leave for the waiting room. I didn't go without a fight, though.

"Are you the family of Claire Davis?" a tall, middle-aged doctor asks.

I fly out of my chair. "Is she alright?" I know I'm invading his personal space, but I don't care. I just need to know how she is.

"Are you her husband?" the doctor asks.

"No, I am." I turn at the offending voice and want to throw him through a damn wall. "I'm Trevor Davis."

"I'll take you back to see your wife." The fucker starts walking off toward the hallway with the doctor but first turns around to smirk at me. It takes all my willpower not to charge at him. I'm only holding back because of Claire.

"Why the hell is he just now getting here?" I ask Evan as I sit back in the chair. I'm seething.

"The hospital wasn't able to get a hold of him right away."

"Right. Where's Brady?" I'm glad the little guy isn't here because he doesn't need to be around all this.

"Trevor's mom has him. Claire had just left her house. Thankfully, he wasn't in the car with her. There's no way he would have survived that." He throws his head back and drags his hands through his hair. He looks worse for wear. I'm sure I'm not any better.

I feel sick. I stand from my seat and leave the waiting room without saying anything else. I just need to be by myself. I'm fucking pissed that Trevor is in with Claire, instead of me. I hate that mother fucker. He's a good-for-nothing man who is now trying to pretend to be the caring husband.

I go to the nearest bathroom and splash cold water on my face. *God, I cannot lose her.* I lean over the sink and breathe in and out. The next thing I know, I'm throwing up in the nearby toilet. I'm sure anyone outside the door is wondering what the hell is going on in here.

I totally fucked things up with Claire and I may never get another chance with her. I don't know if I'll be able to live with that.

I hear a knock on the door.

"You okay, man?" Evan asks when I open the door.

"Yeah, just needed to cool off some. Did the doctor come out again, while I was gone?"

"I went to the front desk because nobody was giving us answers. Douche bag Trevor won't come out and tell us anything."

"Okay. What did they say?"

"The tests they did show there could possibly be permanent brain damage."

I stare straight ahead, not able to comprehend what he's saying to me. I can't respond.

"They're hoping everything will be alright, but we'll just have to wait." He rubs his temples as if warding off a headache.

"When will they know?" I choke out. I'm about to have a fucking breakdown in front of this guy. I can't bring myself to care though. This woman quickly became my life, and I can't imagine a world without her in it.

"Not until she wakes." He pats me on the back and then makes his way back to his wife in the waiting room. Avery and Sierra got to the hospital an hour after we did. I'm glad she has so many people here for her.

❦ 49 ❦

RYKER

"Ryke, wake up." I feel someone shaking one of my shoulders. I slowly open my eyes and see Evan standing in front of me. I'm fucking exhausted. It's been four days since Claire's accident and she has yet to wake up. Along with the head injuries she suffered, she also broke her right leg and her shoulder was dislocated. Thank God, she was hit on the passenger side or she most likely would have died in an instant.

"What's up?" I rub my eyes and see Evan.

"She's awake." *She's awake.*

I jump from the couch I dozed off on. "Can we see her?" I have to see her. They've been letting us visit occasionally, but for the most part, we've had to wait in the private family waiting room.

"Trevor is back with her now." Fucking hell. Of course, he is. The fucker hasn't even stayed here. He's gone home each night and has even been to work. He's put on a nice little act, showing everyone he's stressed and worried for his wife. I can see right through his bullshit.

"Damn it." I sit back down, leaning my elbows on my knees, face in my hands. "I'm about to lose my fucking mind with that asshole."

Evan shakes his head as he takes the seat next to me. "You and me both, bro. I don't even know how to handle him. He's always been a grade-A asshole, but they're legally still married, so he's the only one they'll give information to."

"Fuck, don't I know it." I huff.

"She filed for divorce, ya know?" I turn and look at him, most likely wearing shock on my face. "You didn't know that, did you?"

"No." I shake my head. "I think I really fucked everything up."

"Listen, man. She went through a real rough patch before she met you. I never want to see my sister like that again. It was awful." He shakes his head as if trying to rid the memory from his brain. "She couldn't even get out of bed to care for Brady. She hated me for a long time after I admitted her to the hospital. I didn't think I'd ever get her back." He closes his eyes and takes a deep breath. "Then this shit happened and I was terrified that I was going to lose someone else like this. I couldn't fucking deal with any more tragedy."

I feel like the biggest asshole. While I've been sulking for the last few days, worried about Claire, I never once thought about how her brother felt. She's the only family he has left.

"I'm sorry, man." I leave it at that and we sit in silence until they let us see my beautiful girl.

"MR. PORTER, you can go back to see your sister now." A young brunette nurse tells Evan.

"Come on." He pats me on the back. "She'll want to see you."

We make it to Claire's room and, thank God, Trevor is already gone.

Before we see her, the room is quiet, but then we hear Claire wailing as if pain. On instinct, I push past Evan to her side. She looks up at me, seeming to be lost as she continues to cry.

"Sweetheart, it's okay. Shh." I'm now leaning over her bed, rubbing her good shoulder. She won't stop thrashing around and I'm worried she's going to do more damage to her already beaten body.

"Don't touch me!" she screams and I step back from her, my heart racing. Evan comes around and takes my place. My heart shatters in my chest at the sight of her like this.

"Claire, it's me, Evan. It's okay." He tries to calm her, but she is still out of control. "Ryke, call for the doctor, now!" he yells at me.

I run out the door, looking around for someone to help her, but, of course, no one is to be found.

An older man in a white lab coat finally comes around the corner.

"Sir, can I help you with something?"

"Yes, my girlfriend needs help." The doctor rushes to Claire's room, and in the next moment, Evan and I are being escorted from the room.

"I'm not leaving her!" I shout, but nobody cares what I want. I have no fucking clue what they're doing, but I'm about to lose my damn mind.

"Claire, I'm Doctor Martinez. You were in a bad car accident and it seems you've suffered a pretty rough head injury." That's the last thing we hear before they shut us out.

CLAIRE

I wake, feeling the sweat drip down my body. God, I need a shower. I blink my eyes open and, at first, it's hard to focus on anything. I hear whispered voices and one voice in particular stands out to me. It's rough and masculine, but somehow it makes me feel safe. I have no idea where I've heard it before, but I'm desperate to find out who it belongs to.

"She's awake," a different voice says. I turn my head toward the sound, barely able to move as my neck is stiff as a board.

The voice came from my brother. I give him a small smile as he leans in to give me a kiss on my forehead. Everything is still a fog.

"Hey, sweetheart." This comes from the familiar voice I heard moments ago. A tall man, built of steel, with dark brown hair and beautiful blue eyes stares down at me. I have no clue who this man is, but I'd like to find out.

The stranger tries talking to me, but I'm hardly able to register anything he's saying.

"Where's my husband?" I croak out and grab my throat. I hadn't realized until now that I'm desperate for some water.

"Ryke, her water is on the table." This comes from Evan. The man, Ryke, I guess, lifts the straw to my lips and I suck the water down as if I've been in the Sahara Desert for the last month.

Where the hell am I? I stare around and quickly realize that I'm in a hospital bed. But why?

"Do you know where my husband is?" I ask the good-looking stranger again. I feel kind of bad having these thoughts of this man when I'm a married woman.

He doesn't answer me right away but instead gives me a pained expression.

He shakes his head. "No, sweetheart. He's not here. But we're going to take you to Shayna's until you're ready to go back to Phoenix. Alright?"

"I'm not going anywhere with you!" I shout and then Evan comes back to my line of sight. *Damn, my throat hurts.*

"Sis, do you know who that is?" He points to the man who I am quickly becoming angry with. I just want to find my husband. Damn it.

"No, I don't know him. Evan, please, where's Trevor?"

The dark-haired stranger walks away from the bed and, a moment later, I hear the door click shut. Weird. I don't know who that guy is, but he really needs to pull the stick out of his ass.

I WAKE PANTING. I try sitting up in this godawful bed, but

I'm quickly halted by the restraints around me. I can't move my arm and something heavy lies on my leg.

No. Accident. Head injury. Memory loss. Broken shoulder. Broken leg. Lucky to be alive.

I can't breathe as I suddenly remember all these words being slung at me earlier. I was in an accident? I just want to fucking get out of here, but these assholes are keeping me as their prisoner.

"Hey, Claire Bear," Trevor says as he comes around to hold the hand of my uninjured arm.

"I want to go home," I whisper up at him. *Why do I feel like this man is a stranger?* I'm so confused right now at how I'm feeling and really just want to go home to my own bed. I shouldn't be tired after all the sleeping I've done over the last few days.

"We're gonna get you home soon," he says as he smooths my hair out. I'm sure I look like a damn hot mess after not showering in who knows how long.

"She's going home with us," I hear Evan roar from the door. I turn toward his booming voice and he looks pissed off as hell.

My brother has always been a bit of an asshole, but he'd do anything for me.

Trevor stands so that he and Evan are eye to eye.

"She's fucking going home with me. Her *husband*," Trevor seethes. Why the hell would I go home with Evan? My brother is off his rocker.

"Right. I'm sure that's where she wants to be." Their yelling is giving me a damn headache.

The door creaks open and in walks the dark-haired stranger from before. He looks weary, like he hasn't slept in days. I don't know why this guy keeps coming to my room, but he acts like he knows me. I have no fucking clue who he is.

I massage the side of my head, trying to rack my brain. *Brady.*

"Where's my son?" I interrupt the chaos around me.

"You remember him?" Evan asks, seeming to be surprised.

"Yes, where is he?" A lone tear rolls down my cheek. I hate this feeling. It's as if a huge part of my life is missing, like I don't even know who I fucking am.

"He's with my mom," Trevor says as he squeezes my hand. "She'll bring him home tomorrow so you can see him."

I nod and then lay my head back on my pillow.

Dark-haired Stranger stands on the side of my bed. Is this guy a doctor or something? Because he isn't dressed very professionally. He could have at least combed his damn hair.

"Hey, sweetheart." He takes my hand in his. I look over toward Trevor and see that he's livid that this complete stranger is touching me. Pretty affectionately at that.

"Why do you keep calling me that?" I look back to Trevor. He's still staring at us, looking as if he's going to pounce on this guy if he makes a wrong move.

"That's what I always call you," he whispers. "We were together for a month. And it was the best damn month of my life." I look up at him to see the sorrow in his eyes.

I'm starting to get fucking annoyed. I'm married, for Christ's sake. How is this asshole going to tell me that I had been dating him?

I shake my head in agitation. "No. You've lost your

fucking mind. My husband is standing right behind you, so I suggest you get your damn hands off me."

The man instantly has a look of pain on his face.

"Come on, man. Let's go." Evan grabs the guy and leads him toward the door.

The next second Trevor is by my side again. "Who was that guy?" I ask my husband.

"Just a friend of Evan's. Just ignore him." Trevor chuckles, but I'm confused as all hell and don't find any of this to be humorous.

🎇 51 🎇

CLAIRE

Since the accident, I've been in a lot of pain, but, thankfully, my meds kick in pretty quickly. I'm constantly exhausted and told Trevor I didn't want any visitors. I feel so lost right now. I still can't remember much since before everything happened. The other day at my doctor's appointment, we learned that I lost all memory of the last six months. I didn't realize how old Brady was, and when Lynn brought him to me at the hospital, I completely lost it. I feel like I've lost so much and don't know what I can trust.

"Hey, sweetie." I turn toward the sound of Shayna's voice. I should have known better than to think she'd listen to Trevor.

"Why am I not surprised you're here?" I smile at her.

"Because you know I don't listen to anyone." She leans in and kisses my cheek. "Here, I got you something." She reaches into a plastic bag she carried in with her.

"Not flowers?" I smirk. Shay absolutely hates flowers.

She'd buy me a whole new wardrobe before she gave me damn roses.

"I'm glad your sassy ass is still in there. No. Here." She holds out a jewelry box. Only Shay.

"Seriously, Shay? Jewelry?" I laugh but take the velvety black box from her.

I gasp. "Shay, this is gorgeous." I start to tear up at my best friend's thoughtfulness. Inside is a gorgeous tennis bracelet that has rubies that wrap all the way around it. My birthstone.

"I figured that wouldn't die."

"Uh, you could have gotten me a teddy bear." I snigger.

"Whatever." She rolls her eyes. "How are you feeling? Have you showered since you got home?" She looks at me from head to toe. If anyone else did this, I'd deck them in an instant. But this is just Shay for you.

"I've been home a week. Yes, I've showered. Do I smell that bad?" I raise one of my arms to smell my armpit. "I'm not that bad."

"You're disgusting." She huffs as she sits back in the rocking chair next to my bed. "But really, how are you?" She now has concern etched on her face. She knows I've been frustrated with my memory loss. I've been very sensitive for the last week and every little thing seems to set me off.

"I'm okay. I just feel so weird. Like everyone is telling me what my life was like before the accident, but I have no fucking clue if they're lying to me or not." I huff as I run my fingers through my hair.

She eyes me before she says anything. "And what have you been told that you're not sure of? You know you can trust me, right?"

Shay had wanted me to stay with her after the accident. She said something about how I was going to be staying at her house with Brady, but none of it made sense to me. Why would I stay with her when I have a perfectly good home with my husband?

"Yeah," I sigh. "It's just overwhelming, you know?"

"I can't imagine what you're going through." She gives me a sad look, but I know she won't say much because she knows I don't deal with sympathy well. We have that trait in common.

"Can I ask you a really fucked up question?" I turn toward my best friend and start to get emotional because, honestly, she feels like the only one I can trust right now. I don't know why, but as much as I want this house to feel like home, it doesn't. Trevor has barely been here since last week. He's left me to fend for myself with two broken bones and a fucking brain injury. If Shay knew this she'd kill him.

"Of course," she says softly. I don't see this side of Shay often, but I can tell she's really worried about me.

"Am I in love with Trevor?"

"Oh, um." She turns to look out the window, seeming to be ignoring my question.

"Shay?" She's making me nervous.

She turns back toward me and coughs into her hand. I can tell she doesn't want to say what she needs to which gives me my answer.

"No," she whispers as she shakes her head slowly. "Not for some time." I feel the weight being lifted from my chest. It's a strange feeling but it explains why I haven't felt close to Trevor since I woke up. He obviously doesn't love me either or he would have been here to take care of me. He sure was adamant about me coming home with him.

I stare into space. "I didn't think so. Something has felt off ever since I woke at the hospital. But why was he acting like a freaking control freak when that guy talked to me?" *Dark and handsome.*

Shay hadn't been at the hospital when I woke up, but I told her about everything that took place. How Trevor and Evan fought about who would take care of me. I didn't understand why my brother thought I needed to go clear to Phoenix.

"Because he's an asshole," she pauses, seeming to choose her next words carefully. "He cheated on you," she whispers. I can tell she wasn't sure if she should be the one to tell me this.

I gasp. "What?" I now have tears falling from my eyes. Why the hell did I come home with this man if he couldn't even be faithful in our marriage? "Oh, my God. Are you serious?" I can't stop crying. She comes over from the rocking chair and carefully climbs into the bed with me. "I wasn't living here, was I?" I hiccup.

"No." I look over and see a single tear run down her face.

"Is that why Evan wanted me to go to Phoenix with them?" Not that I could have anyway with all my injuries.

"Yeah." She fidgets with the hem of her shirt. "You were staying in Phoenix for the last several months." She lays her head on my shoulder. "I'm sorry I didn't tell you sooner. I just didn't want to upset you anymore."

"No, it's probably good you didn't." I lay my head back. "If I had been in Arizona, why was I here?"

"You came back because he threatened to try to get

custody of Brady. Don't worry, though. Your brother made sure you have the best damn lawyer in Chicago before he took off. One of his friends from law school."

I suddenly can't breathe. *Oh, my God. I can't lose my baby.*

"I need my baby," I sob. "Shay, I can't lose him." How could Trevor do such a horrible thing to me? He doesn't know shit about taking care of a child. Why would he do this?

"Shh, shh. You're not going to lose him, sweetie" She hugs me gently, mindful of my shoulder. "Why don't I go get him so you can see him? Would you like that?"

I nod. "Yeah. I feel so awful because I didn't even recognize my own child. What kind of mother am I?"

"Claire, you were in a horrible car accident that almost took your life. Cut yourself some slack. Brady knows you love him."

Shay leaves to get my son and I sit back, still not fully comprehending what she just told me. My husband cheated on me and now he's trying to keep our child from me. I have got to get out of here.

52

RYKER

The last three weeks have been the worst weeks of my life. I know I sound like a fucking drama queen, but I miss Claire so damn much and there's nothing I can do about it. Not a damn thing. After she was released from the hospital, I called Evan for the first week to get updates on her. After that, he told me to stop and that he'd let me know if she started to remember me. So, in the meantime, I just sit back and wait. Wait. I feel like I've always been a patient man, but when it comes to this woman, I can't just continue on with my life like she was never part of it.

I've woken almost every night from a nightmare. Even after everything with my mother and with Monica, not once did I lose sleep. This woman quickly worked her way into the depths of my soul and there's no way for her ever to get out. I've faced a lot of pain in my life, but the thought of her not knowing who I am has brought me nothing but numbness. I don't for one second regret my time with her, even if it's all I ever get.

As much as I want her back in my life, more so than that, I just want her to be happy. I know she didn't remember what Trevor had done to her. I told Evan that someone needed to tell her, but all of the doctors she had seen suggested that we let her remember on her own. Sometimes people who wake up from a coma get overwhelmed with all the information thrown at them. The last thing I want to do is overwhelm her, but, damn it. I just want my girl back.

I know I haven't been pleasant to be around and I've even managed to piss off a few customers. I've had some requests to do another live music night, but I just can't bring myself to do it. The last time we had one was the first time I ever saw my brown-eyed girl. I know I'd spend the entire night waiting for her to walk through the door. I'd be vastly disappointed because I know that would never happen.

We were told that it isn't guaranteed that Claire will ever regain all of her memory. She remembered everything up until the last six months before that fucker claimed her. I can never express how grateful I am that her life was spared, but, in a way, it feels like she's gone from this earth. My world isn't spinning without her in it.

"Hello?" I answer after one ring, already knowing who it is. She's been calling me almost every day.

"Anything new?" Sierra asks from the other end.

I huff. "No, I have no fucking clue what's going on." I run my hands through my greasy hair. I haven't taken much care of myself and I know I'm probably starting to smell like roadkill from lack of showering. This is what losing the other half of your heart feels like. I know my friends think I'm insane for acting this way. They say I didn't know her long and that I shouldn't get mixed up with a married woman anyway. If I had the energy, I would have strangled those bastards for having to remind me of that detail. But I can deal with her being married. I just can't handle not having her in my life. I feel like a vital limb from my body is missing, making it near impossible to function.

"This is shit. You know that?" I can hear the heartache in her voice. "She's my best friend and she doesn't have a damn clue who I am."

Having just met Sierra not long before she met me, Claire doesn't remember her either. We've kind of formed a friendship of our own, together mourning for a woman we both love.

"It's going to be alright," I lie. "One of these days, she's going to wake up and realize that the two coolest fucking people on the planet are waiting for her and she'll come back." I wish I could for one second believe the bullshit I'm spewing.

I hear Sierra tearfully chuckle on the other end.

"You are fucking insane, but I hope you're right."

"How's Miles? Do you know when he's coming home yet?" I ask, trying to change the subject. We've talked a few times about her husband who is currently deployed. He hasn't met their young son yet and I know it's been difficult on her.

"Hopefully, next month, but we know not to get too excited because things can always change last minute."

"Well, I can't wait to meet the man who decided to put up with your shit for the rest of his life," I laugh.

"Fuck you," She laughs. "But, really. Call me as soon as you hear anything."

"I will. Talk to you later."

I mindlessly go through the rest of my day, ready to climb back into bed. I know that sooner or later I'm going to have to once again be a productive member of society, but right now is not that time. If I could only wake from this nightmare, everything would be fine. More than fine. They'd be fucking fantastic.

✿ 53 ✿
CLAIRE

Since I got to Phoenix, my injuries have healed, except for my shoulder that I still wear in a sling. At least, I can walk again. My brother has been acting strange, not really knowing how to act when I'm around. I spent the first week here, mourning for a life I left behind in Chicago. Don't get me wrong, I know I don't love Trevor, but it makes me sad that Brady doesn't have his father anymore. Before we left, he threatened me with custody and it was then that I was sure that everything Shay told me was true. It's hard to take everyone's word all the time, not knowing what to believe or who to trust. Obviously, I couldn't even trust my damn husband.

On our way to the airport, Shay asked me if I knew who Ryke was. The name was familiar, but I wasn't sure who she was talking about.

Claire, you called me the first night you met him and I could tell how affected you were by him. You didn't think you could trust him because he was only a player, but you later real-ized that he was much more than that. Somewhere along the line, you fell in love again and I don't think I've ever known you to be so happy. As soon as he found out about the accident, he was on the next flight out and by your side as much as they'd let him and he didn't leave without a fight.

That was when I realized who the dark-haired stranger was that kept calling me sweetheart. I still don't remember him before that, though. When I asked Evan about him, he told me that he'd been bugging the hell out of him to find out how I was doing. It was a nice feeling, knowing someone cared that much. But I still have no idea what happened between us. Did we kiss? Sleep together? I have no fucking clue and it's pissing me off.

"Hey, Claire, I'm back in the kitchen!" Avery yells as I walk into the house with Brady on one arm and his overflowing diaper bag in the other.

"Aby!" Brady yells. As much as I want my own place, I love that my son has developed a close bond with Evan and Avery.

"Hi, Bubba. How's Aunt Avery's guy?" He stretches his arms out, wanting her to hold him. Little traitor. She looks my way, concern in her eyes. "Hey, you okay?"

I nod. "Yeah, I'm just tired." It's the truth. I'm exhausted all the time, but I am thankful that she and Evan have helped me so much with my son.

"You know you can tell me anything, right? Or ask me anything?" She and Evan have both told me several times that they're willing to answer whatever questions I have about the last six months. I can't believe I spent most of them here and don't remember a freaking thing about it.

I sigh. "Will you tell me about Ryke? Shay told me that I was in love with him but had a falling out with him right before everything. Did we break up?"

"Yeah, but it was all from a huge misunderstanding." She takes a deep breath, readying herself for what she's about to tell me next.

"What do you mean?" She's spiked my curiosity. I feel like a huge piece of shit for not remembering the guy. I would really like to go see him, but what the hell would I even say to him? *I'm sorry I don't remember you, will you remind me with that delicious body of yours?*

I remember he had the body of a god, with chiseled assets and piercing blue eyes that would bring any human with a vagina to their knees.

"Uh, I don't know if I should say anything else." She turns away from me, busying herself in the kitchen even though she has absolutely nothing she needs to be doing.

"God damn it, Avery. I'm fucking sick of everyone tiptoeing around me. I'm not going to flipping break!" I feel bad for the way I'm acting, but I just want to know what my life was like. How can I ever get my life back if I have no clue where to start?

"What's going on in here?" I turn toward the sound of my brother's voice.

"I just want to know about Ryke, but nobody will fucking tell me. I forgot I'm a damn toddler that needs to be sheltered." I storm out of the room... like a damn toddler.

I have never felt so lost in all my life and I hope to God that this feeling goes away soon. I don't know how much longer I can live with this. Six months is a long fucking time and I know I'm forgetting some important things. Like I still don't remember catching Trevor cheating, but honestly, that's a memory that I'm all for keeping buried.

But from what everyone has told me, I was starting to find happiness again.

"Knock. Knock." I sit up on my bed and see the door slowly creak open.

"Uh, who are you?" There stands a girl, probably a few years younger than me, with short, dark black hair. She's wearing a pair of cut-off denim shorts with a white wife-beater. She definitely does not lack character, but I have no clue who she is.

"Sierra," she says slowly as if she's worried I'll bolt from her at any moment.

"Do I know you?" I already know the answer to that but ask anyway.

"Yeah." She sits down at the foot of the bed and I decide to join her at the opposite side.

"Are we friends?" It's such a shitty thing to ask someone, but I want to know about all the people who were in my life before. I remember family, of course, and Shay because we were friends for years, but if I had any friends here, I don't remember them.

"Best," she whispers.

I get a stinging in my throat, unable to form words. I've been skeptical about who I can trust, but I know that Evan and Avery wouldn't have let her in their house if I couldn't trust her. She must be someone important to me.

"You live in Phoenix?"

"Yeah, actually you and Brady lived with me and my baby, Auggie."

That's when the tears start to come. I can't believe I can't remember someone who took me and my son in, gave us a place to live.

"Hey, it's okay." She scoots over towards my side of the

bed and wraps her arms around me. At first, I tense at her touch, but I'm immediately comforted by her. It's like my mind doesn't remember her, but my heart does.

Once my tears dry up and I'm calmer, we sit for the next hour and talk about things we did together. Well, she tells me how we met at a psychiatric hospital and we reunited after we went our separate ways. Before today, I had no idea that I had gone through such a rough time after leaving Trevor. I decide I don't want to mourn for him any longer. He's not worth my tears or energy. I'll take Brady to visit him when I have to, but that'll be it.

That night after getting Brady in bed, I lie awake, my mind unable to shut down. I had decided not to ask Sierra about Ryke, even though I was sure she knew him. It seems these two people are the only two I can't remember. Well, the only two important ones at least.

I WAKE WITH A START. I. Can't. Breathe. I inhale and then slowly exhale, but my chest feels like an elephant is sitting on top of it. I feel my long hair and realize that it's drenched in sweat. Then the images start to resurface.

Dark hair. Ocean blue eyes. Bright white smile. Walks at the park. Kissing on the Ferris wheel. Making love on haystacks in an old barn.

My head is pounding. I know the memories should be a relief, but instead they're overwhelming.

I run to the bathroom connected to my room and splash water on my face. I feel like I need to be sick. What do I do now? Approach this man who is practically a stranger? No, he's not a stranger. I'm in love with him.

But if I'm in love with him, how did I possibly forget him? Surely, I wouldn't forget someone so important to me. Would I?

I make it back to bed, thankfully not waking my son during my breakdown. I curl back onto my side, praying that sleep will take me back under, but it never does.

I spend the rest of the night silently crying to myself. How do I get back the life I once had?

54

CLAIRE

The next afternoon, I'm exhausted from my lack of sleep and Brady is extremely fussy. I know he's going to hate me, but I put him in his bed for a nap. He, of course, starts screaming at me. If he could, I know he'd be cussing me out right about now.

"Brady, take a nap and we'll play later, baby." I know my words aren't helping at all as he continues to kick and scream.

But, just as I guessed, his eyes close as soon as his head hits the mattress. *Thank God. This mama needs a break.*

As I walk into the kitchen to grab a bottled water from the fridge, I notice that both Evan and Avery are giving me strange looks.

"Why are you guys looking at me like that?" I could really use a rum and coke right now, but this will have to do.

"What?" Avery quickly asks trying to sound innocent, but I can tell she's up to something. I let it go because, frankly, I don't care right now.

"Let's go watch a movie on Netflix," Evan suggests. I put some popcorn in the microwave and grab another water before parking my ass on their oversized chair. They are snuggled up on the couch. I have to admit, it's kind of weird being here. I'm thankful that they took me in, but I really want to find a place of my own so they can get back to their lives.

Evan finds a sci-fi movie that he's been "dying" to see and when I look over at the couch, I notice Avery is sound asleep. I can't really blame her because the movie is boring as hell. I have no clue what's going on because, once again, my mind is straying to Ryke. I still haven't decided what I'm going to do about him yet.

As I'm about to pass out, there's a knock on the door. Evan stops the movie and gets up to answer it.

"Claire, it's for you," he calls from the front door.

Evan gives me a nervous look before he heads back to the living room. When I get to the door, I see the bitch I never wanted to see again.

"What the hell do you want?" I'm close to grabbing Monica's hair, so I keep both hands on the door. I don't feel like making a trip to the police station tonight. After finally remembering Ryke last night, I soon started remembering finding his ex at his house the last time I saw him. I don't understand why he would have been at the hospital with me, but it really doesn't matter.

"Claire, I know you hate me, but I needed to explain something to you." She looks scared. *Good, she should be.*

"What could you possibly have to say to me?" I bite back at her. I can't believe this is happening right now.

"Can I come in?" When she sees that I'm looking at her like she's out of her freaking mind, she sits on the swing on the front porch. I pull the door shut and stand in front of her.

"Say what you need to, but I'm only giving you five minutes." I'll be proud of myself if I last that long with her.

"I'm not really sure how to tell you this, but your husband is the father of my child." I can't think straight. Did she just say what I think she said? What the hell?

"What?" I gasp. "You slept with my husband?" I yell.

"Yes," she says quietly as she puts her head down. "I'm so sorry." She looks back up at me.

"You're sorry?" I scream again. "How do you even know him?" I hate to know the answer but ask anyway.

"I met him when he visited Phoenix a few years ago and then he met me in London when we were both there. He seemed so sweet back then, but I've recently seen a different side of him."

What are the chances of my husband sleeping with Ryke's ex? This is so fucking messed up.

When I don't say anything, can't say anything in response, she goes on. "I had no idea, Claire. But then I overheard him on the phone telling someone he was upset that he wasn't successful when he tried to kill you." She whispers the word "kill."

I gasp. "What? That's fucking ridiculous. Trevor would never do such a thing. Sure, he cheated on me, but he never got physical with me like that." *Purposely*.

"He was trying to turn this on you because he's worried your divorce will hurt his career. He figured people would feel sorry for him if he were a single father." She pauses as she glances at me to see my reaction. "Claire, I know you have no reason to believe me. But we really need to go to the police about this. I don't want him to come after you and have something worse happen to you."

This is stupid. I don't even know this girl.

"You need to leave." I stand from the swing and, without another word, slam the front door behind me, praying I didn't just wake my sleeping child.

I can't believe what she just told me. There's no way in hell it's true. She just hates me because I was with Ryke and I'm sure she's just a jealous bitch. Well, she doesn't have anything to worry about because now I know he'll never take me back. What would he think if he knew that our exes were sleeping with each other behind our backs?

55

CLAIRE

I want nothing more than to see Ryke, but I'm still worried about how he'll respond to the story Monica told me about her and Trevor. I've made myself sick thinking about it, but after plenty of time to think, I've finally decided that I'm going to go see him.

I'm still reeling over Monica's visit last week, but I try not to let it bother me. She obviously has a sick, twisted mind to play some nonsensical joke on me.

It's hotter than hell outside, so I'm wearing a pair of turquoise shorts with a black tank top and my favorite black pumps. I put my hair into a messy bun. I have to admit I look damn cute.

Once I reach the bar, I sit in Avery's car for a good ten minutes before I gather the nerves to get out. As I walk through the door, I see the place is nearly empty. I take a seat at the end of the bar and wait for someone to help me. Hopefully, *my* someone.

I see him. He's gorgeous. He's wearing dark, worn jeans and a simple gray tee. It fits him like a glove. He needs to shave, but he looks sexy as sin. I want to run my hands through his hair, which is now longer on top. He also needs a haircut, but he's rocking the "just thoroughly fucked" look. I finally get the courage to say something.

"Can't a girl get a drink around here?" His back is to me, but he slowly turns when he recognizes my voice. Once he's fully facing me, he stares as if he isn't sure if I'm real or not.

I give him a half smile. "Hi." I'm hoping to God and all the angels he doesn't tell me to leave because I need to see him. Be near him for a bit. I'm not sure how this will end, but I've missed him like crazy.

"You're here," he whispers, almost sounding out of breath. He's obviously shocked to see me. I want to jump over the counter and into his arms, but I keep my ass glued to my seat.

"I'm here. I've missed you." I'm not sure what else to say to him, but I know I need him back in my life.

"You. You remember me?" he chokes out and my heart cracks in two. Why the hell did I wait so long to come see this gorgeous man? He's obviously missed me. I feel like a bitch for putting him through hell.

Before I can respond, he hops over the bar and I'm in his arms in the next instance. He runs his hands through my hair, staring into my eyes as though I may disappear if he blinks.

"Yeah. I remember." I reach my hand up to his face, caressing the stubble I've always loved on him. "I'm so sorry that it took so long." I have to turn away from him, ashamed.

He grabs my chin. "You have absolutely nothing to apologize for. I was scared shitless that you'd never come back to me. I'm just fucking happy you're here." He studies me, waiting for a response.

"I forgot a lot. It was terrible." I put my head down, but he catches my first tear before it falls.

"I can't imagine how hard that was for you. Not having any idea what was real or not. What about Trevor?" I can hear the hesitance in his voice.

"Shay told me that he cheated on me, so I came back to Phoenix. But soon after I remembered you, I remembered everything else too."

"You remembered me first?" I can hear the emotion in his voice. He's got a death grip on me, but there's no way in hell I'd ask him to loosen his hold on me.

"Yeah," I whisper. "I also remembered finding you with Monica." I look up at him, trying to read him.

"Claire, I didn't sleep with her. I'd never fucking do that to you. I don't care how mad I was that night, I'd never, ever purposefully cause you pain."

"I know." I run my good hand down the side of his face, a part of me worried that I'll lose my memory all over again. "Monica came to Evan's last week."

"What?" He's shocked by this news.

"Yeah. She told me some pretty messed up things."

"Like what?"

"Not about you." I smile. "Well, not really."

"What did she tell you?"

"Um." I don't know if I'm ready to tell him this but decide to rip the band-aid off. "Trevor is the father of her daughter."

I instantly see the shock on his face and pray that he doesn't hate me. "What?" Then I see the realization on his face. "Oh, my God. I knew I recognized him when I first saw him but thought for sure there was no way in hell I'd ever seen him before." He gasps. "He's the one from London?" I nod. "She said the guys' name was Phil."

"Trevor's middle name is Philip."

"It's pretty fucked up that my ex was screwing around with your husband." He stares at me in disbelief.

"Are you upset? I mean, my husband is the reason you got hurt so bad." I put my head down.

"Sweetheart, look at me." I slowly look up, becoming emotional because of his nickname for me. "It's fucked up, but you know what?" When I shake my head, he continues. "It brought me you." He smiles and I smile back.

I let out a deep breath as if I'd been holding it in until I knew how he'd respond.

"I'm really sorry for not coming sooner."

"Baby, you don't need to apologize again, okay? This wasn't your fault."

"Okay, but let me say one more thing." He just looks at me, so I continue. "I should have let you meet my son. That was wrong. I think I knew that you'd never hurt either of us, but I was scared and for that I am really sorry."

"I didn't deserve your trust, but, sweetheart, I hope you'll let me be a part of your life again. I want both of you in it. I know I don't know Brady, but he's part of you, so that makes him important to me."

My heart is a freaking puddle at our feet. My tears are now coming at full force.

"Don't cry, baby." He leans in and lightly brushes my lips with his. It's nothing special but couldn't be more perfect.

"How is Brady?"

"He's good. Getting big. Would you like to meet him?"

He smiles wide. "Yes, I'd love to."

"I need to get Avery's car back to her, but you could come by the house." I hope I'm not assuming too much, but I want to spend more time with him.

"Austin, I need you to close down for me." Without another word, he grabs my hand and we're out the door. I don't think anyone could make me happier than this man.

56

RYKER

A m I dreaming? I was worried I'd never see her again, but she walked into my bar tonight looking like an angel. If I am, I never want to wake up. I desperately want to hold her hand and lean in to kiss her sweet lips some more. But I'm not sure if she's ready so I'm trying like hell to control myself.

When we get to Evan's house, I see the little guy bouncing on his aunt's lap.

"Oh, thank fuck. I had to give him a bath because he got into the garbage can. There was shit all over the kitchen floor. Literally shit." Avery blows a strand of red hair out of her eyes. I want to laugh, but I'm scared she'll kick my ass.

"I'm so sorry," Claire says as she lifts the boy off Avery's lap.

"Sit!" Now, I do lose it. Claire's eyes go wide as saucers at the fact that her son cursed, but it's comical.

"Avery! You can't curse in front of him. He repeats everything!"

"Sit! Sit! Sit!" The boy says again.

"You're a bad influence, so we'll be in the other room." Claire grabs Brady and I follow her into the living room.

"He's into everything now." Claire sets him on the floor and then sits on the couch. "I'm sure Evan and Avery are more than ready for us to move out." She adjusts her hair on the top of her head.

I watch the boy in awe and turn back to his beautiful mother. "Damn, I've missed you." I sit next to her. "Claire, when you decided to go home with Trevor, I thought for sure I'd never see you again."

I look over and see the first few tears leak from her eyes. I know she feels guilty, which is ludicrous.

I grab for her hand.

"I think Monica's visit was the last push I needed, but I hadn't stopped thinking about you since last week when I finally started remembering everything. I'm sorry for not believing you."

"Look at me." I grab her chin and she searches my eyes for answers. "It's ok. I want you more than you could ever possibly know. If you'll let me, I want to show you how much I can love you. You and your son."

"I want that more than anything," she sobs.

"Good." I kiss her nose and she smiles up at me. "Why don't you and Brady come to my house and I'll cook for you?" I ask as I tickle the little guy. He's giggling on my lap and running his hands along my scruffy face. I want them to myself tonight and I'm afraid it'll be cut short if Evan comes home early. I want to start over with this woman, but I also want to get to know her son. If I have it my way, I'll be spending a lot of time with both of them.

"You want us to spend the night with you?" Damn, this woman has me and she doesn't even know.

"That wasn't what I meant." She looks like she's upset with my answer, so I go on. "Don't get me wrong. Of course, you can stay if you want. But if you're not comfortable yet, it's alright." I don't want to rush her into anything she isn't ready for, but, damn, I want to be with her. I'll wait to sleep with her as long as I need to, but it's not going to be easy. I am, after all, only a man. A man who desperately wants this woman.

"I want to stay, if you don't mind." She looks nervous, but she's crazy if she doesn't think I'll agree.

"The lady gets what the lady wants." I lean into her lips. Caressing hers gently with mine. "Later, there will be more where that came from." I wink at her as I stand with Brady.

Claire packs a few things for herself and Brady and grabs his portable bed and highchair. I'm hoping one day soon that I'll have a bed at my house for him. We get into my truck and she immediately grabs my hand, rubbing circles on it. In this moment, it feels like no time at all has passed since I was last with her. So much has changed, yet everything's the same.

57

RYKER

"Where should I put our things?" she asks as we walk into my house, Brady in my arms. It took no time at all for him to warm up to me. I know these two are all I need in life to be content, to be happy. And, damn, am I happy.

"You can set them in my room unless you're more comfortable in the guest room." I sure hope she isn't planning on sleeping anywhere besides my bed with me.

"No, I want to stay with you, but I'll put Brady's things in the other room." I'm surprised but relieved because I want alone time with her after Brady goes to sleep.

I put the boy in his little highchair and get busy in the kitchen.

"Hey, Brady, should we make your mama some dinner?" He giggles and kicks his feet and blows bubbles in response.

"I'll take that as a yes." I put some chicken breasts on the stove, and while they cook, I get busy slicing vegetables for a salad.

"It smells amazing in here," Claire says as she wraps her arms around me from behind. If she's not careful, I'm going to have my way with her right in the kitchen. Forget dinner.

"I hope you like chicken alfredo." I mix together the ingredients for my sauce.

She sticks her finger in the bowl I'm mixing and then pops it into her mouth. She's not trying to be sexy, but the sight is fucking erotic.

"So, tell me, Mr. Allen." *Hard as a mother-fucking rock.* "Are there a lot of women you feed?" I'm not lost on her double innuendo. She turns bright red after realizing what she said. "I meant, do you cook for women often?"

I laugh at her embarrassment. "No, only you." I turn to look at her, so she knows I'm serious. I put the spoon I'm holding on the counter and go over to where she's standing. "Claire, I haven't been with anyone else since you."

"You haven't?" My heart cracks. Does she think I moved on from her? She can't get further from the truth.

"No, I promise you. As scared as I was that you'd never remember me, much less forgive my ass, I was still holding onto hope. I'm so fucking glad I did." I kiss her cheek, my lips lingering longer than necessary.

"How did I forget you?" She gets choked up and it kills me seeing her so upset. I know that, for a while, she'll be emotional like this. It's to be expected after everything she's been put through both physically and mentally.

"Sweetheart, you didn't choose to forget me and you didn't forget just me. You forgot a lot of things. I'm just glad you're back."

"Oh, my God." She leaves my arms and digs through her purse.

"What's wrong?" She's now pulling up something on her phone, leaving me puzzled.

"I didn't call Sierra." She pulls her name up in her contacts and then quickly types out a text.

"Did you just remember her?"

"No." She shakes her head. "I remembered her soon after I remembered you but was nervous to get in touch with anyone right away." She puts her phone back in her purse. "She came over to Evan's before I got my memory back."

"She did?" I ask her. I'm surprised as shit and a little upset that Sierra saw her before I did.

"Yeah. Did you ever talk to her? After I left?" Her voice is filled with pain which rips right through me.

"We talked often actually. She was always calling or texting to see if I'd heard anything from you. I guess we kind of built a weird friendship because we were both missing the hell out of you." She starts to cry again. "Baby, no. I'm sorry I wasn't trying to upset you. We just both were kind of in the same boat, that's all."

She nods her head. I can tell I need to pull us away from this conversation. I want her to enjoy her night. I hold her in my arms and kiss her forehead.

"Now, shall we eat?" She grabs some food for Brady out of his bag. He squeals in excitement when she puts crackers and green beans on his tray along with his sippy cup. We're both eating and talking until we see the smashed green beans in his hair.

"Brady!" She yells. Claire is laidback so it makes me laugh when she tries to scold her son.

"Why don't you go relax on the couch and I'll take care of him?" She gives me an unsure look but agrees. Claire isn't used to other people helping her. I know it was hard for her before moving to Phoenix because Trevor was always gone. And when he was home, he didn't help anyway. I'm not sure how Claire will feel about me helping this much, but she's going to have to get used to it.

"Let's take a bath, little man." Brady claps as I put him in the sink of bubbles.

"Bah!" he yells as he splashes water all over me and the floor. I'm going to need a new change of clothes because, apparently, he thinks I need a bath too.

"Um, what's going on in here?" Claire asks as she walks back into the kitchen. I hope she isn't upset with me.

"Brady wanted a bath," I say coolly without looking away from the boy. He won't hold still, so there's no way I'm taking my eyes off him.

"Right." She chuckles. Her laughs are my favorite sound. Well, and her calling my name when I make her come. *You sick bastard, get your mind out of the damn gutter!*

"Yep. He told me, "Ryke, dude, I need a bath." I wrap a towel around the soaking wet baby. Giving a kid a bath is harder than it looks. I hope she'll let me do things like this for them, for a very long time.

❧ 58 ❧

CLAIRE

I was shocked a bit when I saw Ryke giving Brady a bath. No one has ever helped me like that before. Sure, Evan and Avery have been doing everything they can to make things easier for me, but they're family.

After we get Brady situated in the guest room, I snuggle next to Ryke on the couch. I love my son, but it's nice to have some alone time with him again without anyone else around. I'm glad I worked the nerves up to go see him at his bar, even with the urge to vomit from my anxiety.

"You want to watch a movie?" he asks as he leans in to kiss me.

"No."

"No?" He laughs. "Well, what would the lady like to do instead?" He runs his fingers through my hair and I'm mere seconds away from losing my freaking mind. I missed his touch and I want to ingrain it into my mind, so I'm never without it again. But there's no way I could ever forget anything about him. Sure. My mind couldn't remember him, but my heart and body never forgot him.

"You," I whisper. I can't believe I said that out loud and I'm sure my cheeks are turning eight different shades of red. "Oh, God." I put my face in my hands. I hope I'm not being too forward. I'm not typically like this.

"Don't be embarrassed. I like your dirty mouth." He smirks and pulls my head toward him roughly, instantly devouring my mouth. Our teeth clank together and our tongues dance. I will never get enough of this man. I either need him to touch me or I'm going to need a new pair of panties.

And as if he can read my damn mind he whispers, "Am I making you wet, sweetheart?" I'm going to come from his words alone.

"Yes," I pant. I'm becoming jelly in his hands and can't seem to think of more than one-word sentences. This man is going to be my undoing.

The next thing I know, I'm being lifted from the couch. I wrap my legs around him as he carries me. He's mindful of my injured arm.

Once we get to his room, I slowly slide down his body and our clothes frantically come off. We aren't going slow, not this time. We are both desperate to be with each other again.

"Are you sure about this?" He tucks my hair behind my ear. "I don't want to rush you into anything if you're not ready." This man is so sweet, but I don't want him to be sweet tonight. I need him to take charge of me, of my body. *Woah, girl! Calm yourself!*

"Yes, I'm sure." I quickly strip my shorts off. Well, as quickly as I can with one hand. "More than sure." I'm trying not to fall on my ass, but I can't think straight around him.

He looks me in the eyes once he's standing in front of me in all his naked glory. "I love you, Claire. You know that, right?" When I nod, he goes on. "Never think for one second that I ever stopped, okay?"

"I love you too, Mr. Allen." Instantly, I see the lust in his eyes. I know he always gets turned on when I call him by his last name.

"Damn, woman, you're going to be the death of me." He grabs my naked breast and his mouth finds mine again. I love his hands on me. I can't get enough of his hands.

"Ryke, don't stop." I don't even know what I'm saying because my brain is turning to mush.

His left hand finds me wet and waiting for him. His right hand continues on my nipple. He leaves my mouth and his wet tongue caresses my nipple where he was pulling.

"Bed. Now," he demands as he lifts me and gently puts me on the bed. I've never seen him like this before, but I like this side of him.

I lay on his bed as he stares at me. Typically, I would be uncomfortable, but I can tell he appreciates my body. Stretch marks and all.

The foot of the bed dips and he looks at me with hunger in his eyes. If he isn't inside of me in two seconds, I'm going to explode. He sits in the middle of the bed and lifts me so I'm straddling him. He's so close to being where I need him, yet so far away. His hands caress my sides as he kisses my neck and one of my nipples is suddenly in his mouth. I throw my head back in desire. I can't think straight, my vision blurs, and I'm pretty sure a bomb could go off in the room and I wouldn't notice.

"You are the most beautiful woman I have ever seen." He continues on my breast. He goes to the other one, not allowing it to be forgotten. I've never been loved like this before and he has ruined me for any other man.

"I love you," I pant while he's working on my body.

He pulls away from my breast and looks me straight in the eye. "I have never loved anyone like this before. I'm scared shitless, but I'm going to love you until my last breath and, even then, I'm gonna keep on loving you." His words have a direct line to my soul.

He rocks against my wetness, but he's still not close enough. The bastard is teasing me. I dig my nails into his back and I'm sure I'm going to leave marks on him, but he won't care. If I'm hurting him, he's not complaining.

"Baby, if you don't get inside me right now, I'm going to lose my damn mind." He laughs and pushes me back until my head hits one of his pillows.

"I like when you talk dirty to me." He's still laughing.

"You're an asshole." I swat at his chest. God, his chest is amazing. His entire body is amazing. Now, don't get me started on his dick. *Holy. Shit.* It was a little painful the first time, but I'm so ready for him now. I know I'll feel nothing but pleasure as soon as he enters me.

"Is your pussy ready for me, sweetheart?" *Holy cow. I'm going to scream if he doesn't take me right this second.*

"God, yes! Please stop teasing me, Ryke." He inserts two fingers inside of me and I writhe against them. If I can't have his dick, his fingers are the next best thing. Sweet, sweet torture.

A second later, he's easing himself into me and, Lord

help me, it's incredible. I nearly stop breathing from the desire shooting through my body. This man is a sex god and I'm his goddess.

He lifts me with one arm so he can push further into me. We become one. He tugs on the hair coming loose from my bun and I pull on his at the same time.

"Oh, God! Oh, God!" I yell as he continues to rock into me. I never liked being a "sex screamer," but Ryke makes me want to do things I've never done before.

"You like that, don't you, sweetheart?" He flicks my clit with his thumb. I can't handle the stimulation and immediately come undone, hard. The room is spinning with every thrust he gives. He explodes shortly after I do and we both let out animalistic sounds.

"Claire," he grunts into my shoulder to muffle the sound. "If it's possible to die from sex, I'd die a happy man." He chuckles and I tickle him. I love his sense of humor.

Once we both use the bathroom, we lay in bed together. I'm extremely exhausted and content being in his arms.

🧩 59 🧩

CLAIRE

Ryke and I have been back together for three blissful months. Soon after that, Brady and I moved back in with Sierra, so Evan and Avery could have their house back.

All of my injuries healed entirely and you'd never know just by looking at me that I nearly lost my life.

We're getting ready to fly to Miami this evening for Shayna's wedding. She decided she wanted a destination wedding and they are planning on staying in Florida for their honeymoon. We booked our suite for a few extra days, so we can have a little vacation together. I'm looking forward to some R&R with my man but know I'll miss Brady like crazy.

"If you need anything, please don't hesitate to call my phone or Ryke's." I get done going over everything with Avery before we head to the airport.

"Claire, seriously, leave!" She laughs "We'll be fine. We have phone numbers for every doctor in town if there's an emergency," she mocks me.

"Whatever." I smirk "Thanks so much for keeping him." I lean in to hug her and my brother and kiss my son on the cheek. I want to be alright with leaving him, but I'm not.

"Sweetheart, you alright?"

"I will be. I just haven't left him since the accident."

"Come here." He wraps me in a hug, immediately calming me down. "You deserve some time away and he'll have fun with his aunt and uncle." He kisses my forehead. He always makes everything better. No matter how small the gesture, he always sets off the butterflies inside my stomach. I'm like a junior high girl with her first crush. This is way more than a crush, but I never want the newness to wear off.

We land in Miami around eight and Dennis gets us from the insanely busy airport. We're both exhausted, but I'm too excited to see my best friend to care.

"Hey, bitch!" Shayna yells as soon as we walked through the door of their hotel suite. I will be surprised if her kid doesn't have the biggest potty mouth when he's older.

"Hey, Shay." We hug each other like we haven't seen the other one in ages, even though it has only been a few months. I hate living so far from her, but I can't imagine not being near Ryke.

"Ryke, I have to give you props for getting this girl away from Brady," she laughs as she gives him a side hug.

"She did good." He wraps his arm around my waist and kisses my hair. I fall in love with him even more. He saw me upset about leaving my son but doesn't make a big deal about it.

THE NEXT DAY, the guys go golfing with Dennis's family while the girls head to the reception hall to decorate. Shayna's mom is waiting for us there. I've only gotten to meet her a few times because she lives here in Miami, but I remember her being kind and welcoming. I always enjoy being around other people's mothers because it makes me miss mine a little less.

We spend a good six hours covering all the tables with light yellow cloths and hanging streamers around the entire banquet hall. All of the tables are decorated with rustic looking candle holders that hold floating candles. The clear lights that are strung throughout give the room a romantic vibe. It makes me want to have this again, one day.

When I married Trevor, I didn't get to do any of the planning because he insisted on leaving everything to our wedding planner. I wasn't allowed to lift a finger. He said doing anything ourselves was way beneath us. I was blinded by everything because I was in love. But never again will I let someone force me to be someone I'm not.

"Shay, it's beautiful." I look around the room. My eyes are full of happy tears.

"You'll have this one day." She wraps her arms around me from behind. "If the way Ryke is always looking at you, like he wants to jump your bones, is any indication, you'll be hitched in no time." She chuckles.

I roll my eyes at her. "Shay, you're nuts." I love her for it.

"Thanks for standing next to me tomorrow. I can't imagine anyone else doing this with me." This is a side I don't often see of Shayna. She's usually not serious, but right now she wears a look on her face as if she wants to cry. I've only witnessed this a few times, but it reminds me that, deep down, she does have a soft core.

"I wouldn't miss it for the world."

When we're done decorating, we meet the guys at The Bolivar in Miami Beach. Shayna's parents insisted we go to a five-star restaurant the night before the wedding. She didn't want to have a rehearsal or rehearsal dinner, so they decided to have their families along with Ryke and I. Her dad, the owner of a high-end construction company, can afford to foot the bill for everyone. I just hate not even being able to afford my Caesar salad.

While we're waiting for our food to arrive, I excuse myself to go to the bathroom and decide to call Evan to see how Brady is. As soon as I stand, I become dizzy. The room is spinning. I try not to draw attention to myself because I don't want Ryke to worry. When I get to the bathroom, I splash water on my face. I look at myself in the mirror and see I'm white as a ghost. Suddenly, the room is spinning again and I need to sit before I pass out. I drop my purse and slide to the floor. I hear my phone ringing in my purse, but I don't have the energy to search for it. I look towards the nearest stall to see how far I'll have to go to get to a toilet to puke. I'm scared to stand, so I crawl in my expensive cocktail dress to the stall. If anyone else comes in, they could easily steal my purse, but I'm too concerned about not tossing my insides all over myself to care.

Once I finally make it to the toilet, I lose everything I ate earlier in the day. I hear the bathroom door fly open and I'm suddenly embarrassed.

"What the hell, sweetheart? Are you alright?" Ryke squats next to me on the floor.

"I don't feel well." I wipe my mouth with the back of my hand. I'm in desperate need of a shower and bed. I want to sleep after the repulsive explosion of my stomach. I'm horrified my boyfriend witnessed me like this.

Ryke grabs a few paper towels for me so I can clean myself off. As much as I wish he wasn't seeing me like this, I'm glad he's here to comfort me.

When he comes back in, he rubs my back in circles. Trevor would have been appalled if he ever witnessed me like this. But this is not Trevor.

When I'm feeling somewhat better, I decide to stand so we can leave. I hate myself for ruining Shayna's night, but she insists she and Dennis give us a ride to our hotel. Thankfully, we now have our own room. I wanted to spend a romantic night with Ryke, but I know all I'll be doing is sleeping.

❧ 60 ❧

CLAIRE

I woke three times during the night. Thankfully, I made it to the toilet each time. I hated waking Ryke, but he was by my side without fail.

Oh, no. I grab for my phone and tap my calendar app open. *Fuck.* I don't know why I didn't think of this sooner. This is exactly how I felt my entire pregnancy with Brady.

I throw on some yoga pants and a bra and head to the gift shop in the hotel. Ryke's in the shower, so he won't notice I'm gone.

I quietly open the door to our suite and then I'm careful not to let it slam shut behind me.

We're on the first floor of our hotel, but the gift shop is on the other side of the building. Once I finally make it to my destination, I walk up and down all the aisles, trying to find what I need.

"Is this it for you, honey?" the middle-aged, gray-haired lady asks. I haven't heard such a strong accent since we got here.

"Yeah." I pull my debit card out of my wallet and hand it to her.

"Here, I'll throw in some of this tea for you." She puts a box inside the yellow bag.

"Thank you." I smile at her.

"Of course. It'll help with your morning sickness."

"I'll take all the help I can get." I smile once more and head back to our suite.

When I get back to our room, I slip my clothes off and climb back into bed.

"Morning, sweetheart. How are you feeling?" He walks out of the bathroom in nothing but a towel and kisses my cheek. If I weren't freaking the hell out right now, I would appreciate his wet body more.

"I'm okay. I'm going to hit the shower while I'm feeling better." I'm worried about being sick at Shayna's wedding. Thank God it isn't until this evening.

I grab my things and head to the bathroom. Typically, when he and I stay together, we either shower together or the door to the bathroom stays open. Not this time. I hope he doesn't suspect anything, but I really need privacy right now.

I hold the offending object in my hand, refusing to do anything with it right away. I don't know if I can do this. I slowly breathe in and out and then sit on the toilet.

I pee on the stick and wait. It's strange. Don't get me wrong, I'd love more than anything to have a baby with Ryke, but I'm not sure right now is the best time. At least, I have the comfort of knowing he's not going anywhere.

Finally, after a long, slow, three minutes, I glance over to the counter where the test sits.

Pregnant.

I'm pregnant with Ryker Allen's baby. I'm scared shit-less, but, damn, this kid is going to be adorable.

I hear a knock on the door. "Sweetheart, you alright in there? I haven't heard the water turn on yet. Are you sick again?" As scared as I am, I know he'll be able to calm my nerves.

When I don't answer, I hear the doorknob turn. Apparently, he picked the lock when he became worried from my lack of response.

"Claire, what's wrong? Do you need me to get you anything?" He looks over and sees the test still sitting on the counter.

"Are you?" He doesn't continue his question because he already knows the answer.

"Yes" is all I can manage to say. "Are you alright with a baby?" I still don't look at him. I don't have a clue what expression he has on his face, but I'm too afraid to find out.

He kneels in front of me. "Baby, look at me." He grabs my chin. "You just made me the fucking luckiest man alive. Are you okay with this?" I know exactly why he's asking. I told him before I wasn't sure I could ever go through a pregnancy again after my miscarriage, but I have to have faith everything will be fine. When I nod, he goes on. "I know we haven't talked about this, but you better believe that I'm happy about it. I'm going to marry you one day, Claire Davis. One day very soon."

I knew I wanted to be with this man forever, but we never discussed marriage before. It feels like there are a million butterflies dancing in my stomach. Not because I'm worried any longer, but because I'm so excited to have a life with this incredible man.

"You are?" I whisper. "We've only been together for a few months, so I didn't want you to feel like I've rushed you into anything. I'm so sorry. I must have forgotten to take a few of my pills."

He looks at me with a pained expression. "Claire, you underestimate how much I love you. I'd never think that of you. Sure, this wasn't the order of how I thought things would work out, but who fucking cares? I'm going to make you Claire Allen as soon as this baby is born, hear me? I want the four of us all together on the most important day of my life."

This man. I feel like the biggest bitch for worrying so much.

I stand up from the toilet and jump into his arms. "Ryker Allen, I love you so freaking much. I'm so sorry for worrying. I know you'll be an awesome father, but I just didn't know if you'd want this so soon."

"I want to spend the rest of my life with you and have as many children that you'll let me put inside you." I think my ovaries just exploded.

"I want that too." I smile. "But these two are going to be super close in age, so let's hold off on more for a while." I kiss his nose.

He laughs. "Deal. How are you feeling? Any better?"

"Yeah, actually, I feel great. I think part of it was nerves about taking the test. I'm sorry I should have told you I thought I might be pregnant, but I was a mess."

"You don't need to apologize, but from now on we work through things together, yeah?"

"Yeah." I nod. He leans in to kiss me with a kiss that is full of so much love. It's so hard for me to imagine a time before Ryker Allen.

❦ 61 ❦

RYKER

I'm over the damn moon right now. I could tell that Claire was worried about what I'd think about her being pregnant, but I couldn't be happier. I've already felt like Brady's father, but, damn, it feels amazing knowing this woman is carrying my child.

I grab Claire's hand without saying anything and pull her back into the room. She looks at me with questioning eyes, but I still don't say anything as I lift her shirt over her head. This beautiful woman looks like a goddess. I plan on spending the rest of our lives showing her how incredible she is. I don't know what I did to deserve her, but I'm thankful that she sees the good in me, even though I'm less than worthy of her.

After her shirt is lying at our feet, I turn her around, so I can unhook her bra. I slide the straps down and it joins her shirt on the floor. Her back is pressed against my chest, so I wrap my arms around her and cup her full breasts. She has no idea how perfect she is. She leans her head back on my shoulder, which only gives me better access to her. I pull her hair away from her face and run my tongue along her neck.

"Ryke, baby, please."

"What, sweetheart?" I spin her around so she's looking at me. "I'm going to worship your gorgeous body and then I'm going to make sweet, sweet love to my future wife. How does that sound?" I rub her flat stomach and bend to lay a gentle kiss on it.

"That sounds wonderful," she whispers. "I love you."

"Oh, sweetheart, you have no idea how much I love you." I devour her mouth as I run my hands through her hair. She tugs on my shirt, asking me to take it off without words. I decide to let her have her way and pull my clothes off as fast as humanly possible. I cannot wait much longer to be inside of her.

As soon as we're both completely naked, I lift her onto the bed. I can't take my eyes off the beauty underneath me. She's panting hard and I can tell that she's not going to last much longer. I'm feeling the exact same way. We're both already worked up, so I decide not to waste any more time and gently slide into her.

"You like that, sweetheart?" I ask as I rub her clit. I can't get enough of this woman.

"Yes." She pants some more. She seems to be at a loss for words. I can't say I blame her, if she feels half as good as I do.

I run my hand up and down her right side, stopping at her nipple. After giving it a hard squeeze and getting the reaction I want from her, I lean down and suck hard. Her astounding body immediately comes undone as she lifts herself off the mattress.

"Oh, God, Ryke!" I'll never get tired of her screaming my name when she comes apart.

We spend the rest of the morning relaxing in bed and even make love one more time before we decide to get up.

"How about we go down to the beach for a bit?" I suggest once we're up.

"You just want a reason to see my hot ass in a swimsuit." She winks.

I swat her hot ass. "You better go get yourself ready before I take you back to that bed and have my way with you again."

"You need to behave yourself, Mr. Allen," she says as she goes into the bathroom.

This woman is going to be the death of me.

When we get down to the beach, right outside our hotel room, we both slide our shoes off so we can feel the warm sand between our toes. It reminds me of when I used to come to Florida with my dad and sister growing up. One day, I hope we can bring Brady and the new baby back here. I still can't get over the fact that I'm going to be a father. She has me on cloud nine and I hope to never come back down.

"It's so beautiful," Claire says as she stares out at the clear water.

"I agree," I say looking at her. She has no idea how beautiful she is and that's one of the things I love most about her.

She lets go of my hand and heads toward the water. I'm unable to move because this woman has me in a trance. I watch as she sits in the sand and nearly gets knocked over when a wave comes to shore. I'm several feet from where she's sitting but still hear her giggling. I love seeing her so carefree like this. I know she had a hard time leaving Brady, but she deserves this.

When she couldn't remember me after her accident, I thought my life was over. I didn't think I'd ever be able to breathe again, but, damn, this woman has made me the luckiest goddamn man in the world.

"Hey, handsome." She leans into me as I wrap my legs around her. We came here for her friend's wedding, but I'd give anything to sit here all day with her. We'll be here for the next few days, so I plan on keeping her naked half the time. The rest of the time we'll most likely spend out here. Our hotel is on a private beach, so there are very few other people around.

"You're all wet, sweetheart." I didn't mean for that to sound dirty, but my little vixen chuckles.

"Only for you, handsome." If she's not careful, I'm going to drag her back to bed for the rest of the afternoon.

"Ms. Davis, you better be careful or I'll be forced to take you right here, right now. I'd hate for Shayna to have to bail us out of jail after being arrested for indecent exposure on her wedding day."

She laughs. "Mr. Allen, whatever do you mean?" She turns toward me and bats her eyelashes. She knows she's driving me crazy and she's enjoying torturing me way too much.

"That's it." I quickly stand and toss her over my shoulder as I start running toward the hotel.

"Ryke! Put me down!" She's swatting at my ass, making me run faster.

"If you're going to tease me, Ms. Davis, you will have to be punished." I lightly pinch her ass.

Once we're back in our room, I gently toss her on the bed.

"Ryke, I'm all wet!" she yells and tries to stand up from the bed.

"Yes, I know. That's what got us into this situation, remember?" I waggle my eyebrows at her and start pulling her two-piece suit off her wet body.

"I have sand all over me and I'm getting the bed dirty." She tries again to get up, but I stop her. I lift her over my shoulder and head to the bathroom.

"Ryke!" She laughs as she uses both hands to hit my ass.

If she's afraid of getting the bed dirty, I'll have my way with her in the shower.

❧ 62 ❧

CLAIRE

I stand in the bathroom, fixing my hair into a braid on the side of my head. It's nothing elaborate, but Shayna doesn't like fancy, despite how her parents act at times. The gray, strapless dress I wear hugs my body perfectly. The front dips into a V, showing a good amount of cleavage, which I know Ryke will appreciate.

"Wow, you look gorgeous." He stands behind me, looking at me through the mirror. He's wearing a dark gray suit and it looks amazing next to my dress. The buttercup yellow tie he's wearing matches my jewelry. We look damn hot together.

"So do you, Mr. Allen," I say as I turn to adjust his tie for him. I've never seen him dressed like this, but it's quite a sight. I'm seriously considering ripping the damn thing off him and taking him back to bed instead of leaving like we need to.

"Sweetheart, if you keep talking dirty, we're going to be late and Shayna will castrate me." I laugh at his dramatics, but he's right. Shayna will kill us both if we're late for pictures.

We carefully get into the limo Shayna's parents insisted we ride in. I enjoy all the things they've been doing for us, but there's no way I could possibly repay them.

"You sure you're doing alright?" Ryke asks as he leans in to rub my flat belly. I know he'll be excited to watch my body change during the pregnancy.

"Yes, I'm fine. I promise." I kiss his cheek. Thankfully, after this morning, I didn't throw up again.

The wedding chapel is like a sauna inside, but, thankfully, the ceremony is short and sweet. They invited three hundred people, so it's no small feat. We spend a long hour shaking hands and hugging all the guests before riding in a limo with the best man and his wife to the reception. Shayna wanted Ryke to sit with us at the wedding party table because it's only us and the best man Colton and his wife Audrey. Since I've been so sick, I wasn't able to spend much time with them, but they seem like a nice couple.

Dinner hasn't been served yet, but people are already out on the dance floor acting like drunken idiots. I look over at my best friend, but she doesn't seem phased by the way any of them are acting.

We're served our dinner salads and I suddenly need to pee. I hate to leave my food untouched, but I know I'll wet myself if I don't go now.

"You okay?" Ryke asks as I try to stand.

"Yeah, I just have to use the bathroom. I promise I'm not sick again." I kiss the side of his mouth. He smells delicious tonight with the new cologne I got him for his birthday.

When I get to the bathroom, I notice all the stalls are empty. I take a look at myself in the mirror and I'm glad to see I finally have some color back in my cheeks. I have Ryke's spoiling to thank. He sure knows how to take care of me.

I'm busy reapplying some lipstick after I pee when I hear someone walk in. I look in the mirror and almost fall over in shock.

"There's my beautiful wife." *What the fuck?*

"Trevor? What are you doing here?" I shriek.

"Well, darlin', that wasn't the response I was expecting." He chuckles evilly. "If you recall, the invitation we got was for me and you. I don't think I saw an invite for any white trash." He smirks and I want to punch him in the fucking throat.

"I need to leave." I try walking past him but soon find myself pushed into a stall. "Trevor, please let go of me." I try to talk calmly, but I'm scared to death. I've never been afraid of him, but now I feel the need to get away from him as quickly as I can.

My phone goes off in my purse that lies on my shoulder.

Trevor rips it off me and digs through it looking for my phone. "Ahh, yes. Ryke. That was his name. Fucking lowlife, son-of-a-bitch." He says this without any emotion on his face, which causes the hairs on my arms to stand at attention.

I'm now seeing red. How dare he talk about Ryke like that? I start banging on his chest, not caring how scared I am.

"Let me go and don't you ever talk about him!" I scream.

"Hello, Ryke," he answers my phone. I can hear Ryke on the other end but can't make out what he's saying. "This is Trevor Davis. I'm glad you've enjoyed fucking my wife, but I'm taking her back." *Oh, my god.* If Ryke figures out a way to get in here, he's going to kill Trevor.

After he ends the call, his hand goes around my neck. "I think it's time I finished what I started. I could have fucking cared less that you took off to Phoenix but finding out that bastard had what was mine pissed me off. Why did you have to go sleep with that goddamned piece of shit? How do you think that makes me look? Huh? You don't deserve to be happy. You didn't know I had another family, did you? Yep." He pops the "p" in "yep." "I was fucking her for the last few years and you never even knew. She helped me try to split you and that bar owner up, but now you've ripped her away from me. So now it's time to pay. This time, I think I'll drive you over a bridge so you don't have a chance. Brady will be mine," he hisses in my ear. *Oh, my God.*

"You tried to kill me!" *Oh, my God. Monica wasn't lying.*

I'm revved up on adrenaline and start pounding at his chest in fury. Without thinking, I knee him in the balls, which causes him to fall to his knees.

"You stupid bitch!" he yells as he holds his groin. Then I hear the stall door swing open. *Thank God.*

Trevor is already on the floor, but Ryke kicks him hard in the face, causing him to fall to his back. Blood squirts from his nose, splattering the wall behind him. "Motherfucker! You ever touch her again, I will end you! You're lucky I don't do it now." He pulls him off the floor by the collar of his shirt and Trevor's gasping for air. I don't want him spending his life in prison because of this bastard, but I sickly enjoy watching him beat his ass.

"Ryke, stop!" Trevor's face is turning blue.

He stops and turns towards me, seeing the worry on my face, and roughly throws Trevor back to the floor.

Now, the police are here, thankfully.

"Sweetheart, I'm so sorry. Are you okay?" He looks me over.

"He is the reason I was in a coma. He caused all this fucking pain," I cry. I can't catch my breath as I think about how my husband wanted me dead. I try to wipe at the snot that's now covering his suit jacket.

"Jesus Christ," he mumbles under his breath. He grabs both sides of my head, so I'll look at him. "Everything is going to be fine now. He'll never hurt you again." I can see the anger in his eyes, but he's trying to stay calm for me.

We both turn to watch as my husband is escorted out of the bathroom in handcuffs. My soon to be *ex-husband.*

"I'm never letting you out of my sight again." He squeezes me almost painfully tight. I don't care because right now I feel safe in his arms. As controlling as it sounds, I don't want to be away from him ever again, not after everything that has happened.

After we're questioned by the police, we make our way back out to the reception. I'm slightly embarrassed we caused such a ruckus.

"Claire! Are you alright?" Shayna cries. I hate seeing my best friend crying on her wedding day because of me.

"I'm fine, Shay. Ryke kicked his ass." I chuckle. "My fucking husband is a psychopath." I laugh in shock. This day has been a mess. First, I found out I'm having a baby with the love of my life. But then this. It's been a huge rollercoaster. I'm ready to go back to the hotel and sleep. After cuddling with my guy, of course.

We sit at the table and try to enjoy our meals. I don't want to leave Shayna, but I'm exhausted.

"Go get some rest, Claire. And don't think for one second I'm mad at you for it." She squeezes me tight in a hug and looks at Ryke. "Take care of my girl, alright?"

"I'll always take care of her." Shayna and I smile at each other. I kiss her and Dennis on the cheek and we head back to the hotel.

When we get into the limo, Ryke tells the driver to take us to the nearest hospital. I give him a questioning look. "I know you said you're alright, but I want to make sure. Plus, we need to make sure the baby is okay. Please?" There's no way I can argue with him. This is his child too. Besides, I'm also slightly worried. I can't handle losing another child.

***

"THERE'S YOUR BABY, MS. DAVIS," the young nurse says as she rolls an ice-cold wand on my stomach. It's a bit uncomfortable, but as soon as our little bean appears on the screen, everything else is forgotten.

Ryke leans down and kisses my head, unshed tears in his eyes.

"That's our baby, sweetheart," he whispers in my ear. "Looks like we're going to need a bigger house."

I gasp. "You want to buy a house with me?" This man is too good to be true.

"Of course." He kisses my forehead. "I know Trevor

didn't treat you right, but, sweetheart, you need to get used to me doing things for you."

"I love you, Ryker Allen."

"I'll love you forever, sweetheart." He gifts me with the best panty-melting kiss. Not exactly appropriate, since the nurse is still in the room with us, but that doesn't stop him.

Once we get the all clear at the hospital, we head back to our suite. The doctor told us everything looked great and I'm ten weeks along with a due date of May 15th. We even got to hear our little beans heartbeat. I've never seen Ryke look so proud. He swears we're having a girl, but we won't know for a couple months.

"I'm so happy to be having a baby with you." He wraps me in his arms as we lay on the bed.

"Me too," I whisper. "Are you going to be disappointed if we have another boy?" I laugh.

"Of course not." He kisses my head. "I'd love having two boys." This man melts me every time he speaks.

❧ 63 ❧

CLAIRE

I carefully climb down from Ryke's truck. I was scared to death to drive the beast, but it really wasn't that bad. He's at home with Brady after I told him that I needed to do something today. He doesn't know what, but I'm sure he has an idea. I didn't want to risk him trying to talk me out of it, so I decided to keep it to myself.

I pull the heavy door open that leads to The Espresso Bean. I do a quick scan of all the tables and spot Monica sitting at a corner booth in the back. I got her number out of Ryke's phone. I jokingly asked him about it and he was worried that I'd think something happened between them. No, I'm done jumping the gun in our relationship. That led to nothing but problems.

"Hey, Claire." She smiles up at me as she stirs the coffee in front of her.

"Hey, Monica. Thanks for meeting me." I nervously slide into the booth across from her.

"I wasn't sure what you liked here so, I just got you a

black coffee and they brought out cream for you." She slides the steaming mug across the table to me.

"This is perfect. Thank you." I pour two creams into my coffee and then add a pack of sugar. "I wanted to apologize."

"For what?" She acts genuinely confused even though I was a bitch the last time I saw her.

"Well, for one, I was rude to you when you came over to my brother's house, but also because I didn't hear you out when you tried to warn me about Trevor. You were right." I whisper the last part. Ryke encouraged me to make an appointment to see Desiree. He thought it would be good for me to talk to her after everything that happened in Miami. I couldn't really argue because he was right. I don't want to have another downfall again, so I'll do everything I can.

She reaches across the table and grabs my hand, which throws me by surprise.

"What happened?" This girl is vastly different from the one I saw at Ryke's.

"He showed up at my best friend's wedding in Miami and tried to hurt me, but, thankfully, Ryke showed up before he did anything."

She gasps and puts her hand to her mouth. "Oh, my God." She has a tear running down her face, and I can tell that she really does care.

"He admitted to trying to have me killed. He's currently sitting in a jail cell until his trial." I'm still trying to fathom the fact that my husband wanted me dead.

"Let me know when it is and I'll go with you to testify."

"Really?" I'm not sure how Ryke will feel knowing his

ex is helping me, but she is exactly the witness we need to prove him guilty.

"Of course. I owe you and Ryke for trying to cause problems. I know I'm his least favorite person, but I really do want to help."

I decide not to respond to her because I don't want to sound unappreciative. She really hurt him, but she already knows that. I don't need to add salt to old wounds.

"You don't have to answer me now, you can talk to Ryke first." She pauses and puts her head down.

"What is it?" I ask.

"I thought maybe Kayla could meet Brady." She looks up at me cautiously.

"I think that's a great idea. I think it's important that he knows his sister." I can tell she's surprised by my answer but then a smile lights up her face.

I don't imagine us ever being best friends, but I think I could enjoy spending time with her. Who would have thought?

We talk some more about random things and finish our coffees before making plans to meet up soon with both kids.

I'm not sure what Ryke is going to say about me spending time with Monica, but I want Brady to know Kayla. They both will grow up without their father, but at least they'll have each other.

I leave the coffee shop feeling oddly relieved. I hop up into the truck, ready to see my guys.

64

RYKER

Today, I am fucking elated. We're at Sierra's house gathering the last of Claire and Brady's things before they move in with me. Sierra found out a few weeks ago that Miles will be home tomorrow. Claire was a little hesitant to move in with me since we've only been together for a short time, but she quickly got over it. The thought of having her in my bed every night makes me feel like the luckiest damn man alive. I converted my guest room into Brady's new Mickey Mouse room. Since they've been spending most their nights with Sierra and her son, it was easy to surprise them with it. I also let her pick out new things for our bedroom, so it felt like ours instead of just mine. We'll have to find something bigger before the baby comes, but I've already started looking some.

"Alright, Sier. I think we got everything loaded up." Claire gives Sierra a hug and she starts to cry. Damn pregnancy hormones.

"Thanks for staying with us." Now Sierra is crying.

They act like they'll never see each other again when they'll only be fifteen minutes away from each other.

I walk to the living room and lift Brady in my arms.

"Come on, buddy. Let's go wait for Mama outside." When we got back from Miami, the first thing I did was get a car seat for my truck. It was a bitch trying to figure out which one to get, since Claire wasn't with me, not to mention, trying to put the damn thing in correctly. Thankfully, buckling him in doesn't take a scientist.

"Ike, go!" Brady says from the backseat. He's so smart for his age. I've gotten to spend a lot of time with him since Claire started working at the daycare down the street from my house. We have guy time on the days she's gone. She's also been writing again but won't let me read the book she's working on until it's done. Romance would bore the hell out of me, but I'm damn proud of her.

"We have to wait for Mama." I turn toward the boy and squeeze his foot.

The passenger door swings open and Claire climbs in. We're going to have to get her a car before she gets much bigger or she won't be able to get in and out of this thing.

"Sorry for taking so long."

"It's alright. You okay?" I squeeze her hand. I've done my research on pregnancy and know that women can become very moody. Afterward, it doesn't get much better.

"Yeah, I'll just miss seeing her every day." She rests her head against the back of the seat.

"You can come see her anytime or have her over. Miles comes home tomorrow, right?"

"Yeah, why?"

"Why don't you invite them and Evan and Avery over

this weekend and we'll grill out. It'll be nice to meet Miles and I know you haven't seen much of your brother lately." Her relationship with Evan has been very up and down since she moved to Phoenix, but since the accident, they have grown closer. I'm glad she had them when she couldn't remember me.

"Thanks, baby." She smiles.

When we get to the house, I unload their things into the living room.

"Stay put until I'm done, okay?" I tell her as I run out to my truck. I'm excited to show her and Brady his new room.

I grab Brady's diaper bag and a box for his room, deciding to get the rest later.

I walk back into the house and Claire gives me a questioning look.

"Uh, why can't I leave?" She sits next to Brady who has just climbed up on the couch. Damn, I'm so excited to have them here with me. I just hope I Brady-proofed my house well enough.

"Come on, I'll show you." I lift Brady in one arm and grab her hand.

"What did you do, Ryker Allen?"

"You'll see." I slowly push the door to Brady's room open and, once she has a good view, she gasps.

"Oh, my God! You did this for him?" She squeals and then takes Brady from me.

"Of course, I did. I wanted him to have his very own space here. This is his house too."

I look over at her and she has a tear running down her cheek. And here come the emotions again.

"Brady look what Ryke did for you!" The boy runs into the room in excitement.

"Icky!" He yells and has me and Claire laughing in hysterics at his attempt at saying Mickey.

"That's right, buddy." I lift him into the crib that has Mickey bedding, a fancy one that will later convert into a toddler bed. We'll have to get another crib for the baby.

With Austin's help, I painted the bottom half of each wall red, the top half white, separated by the wood paneling. Mickey Mouse stickers are strategically placed all over the room. A yellow lamp with a red shade sits on a mouse-shaped table next to the rocking chair in the corner. I know Claire likes to rock him to sleep every night, so now they'll have their own special space.

Brady takes it upon himself to climb out of the crib.

"We might have to change that over to a toddler bed sooner than I thought." I chuckle.

Claire laughs.

While Brady continues to roam around his new room, she grabs my arm.

"I can't believe you did this." She pulls my face down to her and presses her lips to mine.

"I'd do anything for you guys and this little one." I rub her now protruding stomach. She still has a while until she delivers, but I look forward to seeing all the changes to her body.

"I love you, Mr. Allen."

"Claire, don't tease me." I peck her nose with a kiss and then join Brady.

"HELLO!" Claire's loud ass friend yells as she comes through the front door. I seriously believe that she doesn't know what a doorbell is.

"Hey, Sier." The two women hug as if it's been months since they've seen each other when it was just two days ago.

"Babe, this is my bestie, Claire."

"I've heard so much about you," Miles says as he wraps my girl in a side hug.

"Oh, trust me. This girl never shuts up about you." At that, Sierra playfully punches her in the arm.

"Hey, man. I'm Ryke." I hold my hand out to him.

"Nice to finally meet you. Thanks for putting up with her while I was gone." He points at Sierra. It's obvious these two are in love.

"Well, she always steals my girlfriend away, so I kind of had to." I wink at Sierra and she mumbles a curse word at me under her breath.

The doorbell rings.

"Hey, Sierra. That's what we call a doorbell." I tell her.

"Oh, shut the hell up. This is Claire's house now too, so I can barge in whenever I damn well please."

"Sorry, man, I can't control her."

We both laugh.

"Can I get you a beer?"

We both head back to the kitchen when he agrees.

"Hey!" Evan yells as he comes into the room, carrying soda and chips.

"Hey, man. This is Miles. The lucky man who gets to put up with Sierra for the rest of his life.

Evan slaps Miles on the back.

"Nice to meet you, man. Thanks for your service." Miles smiles and nods.

Claire comes into the room and hugs her brother.

"Hey, bro. I feel like I haven't seen you in forever." Evan leans down and kisses her on the head as he wraps his arm around her.

"Because you have a damn boyfriend now." He smirks at her and she punches him in the side.

"Whatever. You're just glad we're out of your hair now."

Avery comes into the kitchen.

"Now we can have sex whenever and wherever we want."

"Seriously, Av." Evan rolls his eyes at his wife but then laughs.

"Avery! I do not want to hear that and you know this."

"Oh, come on, seriously? You're pregnant. You guys *obviously* have sex."

"Avery!" Evan covers his ears in disgust. "Did you forget that she's my baby sister. Don't say shit like that."

The guys finish off their beers and then we all head to the backyard. The girls sit with their feet up while they pass Auggie around and watch Brady play.

"Are you excited to be a dad?" Evan asks me as he pats me on the shoulder. Claire and I have discussed it, deciding that we would keep talk of the baby to a minimum while we're around him and Avery. For the last several years, they've been trying to get pregnant without any luck.

"Yeah." I smile wide, not being able to control myself. "I'm going to talk to Claire about adopting Brady once her divorce is finalized."

"That's awesome, man. Hopefully, Trevor doesn't give you guys any trouble." I cringe at his words, knowing there's a strong possibility that he'll try to raise hell.

"Yeah, I know. I'll do anything for those two, you know?" I look over at him as I flip the burgers over on the grill.

"I know. Just take care of them." At that, he pats me on the back again and walks away.

I finish at the grill and the women grab all the side dishes from the kitchen and bring them out to the patio table. Before Claire and Brady moved in, I bought a lot of shit, so this would feel more like a family home. I also set up a small swing set in the yard where Brady can swing and go down the slide. I'm looking forward to watching him and the baby play on it together in years to come.

"Hey, sweetheart," I say as Claire wraps her arms around me from behind.

"Thanks for everything, baby," she whispers and I can hear the emotion in her voice.

I spin around so I'm facing her.

"You don't have to thank me. I don't know what I did to deserve you, but, fuck, I'm so glad I have you.

She stands on her toes and grabs me by the back of the head as she devours my mouth, not caring that we have company.

I can't wait to spend the rest of my life with this woman.

65

CLAIRE

FIVE MONTHS LATER

I pull into the parking lot of the bar. I never thought I'd be a mini-van mom, but here I am. Ryke insisted because it's safer than driving a car with the kids. I let him think whatever he wants.

I open the door and I'm immediately hit with a cool breeze to my face. These pregnancy hormones have me hot and sweaty all the damn time. Thank God I'll be having this baby before summer hits full force.

I know I look ridiculous strolling through the parking lot in flip flops and capris. I've only been in Phoenix for one summer of extreme hell. Sierra laughs at the way I dress, but this mama can't deal with the heat.

"Hey, sweetheart," Ryke hollers from the bar as soon as I walk in.

"Hey, baby." I take a seat right in front of him. Tonight is a slow night, so he doesn't have any customers to take care of right now.

"I'll be ready in a few minutes." He leans over and pecks my lips before running back to his office.

I have no idea why he had me meet him here. He called me this afternoon and had me ask Sierra to watch Brady. This better be good because I'm exhausted and just want to put my feet up.

I decide to walk to his office instead of waiting at the bar.

Ryke's back is to me when I enter the room.

"Whatcha doin' in here?" I ask and he jumps. "Sorry, babe. Didn't mean to scare you."

He holds his chest. "It's okay." He laughs. "Just needed to grab something, but I'm ready now."

"What are we doing? Are you taking me for ice cream? Because I'd love you forever."

He leans in to kiss me. "No, but you'll still love me forever." He smacks my ass as he walks behind me.

"Hey, man. I'm taking off," he tells Austin as we pass the bar. "I'll be in at noon tomorrow."

"See ya, guys." He smiles at us. Austin recently got married to his long-term girlfriend, Amanda. Ryke was his best man.

"Are you going to tell me what we're doing?" I ask again as he helps me up into his truck. "What about the van?"

"We'll come back." He runs around the front of the truck and then gets in and grabs my hand. "You know how you like surprises?" He laughs, knowing damn well that I do *not* like surprises.

"Uh, no." I chuckle. "What did you do?"

"I just want to show you something."

We drive through town, but then I realize that we're headed toward the mountains.

"Baby, where are you taking me?"

He looks over at me and smiles. "We're almost there."

"We're in the middle of nowhere." I look out the window and all I see is desert with a few houses scattered throughout. I have no clue where the hell he's taking me.

Finally, he turns on his signal for no reason at all, as we're the only people out here.

He turns down a long drive-way that looks like it belongs to a house, but if it does, I can't see it yet.

Once we're reaching the end, I notice a light from ahead. Then it comes into view. The most gorgeous, two-story, western-style home. The house is built of stucco like every other one in Phoenix, but it has a unique vibe to it.

"Babe, what are we doing here?"

He parks the truck. "I'll show you."

He runs around to my side to help me down. Being enormously pregnant makes it near impossible to get in and out of his truck.

"Doesn't someone live here?" We continue toward the house, but he doesn't answer my question. "Babe?"

He pulls me up to the beautiful wrap-around porch.

"Yes, someone does live here." He gives me his signature smirk.

"Who?"

"Us." He smiles from ear to ear.

"Oh, my God! Seriously? You bought this house?" We only talked about buying a house once and I honestly kind of forgot about it.

"Yes." He gets down on one knee and my heart leaps

from my chest. "This is where I want to bring my beautiful bride home to." He reaches in his back pocket and pulls out a beautiful, white gold ring, with a heart-shaped diamond surrounded by a circle of diamonds. It's gorgeous. My knees nearly buckle out from beneath me. "Will you marry me, sweetheart?" He looks both nervous and excited at the same time.

"Yes!" I join him on the ground, tackling him in a kiss.

He laughs at me. "Careful with my baby."

"The baby is fine." I grin. "Where's my ring?" I reach for his hand, acting like a greedy child.

"So grabby." He swats at my hand. He helps me up from the ground and then grabs my left hand before sliding the beautiful band on my finger.

I hold my hand out to admire it and then wrap my arms around his neck.

"It's perfect," I whisper into his ear as I nuzzle into him.

"You're perfect, sweetheart." He kisses my cheek. "I want to spend the rest of my life in this house with you." He gives me an intoxicating kiss and I know that I'll never tire of this.

He pulls away from me.

"Let's go see your house, sweetheart."

He walks me through the front door and I get eager thinking about my future with this man.

❦ 66 ❦

CLAIRE

"Come on, Claire, we just need one more good push," Doctor Eckman says calmly.

"I can't!" I yell. I'm in so much pain and can't wait to get this baby out of my freaking vagina. *How could I have possibly forgotten how godawful this was?* I guess if women remembered every grueling detail about childbirth, they wouldn't do it again.

"Yes, you can, you're doing great." *Easy for him to say.*

"Yeah? How many times have you pushed a baby out of your vagina, huh?" I'm totally being a bitch, but how can he possibly know how much this sucks?

"Claire, be nice," Ryke whispers into my ear. "You got this, sweetheart." I'm sure I've just embarrassed the hell out of my fiancé, but I couldn't care less right now. He's the one who got me into this situation.

Thankfully, the doctor decides to shut his damn mouth, so I can focus on getting this kid out of me.

I've just had the hardest workout of my life, but then I

hear the sweetest cries and I suddenly forget how exhausted I am.

"It's a girl!"

I look over and see tears on Ryke's face. I've never seen him so happy before. After much arguing, he finally agreed to not find out the gender of the baby. I have to say it was difficult not knowing, but now it's totally worth it, seeing how thrilled he is.

"We have a girl, sweetheart," he whispers in my ear in a croaked voice. "She's beautiful, just like her mother." He leans in and kisses my sweaty forehead.

I've never been more content in all my life. This man came into my life when I was at my lowest, but he saved me. I don't know how I'll ever repay him for that, but I'll spend the rest of our lives trying.

❧ 67 ❧

CLAIRE

ONE YEAR AFTER ENGAGEMENT

"Look at you Mama, all hot and sexy!" Avery shrieks as she walks into my make-shift dressing room at the church.

"Av, calm down." I smirk at her and then lean in to kiss her on the cheek, careful not to ruin my newly applied makeup that Sierra did.

I turn back toward the mirror to admire myself. The simple mermaid floor-length gown is covered completely in lace, its train pooling at my feet. My mother's dress was very similar and it was my way of having a piece of her here with me today. Between the capped sleeves, the neckline dips low, showing a bit of cleavage that Ryke is sure to like. It's beautiful and timeless.

Around my neck lies a white gold chain that holds both my parents' wedding bands. I choke up at the thought of not having them here with me today, my dad not able to walk me down the aisle. Thank God for my brother.

I twirl around in circles, my three best friends laughing at me.

They all wear deep purple, knee-length dresses with black heels. I decorated flip flops for all of us to change into at the reception.

I carefully bend over and lift each of their bouquets from the box. They'll each carry a bundle of white roses. My bouquet the color of their dresses. Elegant, yet simple.

"Here, girls." I hand them each their flowers and they "ohhh" and "ahhh" over them.

"They are gorgeous," Sierra says as Avery goes to answer the knock at the door.

"Hey, sis, you about ready?" Evan walks in and stares at my dress, tears starting to form in his eyes. This is something I rarely see, so it shreds me to pieces when I do.

I let out a big breath. "Yeah, I think so." I smile at him through the mirror.

"He's out there driving us all fucking crazy, so you better hurry your ass up before Miles and Austin kill him."

I laugh, having no doubt about him having nervous energy. He was the same way at the hospital when we had the baby.

"Alright, let's go then." I hug each of my friends and then lace my arm through Evan's.

I can't believe I'm finally marrying Ryker Allen.

ॐ 68 ॐ
RYKER

I can't believe this day is finally here. I'm marrying my best friend and the mother of our children. Yes, you heard me right. Once Claire's divorce was finalized and her ex was shoved into prison for paying someone to kill her, he signed over full parental rights of Brady and I adopted him right away. After he admitted to trying to kill her, we found out that he had hired a friend to run her off the road, but the idiot ended up killing himself instead. For whatever fucked up reason, Trevor thought he'd actually get custody of Brady. Over my fucking dead body. It makes me sick for the little guy, but, thankfully, he doesn't know any better.

I'm also the father of a beautiful little princess named Aria. Thankfully, Claire's pregnancy was uneventful with minimal sickness after our trip to Miami. She's now a full-time stay-at-home mother while I still work at Ryke's. Since I now have a family, I decided to change the bar into a partial restaurant so my children are able to visit me. I didn't want them around a bunch of drunk idiots, so we only have a small bar separated from the rest of the building.

Over the last year, Claire has developed a relationship with Monica. At first, I hated it because I didn't care for her to be around my ex, but they've really helped each other. They both were hurt by Trevor Davis and Claire wanted Brady to grow up knowing his sister. Monica has recently gotten into a relationship with a guy she met at counseling. As fucked up as it sounds, I'm proud of her.

Evan and Avery just found out last week that they are expecting their first child. Claire is over the moon for them and thrilled about being an aunt.

Miles, Sierra's husband came home last year and they are now also expecting their second child. Claire has already informed me that her "baby factory" is closed for the next couple years. We'll see. Seeing her with our children makes me feel like the fucking luckiest man alive. I'd loved to put ten more in her if she'd let me.

I now stand at the front of the church waiting for my bride. I see the doors open in the back of the room. My beautiful girl is in a simple white lace, floor-length dress. A purple bow sits perfectly under her breasts, at my request. It's always been my favorite color on her. Her veil drapes over her face, but it doesn't hide her beauty. She's stunning. Brady stands next to me with Austin and Aria is cradled in Avery's arms. My dad, Gail, Becca, and Justin sit in the front row, promising to help with the kids if we need it.

We repeat our vows to each other and the minister pronounces us husband and wife. Before I'm even told to kiss her, I grab my wife by the back of the neck and crash my lips to hers. She giggles when I finally let her go. She wears the biggest smile on her face I've ever seen.

She always says she's unworthy of my love because she feels like there is nothing for her to give me in return. She's given me more than she'll ever know. She revived me.

The End

Want more? Stay tuned for Evan and Avery's story in Renewed!

ACKNOWLEDGMENTS

First and foremost, thank you to my wonderful hubby who didn't think this writing journey was completely insane. I couldn't have done any of this without you. Love you, babe!

My two amazing kiddos who put up with me working on the weekends while they were home.

My BFF, Amanda for reading my book even though it made you blush ;)

My parents for believing in me. I miss you guys every day!

MA Foster, Kim Deister, Trenda London, Andrea Galante, and Jessica Ames. Your guidance has made this book everything I could have possibly wanted it to be.

ALL of my Beta readers!

All the amazing authors I've met on this fun and exciting journey and put up with my obnoxious questions.

My AWESOME reading group who has supported me from the beginning! You all seriously complete my days.

My new friends, Missy and Valerie for making me laugh every day and believing in this first-time author.

Last, but definitely not least, my readers! Thanks for taking a chance on this new author!

ABOUT THE AUTHOR

S.E. Roberts was born and raised in the cornfields of Central Illinois, but now lives in sunny Arizona with her husband, two children, and her rescue cat, Stanley. When she isn't spending time with her family, she enjoys writing steamy romance, reading, and sipping on iced vanilla coffees. She continues to dream up her characters with the assistance of rocky road ice cream.

facebook.com/serobertsromance

twitter.com/authorSEroberts

instagram.com/authorseroberts

Made in the USA
Monee, IL
12 March 2021

62554651R00213